A LONESOME PLACE FOR MURDER

ALSO AVAILABLE BY NOLAN CHASE

A Lonesome Place for Dying

A LONESOME PLACE FOR MURDER

AN ETHAN BRAND MYSTERY

Nolan Chase

NEW YORK

Books should be disposed of and recycled according to local requirements. All paper materials used are FSC compliant.

This is a work of fiction. All of the names, characters, organizations, places and events portrayed in this novel are either products of the author's imagination or are used fictitiously. Any resemblance to real or actual events, locales, or persons, living or dead, is entirely coincidental.

Copyright © 2025 by Sam Wiebe

All rights reserved.

Published in the United States by Crooked Lane Books, an imprint of The Quick Brown Fox & Company LLC.

Crooked Lane Books and its logo are trademarks of The Quick Brown Fox & Company LLC.

Library of Congress Catalog-in-Publication data available upon request.

ISBN (hardcover): 979-8-89242-302-1
ISBN (paperback): 979-8-89242-314-4
ISBN (ebook): 979-8-89242-303-8

Cover design by Jerry Todd

Printed in the United States.

www.crookedlanebooks.com

Crooked Lane Books
34 West 27th St., 10th Floor
New York, NY 10001

First Edition: August 2025

The authorized representative in the EU for product safety and compliance is eucomply OÜ Pärnu mnt 139b-14, 11317 Tallinn, Estonia, hello@eucompliancepartner.com, +33757690241

10 9 8 7 6 5 4 3 2 1

For C.R.

1

"For want of a damn nail."

Ethan Brand had been stalking across wet grass for half an hour, searching for the old man and the horse. The pasture was uneven, spongey from a week of summer rain. His shoes and the cuffs of his pants were soaked. Every uphill step sent an ache through his repaired foot and ankle.

Ahead of him, Brenda Lee Page halted and turned. "Did you say something?"

Ethan hadn't realized he'd spoken out loud. All the same, he was grateful for the pause. Judging from the sweat on Brenda Lee's upper lip, she was, too. Ethan Brand was Chief of Police for the town of Blaine, Washington. Brenda Lee Page was his most senior officer. They'd worked together for twelve years. While Ethan considered Brenda Lee a friend, there was a competitive edge to their friendship—even down to who could walk fastest over a wet patch of grass.

"I was thinking of that old Ben Franklin quote," Ethan said. "*For want of a nail, the horse was lost.*"

"The shoe," Brenda Lee corrected. "*For want of a nail, the shoe was lost. For want of a shoe, the horse was lost.* The horse loses the rider, the rider the battle. I don't remember what comes next."

"The kingdom, I think."

"*And all for the want of a nail.*" Brenda Lee turned and scanned the clouds, a pretext for wiping her face with her sleeve. The sky had the look of quilted satin and there was a breeze blowing in from the ocean. It would rain again soon. "What brought that to mind? Buyer's remorse already?"

"Nobody's buying," he said. "We're just here to take a look at a horse."

"You don't walk onto a car lot, Ethan, unless you're thinking of buying. And why ask me?"

He shrugged. "You're an animal person."

"I'm a dog person," Brenda Lee said. "And a 'sleeps in on her day off' person, too. Why all of a sudden do you want to buy a horse, anyway?"

She resumed walking, handling the incline with ease. Ahead of them the ground rose steadily in a grassy hillock. To the north lay a stand of Douglas fir, beyond that the Forty-Ninth Parallel. The pasture ran east along the border.

"For the kids," Ethan said, once again falling behind. "It's hard to explain."

The idea had been building over the summer. During the school year, the boys lived with their mother in Boston. Ethan had them for July and the first part of August. Back in their old room in the one floor house they'd all shared before the separation.

At first the three of them had been shy together. Ben and Brad were eight and ten. They'd outgrown their bunkbeds. They missed their mom and friends. Ethan had taken them boating and camping. They'd dug for razor clams and took in the Puyallup Fair. On the days he was needed at the station, the boys came with him, hanging out in the muster room or his office.

The visit had nourished Ethan's heart in a way he hadn't quite realized he'd needed. Yet it had been unsatisfying as well. The boys enjoyed the trips and activities, but in the downtime their attention had been elsewhere. Both had tablets and phones, with safety features his ex had patiently explained to him. Between calls and texts and games and internet videos, the devices had been out more than away.

A different generation, Ethan reminded himself. It was good the boys stayed connected, that they knew how to function online. And didn't he have his work phone with him at all times? When he asked them to put their gadgets away, they complied with minimal fuss.

Despite that, Ethan felt their lack of engagement with their surroundings. All his life this had been something he cultivated, first as a child dropped into the wilderness by his father, then as a Marine and an officer. His most sacred duty as Chief of Police was to prevent violence. Situational awareness was critical for that. To be truly present in the world *mattered*.

Blaine was a small border town with a population of less than six thousand. It rained more than a third of the year, about average for the Pacific Northwest. Compared to Boston, as a cultural hub, Blaine wasn't much. Yet it was home. Months spent trekking through the Helmand Valley in Afghanistan had given him a new appreciation for rain and ocean, evergreens and beaches, for small towns and the people who lived in them. He hoped he could pass on a little of that to his sons.

One afternoon he'd taken them for ice cream at the Railyard Café, an old caboose refurbished into a snack shack near the water. A truck pulled up, towing a sleek horse trailer. Instantly the boys were fascinated. They watched as the driver fed peppermint Life Savers through the gunmetal slats of the trailer. She saw them watching, smiled, and offered to let them try. Ben had dashed up to the trailer immediately. Brad, more cautious, had followed only after his brother's hand re-emerged from the animal's mouth unharmed. For those moments, the digital realm had fallen away.

"I want my kids to know there are things in this world worth showing up for," Ethan told Brenda Lee.

"And a horse is a way to do that?"

"Maybe." The only other time they'd been as enthusiastic was when he pointed out the blue-eyed coyote that sometimes crossed his property. The boys had been astonished and delighted when a pair of sand-colored pups emerged from the red currant bushes and followed their mother across Kickerville Drive.

"Chickens would be cheaper," Brenda Lee said. "Plus you'd get eggs."

"Bit harder to ride, though."

Brenda Lee reached the crest of the hill first, Ethan loping after her. The land smoothed out below in a strip of green. In the middle of the pasture was a weathered gray shed with double doors. About equal distance between the shed and the trees, an old man sat on the ground with his legs straight out in front of him. He was staring at a torn and disturbed patch of earth. Ethan recognized him as Mac Steranko.

"Something's wrong," Brenda Lee said. She broke into a jog, heading down toward the scene.

With a grunt of pain, Ethan followed.

* * *

"She's a beaut," Nettie Steranko had told him over the phone. "Chestnut mare with a broken blaze. Fourteen hands, so on the small side, but that's a plus if you got kids. Good ground manners, too. And as pretty a gait as you'll see. Mac told me if he was twenty years younger he'd keep her for himself."

The Sterankos had been horse traders for more than sixty years. Nettie had a keen eye for bargains and a love of haggling that bordered on bloodlust. Once, when Ethan pulled her over for speeding in a school zone, Nettie talked her way out of a ticket by claiming she was late for work. Only after she pulled away did Ethan recall that the Sterankos were self-employed and set their own hours. Mac worked with the horses, as confident in the saddle at eighty-two as he'd been at eighteen. Something to aspire to, Ethan thought, finding a thing you loved that much.

"What's a broken blaze?" he asked. "An injury of some kind?"

Nettie's laughter was mocking but warm. "Her markings," she said. "A white stripe on her face we call a blaze. If it's not continuous, if it's broken into patches . . ."

"Got it."

"Her mother had the same markings. Munequita out of Agua Caliente. She was sired by Anything for Billy. There's Breeders' Cup blood in her, you go back far enough. As to her own record, well, one-three-two with thirty-four starts. Showed real promise in her younger days, but who among us didn't?" Again that easy laugh.

"What's her name?" he asked.

"Trim Reckoning. You come and meet her Sunday, Ethan. I guaran-darn-tee love at first sight."

Ethan knew the conversation wouldn't end until he agreed to take a look. Knowing little about horseflesh, and fearing Nettie would have him signing papers before he knew what he was getting into, he'd asked Brenda Lee Page to come along. No small request: Sunday was her day off.

"Terry was making French toast," Brenda Lee said on the drive to the farm. "I'm giving up breakfast in bed because you're worried an eighty-year-old woman is trying to fleece you?"

"No," Ethan said, "I'm worried she already has."

When they arrived at the farm, Nettie Steranko was sitting on the front steps of the weathered two-story house, phone held to her ear. She was dressed in a red checked shirt and black jeans with tasseled leather moccasins. Beneath her steel hair, the laugh lines of her face were gathered in an expression of worry. Her husband and the horse weren't in sight.

"Mac's not picking up," she said. "He took your mare out for a quick hop, just to get the wildness out. Should've been back an hour ago."

Ethan wondered exactly how wild the horse was. "Could be he forgot to charge his phone."

"I suppose." Nettie didn't sound convinced. "Could I beg a favor, Chief? I'd go myself only on account of the gout."

What else could they do but check it out? Nothing could ever be simple.

* * *

Now, as he picked his way down the soggy hillside, Ethan got his first look at Trim Reckoning. The mare's coat was a dark chocolate at the withers, lightening to a glossy cinnamon around her belly. A startling white streak on her forehead tapered to a thin slash between her eyes, breaking off at the bridge of the nose, then picking up again close to the nostrils. Her reins dangled over the empty saddle. She was trotting along the line of evergreens, as if considering making a break for Canada.

He noticed the horse's canter was uneven. She seemed to be favoring one leg. Ethan could relate. Fragments of his left foot had remained behind in Helmand Province, the result of an IED. He got around now with the help of a heel plate and fitted prosthetic. It balanced his stride, but there was discomfort, sometimes pain, especially over uneven terrain.

Mac Steranko remained seated. As they approached, he held up his hand, either in greeting or in warning. Brenda Lee reached the old cowboy first.

"Anything broken?" she asked.

"Don't think so, knock wood."

"Can you stand?"

He took her arm and allowed himself to be pulled to his feet. Miguel Steranko was short and compactly built, dressed always in denim, from jeans to snap button shirt to fleece-lined vest. His snow-white hair was a little too long to be fashionable. Born in Mexico to a Ukrainian family, Mac walked with a mild stoop as a result of injuries from his rodeo days. Ethan was glad he seemed okay. There was a toughness to the old man, matched only by his wife. The Sterankos had seemed invulnerable to him as a child, conjured up from an earlier time. Frontier people, somehow outside the modern world.

"Did she throw you?" Ethan asked. If the horse could toss a rider as well seasoned as Mac, how could he let his kids anywhere near her?

The old man shook his head. "Stumbled is all." He spotted Trim Reckoning and made a sound with teeth and tongue, somewhere between a click and a kiss.

Brenda Lee was inching closer to the patch of torn earth. Blades of grass were pasted to her leggings. Her hiking boots sunk in the turf with each step. She adjusted her glasses, squinting down at the spot. "Moles?"

"Most likely." Mac wiped his hands on his jeans. "Guess I was lucky. Fellow I knew broke his tailbone stepping in a gopher hole. He and the big bay he was riding went ass over teakettle. Got hisself an office job after that."

Ethan pointed at Trim Reckoning. "Is her leg all right?"

"Hard to say. Not bleeding, and I didn't hear a break. Still, it was a bad hop."

Mac nickered at the horse again. In a sing-song voice he called to her, "Hey-o little old gal." Trim Reckoning's ears perked up.

The horse took a few steps toward them. Her eyes, large and amber-black, settled on Ethan with cool curiosity. He hoped she wasn't in pain.

Brenda Lee crouched and prodded at the hole. "Moles didn't do this. See how the soil is pushed down instead of up?"

He tore his attention from the horse and saw that she was right. The depression was half a foot long. Ethan had seen a polo game once, and this looked like the divots left by the players' mallets, only larger. Brenda Lee peeled back the scrap of turf.

"Ought to be careful," the old man said, and at that moment the ground gave way.

The collapse was swift. Brenda Lee was bent over, jabbing at the earth. The next instant an entire green shelf had dropped away, carrying her out of sight. Ethan bolted to the edge of the rapidly enlarging hole but felt something snag the back of his jacket. The fabric tore. Mac Steranko was restraining him with surprising strength.

Spooked, the horse bolted in the direction of the trees.

Ethan struggled free of Mac's grip. He approached the edge, called Brenda Lee's name. To his relief, he heard coughing.

The hole had enlarged to a trench, maybe six-feet deep and longer than it was wide. He could see the heels of his officer's hiking boots resting on something dirty and orange. A tarp, from the looks of it.

"A tunnel," Brenda Lee shouted up. "Human-made, looks like."

He moved so the thin overcast sunlight fell over his shoulder. The tunnel was low-ceilinged. In places it had been braced with two by fours. The earth had worked on the wood for years, and what was left was rotting. All it had taken was a few steps from a horse to cave in the ceiling. One small hoof for mankind, he thought.

Ethan had cleared tunnels in Helmand. Many were left over from the Soviet–Afghan war, hollowed-out crevices in the rocks, barely large enough for a man. But large enough to cram an explosive or other trap. Tunnels were always a danger.

"I'll get you out," he said, looking toward the shed. Maybe there was rope inside.

"Give me a minute. I want to see where it goes."

"Famous last words."

Brenda Lee was crawling further in. Soon her boots were lost in the darkness.

"Strong-willed lady," Mac observed.

"Don't have to tell me." A year ago, Brenda Lee Page had been shot in the line of duty. She'd hurried through rehabilitation, determined to come back at full strength. And she had.

"Anything?" he called down.

No immediate answer. Feeling useless, Ethan decided he'd phone Nettie. At least she could stop worrying about her husband. And then a sharp note of surprise echoed out of the tunnel, a sound he'd never heard his senior officer make before.

"Ethan, there's a body down here," Brenda Lee called. "And it looks like it's been here a while."

2

The dimensions of the tunnel allowed for one person to crawl. No room for turning around. Brenda Lee Page had to shimmy back on her palms and knees to reach the collapsed opening. Boots came in view, then leggings, then her blue Patagonia jacket. Smudges on her brow and nose, clothing caked in rich Washington State earth. Her glasses hung askew. Brenda Lee stood and shook crumbs of dirt from her hair.

"You're paying my dry cleaning bill," she said.

"Anything else down there?" He offered a hand but she vaulted onto the grass and swung her legs over.

"Dirt and a lot of it. The body's about thirty feet from the collapsed part. I'd estimate he's been down there for several years."

"He?"

"The clothes. Men's boots and a chain wallet." Her hand sliced the air in a northerly direction. "The tunnel goes in a straight line. I didn't see an exit."

Ethan turned to Mac Steranko. "You know anything about this?"

The old man glanced down at the vent in his pasture. "Damnedest thing I've seen."

All of a sudden there was too much to do. Preserve the scene—but what *was* the scene, at this point? How far did the tunnel go? Was there a starting point, an end? They would need backup, need to call in forensic technicians, which meant alerting the Whatcom County Sheriffs and the Washington State Patrol. The Border Patrol, too. They would need something to keep the rain out of the hole. And how would they get the remains out without collapsing more of the ground?

A body in a tunnel fit the definition of "suspicious death." That didn't mean it was necessarily a homicide, but they had to treat it as one until they found evidence to the contrary.

Trim Reckoning had shied away from the opening in the ground. The horse was pacing a short distance from them. An injured mare at a crime scene was one variable too many. "Think you can catch her?" he asked Mac.

"If she wants to be caught."

"Calm her down, see how the leg is. If she can walk back to the barn, put here there, and if not we'll call a vet. You need a phone?"

The old man shook his head. "Mine's in the saddlebag."

Ethan looked south, past the toolshed to the edge of the Steranko property. "We'll need an access route for vehicles. Where's the best spot?"

Mac pointed out a section of fence close to the road. "'Tween those posts is a gate. Don't tell the stock."

"All right. We'll need to talk more about this. With Nettie, too. It's important you don't speak to your wife about this before we do."

Mac looked at him, confusion on his face. Genuine hurt, as well. "Are you saying me and Nettie are suspects, Chief?"

"At the moment all you are is two people with a hole in your field," Ethan said.

They both knew the real answer. Until proven otherwise, everyone was a suspect.

* * *

Blaine's police department was as small as the town itself. In addition to Brenda Lee, there were only a handful of full-time officers. Ethan spoke to the civilian administrator, Jon Gutierrez, and told him to get hold of them all.

"Copy, Chief." Jon's voice was even-toned and energetic. A professional actor's voice. In his downtime, Jon and his husband organized the town's amateur theatricals. "Heck and Mercy are on patrol, and Mal and Brenda Lee have the day off."

"They did. Brenda Lee's already here. Tell Mal it's all hands on deck."

"Copy."

"Got a pen? We're also going to need barricade tape, tent pegs, a tarp as big as you can find, a canopy, evidence kits, and a camera with a decent flash. They're going to drive over the Steranko property, so they should take the four-by-four."

"Quite a grocery list, Chief."

"Anyone asks, tell them we have a . . ." Ethan couldn't think of the proper term.

"A rapidly developing situation?" Jon suggested.

"Perfect. Tell them that."

"Will do, Chief. Anything else?"

"Coffee and donuts wouldn't be out of line."

"That went without saying, Chief."

Brenda was on the phone with Lt. Moira Sutcliffe of the WSP, arranging for technical support. Blaine had good relationships with the larger and better funded state and county departments. But issues of jurisdiction could be knotty. Moira's team was larger and more skilled, facts she didn't hesitate to remind them of. It could be hard to get the proper amount of support, neither more nor less.

Ethan looked at the shed. A direct line could be drawn from the structure to the hole and onto the border. That couldn't be coincidence. On the other side of the fir trees was Zero Avenue, tract housing and farmland. Canada didn't look any different from here. If the tunnel reached that far it would be roughly a mile long.

Drugs were the obvious reason, but not the only possibility. Prescription pills that were cheaper in one country could be shipped and sold in another. Cigarettes, too, or whiskey. Blaine and the surrounding coastline had been prime bootlegging territory back in the days of Prohibition. And something was always prohibited.

Guns and explosives were another terrifying possibility. Cash, too. Or the cargo could be human. For a fee, people known as snakeheads or coyotes could arrange to bring people over the border. Sometimes this was only the pretext to another crime—robbery, enslavement, or murder. Was that how the body had ended up in the tunnel?

He was getting ahead of himself. Ethan walked toward the shed to see if he could find an entrance.

The structure was aluminum, originally painted white, grayed by weather and neglect and pitted with brown streaks of rust. No padlock. Grass had overgrown the track of the sliding doors, and Ethan muscled them open with difficulty.

The interior didn't look like it had been disturbed in years. Not by humans, anyway. Bags of fertilizer and grass seed, the plastic ripped open by critters. Spiderwebs dangled in dark banners from the ceiling. The shed had been insulated with sheets of Styrofoam, now crumbling and dirty.

He shifted yard tools out of the way. Propped behind a roto tiller was a large piece of foam, rotten and brittle with age. Had someone once slept in here? Ethan wondered.

The floor of the shed was a carpet of rubber auto mats. Ethan hurled shovels and adzes through the doorway, hearing the tools thump on the grass. His fingers peeled up one of the mats, cold and streaked with silver snail trails. He flung this out the door as well.

Below the mats was a sheet of filthy plywood, cut to the dimensions of the shed. Mice and other critters had nibbled at the edges, and in spots the moisture had rotted the wood to splinters. In its past life the flooring had been a signboard, judging from the faded green and white paint. He could make out the letters *E* and *V*.

A Green River soda tin, a set of rusty tent stakes. Ethan worked faster now, tossing the shed's contents aside, whipping the floor mats out the door. The sign below revealed itself. *WELCOME TO WASHINGTON, THE EVERGREEN STATE.*

He was looking for an opening large enough for a person, something not made by animals or time. It stood to reason that the tunnel would line up with the shed.

There.

Beneath the mats in the back left corner, he could see where a square of the sign had been carefully sawed out and fitted back into place. He dug fingers and nails into the gap, wedging it up, realizing as he did that this would be the ideal spot for a tripwire. An IED triggered by the opening of the tunnel—

But there was no wire. The wood came out cleanly. Soon he was staring through a neat square in the floor, just wide enough for a grown person to fit through.

"Find the entrance?" Brenda Lee called from the doorway.

"Or the exit."

"The body's on its stomach facing north, so I'd say he was heading in that direction." She ran fingers over the Styrofoam, a chunk breaking off. "I don't see Mac and Nettie as drug runners or human traffickers."

Ethan didn't either, but had to admit that would make them ideal for the task. Who would suspect a pair of octogenarians?

The tunnel gave off a smell of soil and mulch. No ladder going down. Ethan could see the framework of timber shoring up the sides. How long would the structure hold? He turned on his phone's flash and secured it in his breast pocket.

"You're not going down there?" Brenda Lee said.

"Never assign a task you wouldn't do yourself."

With a steadying breath, he lowered himself into the dark.

The floor of the tunnel had been lined with strips of tarp and sheet plastic. His hands passed over small pools of water and debris. The beam of the flash cut downward, only lighting up a few feet in front of him. Beyond that he could see the gray sunlight of the collapsed section.

At five-foot intervals, crudely carpentered support timbers ran along either side and over his head. His shoulders barely cleared them. After twenty feet or two, the wooden reinforcements began to be spaced farther apart. Unfinished, he thought. Maybe the builder had run out of time or materials. Maybe they'd gotten lazy. Or perhaps the builder was the dead man in the tunnel. A heart attack, a gas main, suffocation—a number of unpleasant ways to go.

Digging one's grave without knowing it.

The gray light of the opening grew more prominent, falling on a mound of dirt and grass. As he crawled toward it, his fingers touched something metal and cylindrical. A shell casing, he realized. Ethan pocketed the casing and continued.

Calling Brenda Lee's name, he passed over the rubble at the opening. No plastic sheeting after that. No more wooden supports. The tunnel ended a few feet past the body.

Timberland boots, size 11, he'd guess. A nylon jacket, maybe an XL. The fabric hung loose over the emaciated corpse. The parts of the body that had been clothed had decomposed at a slower rate. The hands were missing bones and the head was a broken skull with wisps of hair. A decade was about right. The earth and everything in it had been at work on the corpse for years.

He waved the phone over the body, taking pictures from a variety of angles. Hopefully a few would turn out. Ethan wasn't much of a photographer, even with ample light and above ground.

Carefully he unsnapped the wallet's chain from the belt loop. The smell of the dank leather was strong. Something familiar about the stitching. Nothing else in the pockets, no phone, no keys. No firearm that he could see.

Here lies a man, Ethan thought. Circumstances and choices and plain bad luck had led him to this end. His fate, if you wanted to get philosophical. In Ethan's own profession, the manner in which a person died was funneled down to one of five options: natural causes, suicide, homicide, accident or undetermined. A shell casing alone wasn't proof that the body in the tunnel was the result of a homicide, but it tipped the scales of probability in that direction.

He turned the flash off and retreated back down the tunnel in darkness, feeling along with his knees and hands. At the opening he stood up and accepted Brenda Lee's help onto the grass. Rain pelted his hair and face. A good feeling after the confines of the earth.

"Found this," he said, handing her the shell casing. The dirty brass jacket of a .45 ACP round.

"So it's murder."

"I think so."

She pointed at the shed, the contents spilled across the grass. "Somebody was living out here at one point. There's a sleeping bag and an old camp stove behind the tools. A stepladder, too."

Brenda Lee had wiped her face, but her clothes were still smudged with earth. Ethan realized he must look the same. "Don't think dry cleaning's gonna cut it," she said.

Over the hill he saw running lights. A Blaine PD Explorer bounded across the grass, Hector "Heck" Ruiz at the wheel. Beside him sat Mercy Hayes, the newest addition to the department. No doubt Malcolm Keogh was on his way.

Ethan wiped his hand on his shirt before opening the wallet. A few soggy bills, a driver's license issued to Tyler R Rash. The name resonated.

Brenda Lee examined the license. "You know who he is, or was?"

"I do, yeah." Ethan felt a tightness in his stomach. A feeling he'd almost forgotten.

A photo was wedged into the billfold. An old Polaroid, the image faded in the corners. Time and damp had left the faces in the photo hard to recognize. But he recognized them all the same.

The photo showed a teenager with dirty blond hair and the proud beginnings of a mustache. Next to the teen, holding a bottle of High Life, was a dark haired man in his thirties. The man's features were handsome but stern. At least Ethan had always thought of them as stern. Both of the faces were grinning.

"Which one is Tyler Rash?" Brenda Lee asked.

"The teen." Tyler had been three years older than Ethan himself. The corpse in the tunnel was an adult, which squared with his timeline. "It's an old photo, almost thirty years. I'm amazed Ty held onto it."

"What about the other guy? You know him, too?"

Ethan Brand wasn't sure he ever really knew the man. But he nodded. The feeling of tension in his stomach had only grown.

"That's Jack Brand," Ethan said. "My father."

3

For a moment they didn't speak. As the Explorer scudded down the hill, it came alongside Mac leading Trim Reckoning. The vehicle braked. Ethan saw Nettie Steranko in the back seat. She leaned across Heck Ruiz to exchange words with her husband.

A crime scene was a fragile thing. Dealing with a dead body was similar to dealing with a sick body—the first rule was to do no harm. And harm was being done every moment they stood here. Witnesses were conferring with one another. Rainwater spatted the tarp at the bottom of the opening. Brenda Lee waited for his explanation.

"Tyler Rash lived with us a little over a year," Ethan said. "He and I were friends. We lost touch, though, after my father died."

"There's more to it than that, isn't there?"

He nodded. The stomach pain hadn't lessened. A feeling he associated with being helpless. Vulnerable. Ethan willed it to pass.

"I know your dad went missing when you were young," Brenda Lee said. "Presumed dead. Some kind of outdoorsman, wasn't he?"

"A survivalist."

That was an understatement. Jack Brand believed in self-reliance. Had made a religion of pitting himself against nature.

Every year he would have a pilot fly him to a remote campsite, always a different location. He'd stay for weeks, sometimes months, before coming home.

And then one year he didn't come home. The pilot had returned to the campsite and found no trace of Jack.

Ethan had been fifteen. He and his mother organized search parties, hired local Indigenous trackers and a diving team with sonar. Twice they'd searched the surrounding wilderness and sounded the depths of the lakes. All to no avail. Jack Brand's fate, his final resting place, was unknown. A part of Ethan felt his father would have wanted it that way.

Nearly thirty years had passed since then. Ethan still had no perspective on his father. The course of his own life—from college to the Corps to the department, with a few bumps along the way—had been shaped as much *against* Jack as *by* him.

That was the bond Ethan shared with the dead man in the tunnel.

Brenda Lee waved at the Explorer, directing Heck Ruiz to park at a distance from the tunnel. Who knew what else was buried here?

"I take it I'm leading the investigation," she said.

Ethan nodded. "Better that way." Even if Brenda Lee Page wasn't the most experienced officer, a death investigation demanded objectivity. The photo and license had shot his objectivity to pieces.

"We'll have to talk about this in detail, you know." Brenda Lee smoothed a dirty hair off her forehead. "The whole story, with nothing held back."

"Deal."

"Heck and Mercy and I can secure the scene. Why don't you take Mac's statement?"

The old man was nearly at the top of the hill. Ethan wasn't looking forward to the trek back across the field, but if the injured horse could make it, he could, too.

Brenda Lee found a clean spot on her shirt and wiped the lenses of her glasses. "Feels nice giving you orders, Ethan. Natural. We should do this more often."

* * *

The rain was a soft but steady accompaniment. Just spitting, as people said. Of course, what counted as spitting in Washington State would be considered a minor monsoon to someone from Arizona or New Mexico. Ethan buttoned the collar of his damp shirt.

He caught up to the horse trader on the other side of the hill, in time to see Mac extract something from the saddlebag. It turned out to be a hat. Ethan would have expected the old cowboy to wear the ten gallon variety, but it was a plain blue ball cap with the Olympia Beer logo on its foam front.

"Nettie worries I'll catch cold," Mac said. "Now you can tell her I kept my head covered."

"What did you say to her?"

"Told her I was okay and explained about your horse. The woman tends to fret."

Mac kept a grip on the bridle. Trim Reckoning matched his pace. Ethan could feel the animal's breath. Despite her injury, the large dark eyes were calm.

"How is she?" he asked.

"Short distance like this she'll be okay. What lames a horse isn't the injury, it's the compensating, working the other limbs harder to make up. Wears them out that way."

Ethan didn't answer, knowing firsthand what the old man was speaking of.

"My fault, I guess," Mac said after a while. "Figured a jog around the pasture would wake her up. Aimed to be back before eight, since you were coming by at nine."

"Why would that be your fault?"

Mac adjusted the brim of the cap. "You won't repeat this to the missus, will you?"

"What were you up to?"

"The hill," Mac said. "Nettie doesn't approve of me opening up on the way down. Letting the horse run. Foolish at my age—but hell, what am I drawing breath for if I can't get the blood going every now and then?"

"So you raced down the hill?"

"That little mare has spirit. All I had to do was loosen up and hold on. Figured we'd circle the shed and take 'er easy on the way back. Only she took that bad hop, and when I reined up, she threw me."

"Tell me about the shed," Ethan said.

"We put it up, Nettie and me, oh, got to be forty years ago. Figured we'd have a real outfit someday. Trailers and RVs for the hands, maybe a bunkhouse. Didn't quite work out. Now it just holds what we can't fit in our basement."

"Someone was living out there."

"Oh, not for years and years."

"Was it Tyler Rash?"

The name caused the old man's jaw to clench. Disappointment, maybe. Or regret.

"We tried with that boy," Mac said. "Like your folks did."

"When did you see him last?"

"My age, all the years kinda seem the same."

"Give it a try, sir," Ethan said. "Could be important."

Mac took his time, working it out by the memories of who was president, what color the house was trimmed that year, the make and model of Ty's car. An old white hatchback Mustang.

"Fourteen years ago," he said with confidence.

"How long did he stay?"

"Less than a year. Ten months, maybe."

"Why'd he leave?"

"Couldn't tell you that. You know what Ty was like."

Ethan nodded. "Ty lived with you after he left us, didn't he?"

"That's right. He liked the shed better than the house. Nettie fixed it up for him. Think he felt safe out there. When he left, we didn't hear from him for ages."

"Until fourteen years ago?"

"That's about right. One day he just showed up in that Mustang. Asked could he stay in his old digs for a little while. Paid us rent—I mean, he chipped in a few bucks room and board."

"I'm not the IRS," Ethan said. "Did Ty pay cash?"

"Always. First of the month he'd leave an envelope tucked under our back door mat."

"And that's when he built the tunnel?"

Mac scowled at the ground. "Never knew the damn thing existed till that mare stepped wrong."

Beneath the brim of the hat his face was wet. Maybe that was only the rain. Mac Steranko stared at the farmhouse rising out of the field in front of them.

"We tried with that boy," he repeated. "Some folks can't be helped. Hard lesson to learn, isn't it?"

"I don't seem to be able to learn that one myself," Ethan said.

* * *

In the stable next to the farmhouse, Ethan helped Mac ice down Trim Reckoning's leg. He watched the old man massage the muscles before applying a heat pack. Mac spoke to the horse as he worked. "That's a good girl. Gonna get some special shoes on you. How's that sound?"

There were two other horses in the nearby stalls, a large white Arabian and a small paint. The roof had buckled and warped in places. Water drizzled down into a bucket in an empty stall.

"I'm gonna call the horse doctor and my farrier," Mac told Ethan. "I'll make sure to keep all the receipts."

A bizarre comment, until Ethan remembered that this morning he'd been considering buying the horse. Funny how death made the rest of life seem like the distant past.

The front gate of the property was unlatched. He saw where the Explorer had crossed from the gravel driveway onto the field. Ethan walked back to his truck. The ancient brown Dodge had been his mother's, and was far too beat up to justify keeping it on the road. But he did, year after year. Every dent and ding was familiar, and he knew every song on the cassettes in the glove box. In a world that kept changing, familiarity had its benefits.

Covering the seat with an old supermarket flyer, Ethan turned the heat on. He pressed play on the stereo. Alan Jackson, "Summertime Blues." And then some, he thought.

Following the Explorer's tracks over the pasture, he contemplated what a difference fourteen years could make. So many of the good things in his life hadn't occurred until later. His sons, the best years of his marriage. Hardships too, of course. The separation. Loneliness. The bitter put the sweet in perspective, and together they made up a life.

Someone had robbed Tyler Rash of that. Whatever Ty had or hadn't done, an unfair sentence had been executed on him. Ethan owed it to the man to find answers.

* * *

When he returned to the field a large gray canopy had been erected over the opening. His officers wore rain gear and were busy. Mercy Hayes was documenting the contents of the shed. Heck Ruiz had found the fence's gate and was busy widening it, peeling back a section of heavy gauge wire, creating direct access from H Street onto the property. Brenda Lee Page was talking with Nettie Steranko.

As Ethan approached, he overheard Nettie working out the timeline of Ty's second stay with them. Her process was almost identical to her husband's. Ethan wondered if their marriage had lasted because they reasoned along the same lines, or if the years had drawn them closer in the way they thought. Maybe both. His own marriage had lasted almost a decade, and if anything, Ethan Brand and Jasmine Soltani thought more differently about things now.

"Why the shed?" he heard Brenda Lee ask. "Why not rent out a room in the house?"

"Ty always needed his own space. People thought he was half-wild, but some folks just need room to get a handle on the world."

"Did he help you and Mac with the horses?"

Nettie smiled as if Brenda Lee had made a bad pun. "I think the nags spooked him. Up close, that is. Ty loved watching them from out here."

Ethan quietly took position beside Brenda Lee, not wanting to interrupt the questioning. The old woman looked at him, anxious and sympathetic.

"I'm sorry," she said.

It took him a moment to understand that she was offering him condolences.

Brenda Lee handed her the photo. "Can you identify where this was taken, ma'am?"

"The day I can't I'll be in deep trouble," Nettie said. "I'm the one that took it. That's our house. Jack was over to celebrate Ty's eighteenth. This would've been taken a few months before Jack disappeared."

"So they were friends?" Brenda Lee asked. "Pardon me for saying, but that seems a bit peculiar given their ages."

Nettie shook her head. "Not at all. Before Ty stayed with us he lived with Jack and Agnes. More than anything, that man loved being in the wild. Ty had those same inclinations."

Nettie smiled at the recollection, holding the photo close to her face. Her expression was dreamy.

"Ty had a real knack for outdoorsy stuff. Jack taught him how to live off the land. He mentored that boy. They were kindred spirits. In fact, Jack used to call him the son he never had."

Nettie's smile burst as she realized what she'd said.

"Lord, I'm so sorry, Ethan."

He felt Brenda Lee looking at him. The words had stung. Only the truth could hurt that way.

4

By late afternoon forensic services had arrived. Two State Patrol evidence vans detoured onto the field through the break in the fence, carrying technicians in Tyvek bunny suits. The techs praised Ethan's officers for their work preserving the scene, then kindly asked everyone to clear out.

Ethan left Mercy Hayes to stand guard. He told Brenda Lee they'd meet later, at Lucky's Café, to discuss Tyler Rash. There were reports to write, and Ethan had a department to manage. But first they needed showers.

The tunnel didn't seem to reach the border. Yet the fact it was so close to Canadian soil meant the RCMP should be included. The DEA and ICE had already been called, adding more bodies to tomorrow's briefing. He'd need to arrange coffee and snacks—the sheriffs and commanders could get testy if there wasn't food.

A hole in the ground that went nowhere. A body left at the end. Once Tyler Rash's remains had been removed and autopsied by the medical examiner, perhaps they'd yield a clue as to why he'd been killed. None of the possibilities were particularly pleasant.

The extreme northwest corner of the continental United States was home to several smuggling rings. The closest to Blaine was run by the McCandless family, who lived just outside the city limits. Could Ty have run afoul of the clan? Seth McCandless would have been running things fourteen years ago. Both Seth and his brother Jody were currently in prison. At present their sister oversaw the family business now. Sissy McCandless was the smartest of the three. She kept a low profile.

The killing could have been personal. Or self-defense. Or an accident, Ethan supposed. After all this time, it would be hard to find definitive proof.

No one said the job would be easy.

* * *

Blaine's police station was headquartered in a one-story brick building with a clapboard front. The side was water stained and in need of a wash. In the summer the building retained heat; in the winter it allowed chill air to seep in. Whatever the weather, you could count on the station to be equally uncomfortable.

"Messages?" he asked Jon as he passed the front desk.

"A whole bunch, Chief."

Most of them pertained to Blaine's upcoming election. Mayor Eldon Mooney was running for another term, and hoped to organize an event "that shows our offices' strong mutual support." Ethan Brand hadn't felt much support from Mooney. It didn't help that his first act as chief had been to fire the mayor's nephew. An unavoidable decision, given that Cliff Mooney was corrupt, brutal, and incompetent. Still, it was never good to make an enemy of a mayor.

Mooney's opponent was Arlene Six Crows, a lawyer and city councilor. Arlene had called to discuss Ethan's role in her campaign. He hoped his role would be limited to moral support, perhaps a donation or two. Politics wasn't his strong suit, and neither was public speaking. Still, Arlene was a friend, and she'd be a good mayor. Ethan would help if he could.

Gus Murphy from the Sheriff's Department had called to ask if tomorrow's meeting would be catered. Like locusts, he thought. It was already starting.

"Any word from Mal?" he asked.

Mal Keogh was the department's most technically proficient officer, as well as the former chief's son. He hadn't showed up at the crime scene, and wasn't in the office now.

"He's not coming in today, Chief." Jon looked reluctant to relay the message. "I stressed the importance and the unusual circumstances."

"What did Mal say to that?"

"'My day off is my day off.' His words, Chief, not mine."

Ethan kept from expressing his disappointment. Maybe Mal had been indisposed, or too far out of town to get back. He didn't want to doubt the young officer's commitment. Mal's father, Frank Keogh, had been Ethan's mentor. Growing up the chief's son couldn't have been easy.

In his office he changed into his spare uniform, then attempted to deal with the unfinished tasks waiting on his desk. The officer fitness reports were already overdue. Ethan had been chief of police for just over a year and still hadn't evaluated his force. The thought of passing judgment on his former coworkers didn't especially thrill him. The job of chief had more dimensions to it than he'd anticipated.

He wrote up his preliminary report on the morning's events, including the circumstances that brought him to the property. *Officer Page accompanied me to offer her opinion on the possible purchase of the aforementioned horse.* Embarrassing to write. Why had he been so captivated by that idea?

The dead man in the tunnel was now in transit to the basement morgue of Bellingham General Hospital. The Whatcom County Medical Examiner, Dr. Sandra Jacinto, would perform the autopsy tomorrow. For Ethan, a tangled mess of memories and emotions had been unearthed along with the body. *The son he never had* . . .

As Ethan left the station to meet Brenda Lee, Jay Swan fell in step beside him.

"Is it true there's a tunnel with a body in it on the Steranko property?" Jay asked.

"Can't confirm nor deny. It's 'nor,' right?"

Jay covered crime and municipal affairs for the *Northern Light*. They also updated the website and recorded a weekly podcast. Jay was a good journalist, and usually fair, but wielded something of a purple pen. Pulitzer dreams, he supposed. Ethan remembered when Jay used to babysit his sons.

"What can you tell me, then?" The flap of Jay's messenger bag was open, their hand clutching a sound recorder attached to a directional mic.

"A situation is developing," Ethan said.

"That doesn't do me a lot of good, Chief."

"Me neither."

He crossed H Street, passing by the decommissioned cannon that was part of the city's memorial to fallen soldiers. As he neared the gas station he spotted a row of choppers parked at the curb. Five men in chaps and leather jackets were gathered around one of the pumps. They were crowding a woman as she filled the tank of a black SUV. They weren't getting ugly or violent, but they were loud, and beginning to push their luck.

Up close he saw the five weren't outlaws. Weekend warriors, middle-aged and white-collar types. Canadian tags on their bikes. Probably gassing up in Blaine before hitting I-5. He approached, keeping them all in his line of sight.

"Those bikes are going to tip over," he said. The quintet gave off a sour smell. At least one of them had been drinking beer. Or bathing in it.

"Bikes look fine where they are, buddy." The largest of the group had a forked beard. Strands of lettuce or cabbage caught in the whiskers.

"You misheard me," Ethan said. "I didn't say they might fall over. I said they're going to fall over. You have less than two minutes."

"That a threat?"

"Prognostication. Good word, isn't it? Know what it means?"

"What?"

"It means you have one minute now."

The leader grinned, held his hands up in exaggerated innocence. "We were just asking the pretty lady if she knows where we could all get a drink."

The woman twisted the cap onto her gas tank and closed the flap. Her expression wasn't fearful. In fact she seemed amused. She was striking, her dark skin complimenting dark red hair, eyes hidden behind wayfarer shades. She wore a skirt and tall boots, a plum colored blouse beneath a black three-quarter raincoat. On the passenger seat of her vehicle, Ethan saw a tan cowboy hat.

"Do you know these guys?" the woman asked him.

"Familiar with their type."

"Do you think they know they're on camera right now? Or that a law enforcement officer with a standard issue sidearm could put two rounds in each of them without pausing to reload?"

The leader's grin dropped off his face in rapid time.

"The extent of their ignorance hasn't been determined," Ethan said. To the quintet, he added, "She's right. My standard issue sidearm prefers to stay holstered."

"Mine doesn't." The woman shifted the breast of her raincoat, exposing an automatic pistol hanging from a shoulder rig. "These are very tough, very bad men. Who's to say they're not carrying controlled substances?"

"We're not," the leader said.

"Want to prove it? Spend forty-eight hours naked in a cell, waiting to see what you pass?"

The group had backed away toward the curb. Soon Ethan heard the mechanical flatulence of the motors. The procession of bikes swung onto the ramp for the interstate. The noise faded.

Ethan glanced at the law enforcement decal on the SUV's license. "FBI?" he asked.

"Close. You're local, I take it?"

"About as local as they come."

She extended a hand. A strong grip, clear polished nails. A silver band on the wrist. "Vonetta Briggs," she said. "How did you know I wasn't planning to run off with the Wild Angels?"

"Finely honed intuition. Plus I attended a law enforcement seminar once."

"Yeah?"

"Almost stayed awake for the whole thing."

She smiled, opened her door but didn't seat herself. "The assist wasn't necessary but I appreciate the gesture."

"What are you in town for?" Ethan asked.

"This a professional question?"

"Sure."

Vonetta Briggs pointed at the pump. "Just gas, for now at least. I'll have my office inform yours if that changes."

"Please do," he said. "Welcome to the Peace Arch City."

* * *

Walter "Lucky" Luk had decorated the walls of Lucky's Café with historical photos of the Chinese community in Washington State. Ethan liked gazing at the images of logging gangs, railroad crews on their break, merchants posing defiantly outside of their simple wooden storefronts. It was a reminder of how complex and left-handed history could be, and how people could endure. Lucky's Café served good coffee and Chinese-American cuisine. It was also close to the station.

As Ethan entered, Mei Sum placed a coffee cup in front of the stool on the end, his usual spot. The teen moved the lucky cat statue so Ethan had a view of the magnetic chessboard. Mei had been teaching him the game for two years now, defeating him match after match. Ethan had gone from a poor chess player to merely a lousy one. He still had yet to beat Mei.

"Heya, Chief," she said. "Figure out your move yet?"

"Hasn't been at the front of my mind."

"Doesn't much matter, you're beat in two moves anyway."

"That's what you think," Ethan said.

Mei gave an I-warned-you shake of the head and took his order. Buddha's feast, red-eye gravy, steamed rice and a second cup. He was breaking his rule by drinking coffee after noon. But then it had been a broken rule kind of day.

As usual, Brenda Lee was prompt. She had changed into her uniform and wore the department's all-weather jacket over top. She took her time settling into the seat and looking over the menu. Ethan was still contemplating his move.

"Just admit it's over, Chief," Mei said.

He examined the board, trying to see the danger ahead. Brenda Lee settled on wonton soup. His senior officer slapped her heavy-duty notebook on the counter and uncapped her pen.

"Tyler Rash," Brenda Lee said. "Tell me everything."

"Where do you want me to start?"

"From the top, and don't leave out the tough parts."

If I did, Ethan thought, there'd be nothing to tell.

5

"What direction?" his father said.
"South. I think."
"You think? Are you trusting your life to 'think' now?"
"No sir."
"So what direction are we heading?"

Jack Brand had been driving for an hour. The truck had left asphalt for gravel about twenty minutes ago, and now seemed to be rolling over bare earth. Ethan could hear the snap of branches, feel the tires shudder over uneven ground. The blindfold was tight, cutting into the skin above his eyes.

He tried to reason out the direction. It had been past midday when they left Blaine, the sky clear. The windows of the truck's cab worked as lenses, baking the back of his neck and his right shoulder. That meant the sun was behind them, which meant they were traveling—

"Southeast," Ethan said. "I'm sure."

In response, his father executed several sharp turns. The truck bounded and Ethan's knee smacked the side of the door. The worst part was not knowing when the ground would dip or rise. He couldn't brace himself. Only endure.

"How about now?" Jack said.

Ethan could no longer feel the sun, which meant they were likely under a thick canopy of trees. Gaining in altitude. He tried to envision a map of the area. The mountains were where, exactly?

"Still southeast."

The inside of the cab smelled of stale beer. The truck rumbled and finally stopped. A jingle of keys as his father killed the engine. They sat silently for a moment. Then he felt cold steel against his cheek. The blindfold was cut off. Ethan blinked.

They were in a grove of impossibly tall redwoods, which let in only a smattering of light. The undergrowth was dense, ferns and snakes of ivy, small pools of water with electric green swirls of algae. A rotten trunk loomed, shelf mushrooms jutting from its side.

"Out of the truck," his father said.

Jack had a beer in hand. He opened the gate of the truck and lifted out a green knapsack. Ethan watched his father close his eyes, inhale the smell of the woods. Almost instantaneously Jack seemed to relax. The knapsack was shoved into his son's hands roughly, but with affection.

"Listen carefully, Ethan. I'll be back tomorrow at oh eight hundred. I'm leaving you a knife, a tarp, a book of matches and some liver for your supper. Don't eat any foliage—'specially not those mushrooms. Next time I'll teach you what's safe and what's not. First priority?"

"Fire. Shelter."

"Which is it?"

"Shelter."

"Correct. Make yourself a shelter and *then* get your fire going. A small one. Don't use green wood and don't use more than you need. Understand?"

Ethan nodded.

"I'll tell your mother you're sleeping at a friend's. She wants you to be a good little gentleman, a productive member of society. That's all well and good, but I'm trying to teach you how to survive when society disappears—and sooner or later, Ethan, it will."

His father tousled his hair. Jack Brand seemed almost embarrassed by the gesture. He finished his beer.

"There's a lot you need to know about the world. For now, focus on the essentials. Shelter and fire. Eight o'clock sharp tomorrow, you'll be packed and ready to go. The site will look the way you found it. In the future I'll expect you to make your way back on your own. Any questions?"

Ethan made a quick inventory of the contents of the pack. The meat was wrapped in butcher paper. It smelled gamey. Matches, the tarp . . .

"No knife," he said.

From his back pocket, Jack produced a small clasp knife. He handed it to his son.

"You're learning," Jack said. "Just because a person says a thing doesn't mean they'll do it. Like the man says, trust but verify."

"Are there bears out here?" Ethan asked.

"You tell me. Are there?"

"Black and brown." He tried to remember what he'd read about their habitat. An image came to mind: a lumbering creature the size of the truck, its fangs bared, leaping from the bushes the moment his father left. Ethan felt a stab of anxiety in his stomach—the first time he'd ever felt that constricting pain.

"Remember," his father said, climbing into the truck, "there's no such thing as lost. Unless you panic."

Ethan Brand was thirteen years old.

* * *

The tarp was threadbare and full of holes. Ethan sat beneath the fallen tree and wrapped it around himself. Every sound set him on edge. Bears were out here. Coyotes too, and wolves. Monsters. If he started a fire they'd be drawn to him. So he sat, chilled and uncertain, using the tarp as a cape, waiting for the sun to drop and then rise again.

As it grew dark, though, he remembered this was a test. His father would know if he failed to make fire and shelter. Ethan stood and kicked twigs and small branches into a pile. He strung up the tarp over the log to form a wind-break. His hands were cold. The matches flared out before they could share their flame with the tinder.

What if his father never came back? What if Jack got lost, or something happened to him? Where did the test end and normal life start up again?

Maybe it wouldn't, and he'd have to figure it out for himself.

Ethan got the fire going. He balanced the piece of liver on a forked branch. The green wood popped and smoke blew south. The smell of the meat might attract critters, but the fire would keep them back—so he hoped.

A branch snapped somewhere beyond the fire. The shuffle of dirt and dead leaves. Footsteps. An animal approaching. Ethan opened the blade and held it ready, the branch in his other hand. A fight to the death was coming.

But the animal was a boy. A teenager, taller than him, dragging along something that gave off a metallic squeak. The boy approach the fire and nodded.

"Hey," Ethan said, unsure what else to say.

"Hey."

The kid was thin, with blond hair and faint chin whiskers. He wore an AC/DC shirt with a ripped collar, and the dirtiest pair of jeans Ethan had ever seen. He was dragging a rusty bicycle with only one tire. He pointed at the meat.

"Can I have some?"

Ethan handed him the branch. The kid took a large bite, chewing, not caring it came straight off the fire. As if he hadn't eaten in days. Steam escaped his mouth between bites.

"You live out here?" Ethan asked.

"Uh huh."

"Ever see bears?"

"Sure. Tons." But the kid was grinning.

They took turns feeding the fire. As it grew darker, the kid produced a tin of flake tobacco. Ethan had never taken snuff. He took a pinch and sneezed, feeling sick. The kid seemed amused.

"Nice knife," the kid said. "Can I see it?"

"My dad says not to hand a weapon to someone you don't know."

"Smart." The kid prodded the fire. "I'm Tyler."

"Ethan."

"We know each other now."

"Yeah."

"Ever seen a Playboy?"

"No. You?"

"Yeah."

They slept sitting on either side of the fire. In the morning Ethan's father returned and took them both home.

* * *

"You're thinking about that girl."

"No sir."

"Don't lie to me. Your head's not in this."

"No sir."

"Then explain why you lost."

Every part of his body hurt. They'd been fighting on bare earth, and Tyler Rash had thrown him twice. Wrestling, his father called it, but there were no holds barred. Ty loomed over him, proud of his victories but trying not to show off.

The fact was, Ethan *had* been thinking of that girl. Girls were all he thought about these days. One rainy afternoon, Leona Marsh had shared her umbrella with him. They'd kissed a day later. He suspected he was in love.

Love wasn't something Jack cared about.

"He's bigger than me," Ethan said.

"What else?"

"Stronger."

"Any other excuses?"

Jack leaned against a birch, officiating with a can of High Life in hand. His tone wasn't mean. It was soft, almost kind. Only a faint trace of mockery beneath the words. That made them hurt all the more.

"No sir," Ethan said, willing himself to stand.

"Do you think bigger and stronger doesn't exist out in the world?"

"No sir."

"You think you're special enough to skate through life without adversity?"

"*No sir!*"

"Then what are you gonna do about it?"

Lunge. Ty was ready for him, though. The two collided, arms locked above their heads, struggling for advantage over the dirt. Nothing else existed for Ethan. Not pain or exhaustion, not the call of birds in the trees. Not even his father. He felt Ty grab his shirt and twist at the waist, getting ready for another hip toss. Ethan dug in, muscles screaming.

Then Ty was falling and Ethan was following him down, pinning his shoulders. In desperation Ty grabbed at his face, fingers digging into his flesh. Ethan held on, grinding Ty's shoulders into the dirt.

"Let him up," Jack said.

Ethan heard his father but didn't obey. Every cell in his body was after blood. He was victorious, for the first and only time.

"I said enough." Jack kicked his shoulder, sending Ethan to the ground. He lay there, chest thirsting for oxygen, his heart a steady trip of thunder.

He'd won.

Instead of congratulation, though, his father inspected the battleground. Jack bent over a deep rut where the heel of Ty's sneaker had dug into the soil.

"He tripped," Jack said.

"No he didn't."

"Arguing with me?"

"He didn't trip. I won."

"You want to claim a tainted victory?"

"*I won.*" Ethan knew there was no benefit to arguing. Fairness was something that only mattered sometimes to Jack Brand. The contest was over, and what did it matter who won?

Yet it did matter to him. Beyond fairness, beyond reason. His father could march him over hell and gone, and he'd never yield.

Jack turned to Tyler Rash. The older kid was already on his feet, wiping a trickle of blood from his mouth. "Did you trip or did he pin you?"

Ty spat. He looked down at Ethan.

"I didn't trip," he said.

His father kept his first aid supplies in a Senator tobacco tin. He patched the boys up, rubbed liniment on their bruises. Later they sat around the fire, sore and smelling of camphor, passing around a bottle of rye. The liquor burned Ethan's tongue, but he liked it. His father told them stories about fights he'd been in or witnessed.

Ty had pulled out his tin of snuff, offering it around. Jack swatted the tin from his hand. "Too much of that'll bung up your nose."

"Yes sir."

"Keep the tin, though. Nothing better for a first aid kit."

After his father fell asleep, Ethan helped Ty gather the spilled flakes back into the tin.

"I don't know if I slipped or not," Ty confessed.

"That's OK," Ethan said. "I *was* thinking of girls."

* * *

"A date?"

"Yes sir."

"You're giving up your training for a date."

"A dance," his mother interrupted from the kitchen. "It'll be chaperoned, Jack."

"I don't care about chaperones. What I care about is—"

"We know, we know." Agnes Brand entered the dining room carrying the chicken. His mother had been a popular, beautiful girl. Ethan inherited her features and slender build, as well as a love of old books and gardens. Her sense of humor, too. "He's a child, Jack. So is Ty."

"Ty wants to go. Don't you?"

Tyler Rash looked up from his plate, mouth full of mashed potato. He nodded. Ty always ate as if the food might disappear. Once it was inside him, it seemed to. He hadn't filled out since coming to live with them, and he'd grown another inch.

Ethan had spent a week working out how to ask Leona Marsh to the dance. He'd written out his speech and asked Ty for editorial advice. Ty had suggested taking out the second "please," but otherwise didn't offer much help. Though older and clearly interested in girls, he was skittish around them. Around everyone, really, other than Ethan and his folks.

"He can miss one trip," his mother said. She was pleased her son was taking an interest in the opposite sex, and it amused her to defy her husband. Jack was in the minority for once. "There's more to life than chopping wood and foraging for mushrooms."

"This isn't education he'll get anywhere else. Our son's not prepared. He's—" Jack hesitated, as if working himself up to admitting something painful. "Weak."

Ethan hadn't touched his food. That tightening of the stomach had never gone away, really. He felt hurt and hate in equal measure, and he knew he'd caused the same feelings in his father.

"There are other types of strength," his mother said.

"Look at him. The hair, the clothes. He's never taken a word I said seriously."

"That's simply not true. He's tried."

"Trying gets you killed," Jack said.

Ethan met his father's stare. "I'm not going."

"You sure about that? Can't walk this one back, son."

"I'm never going with you again."

For a second, his father's face contorted with pain. Jack truly believed in the gospel of survival. In his mind, he was preparing his son for a harsh and unforgiving world. Ethan wondered how his father would react.

But his father didn't react. Jack ate his dinner in silence. He cleared the plates and loaded the dishwasher. Later on, Ethan and Ty lay in their sleeping bags, listening to his parents argue into the night.

He wished Jack Brand wasn't his father. He also knew the kid on the other side of the room was wishing the very opposite.

* * *

A year later:

Snow on the ground and the sun falling fast. Still the boys marched, neither willing to be the first to stop. Stopping meant admitting defeat. Worse, it meant admitting Jack was gone.

Ty's snowshoes glided easily over the frozen ground. Ethan felt the cold deep in his chest. His jacket and gloves weren't meant for a Canadian winter.

Another hour. Now the sun was only a suggestion of orange over the crest of the mountain. The shadows of the birch trees were growing longer. And miles yet to go, Ethan thought.

If they turned back now, it would be night when they rejoined the others. His mother and the volunteer searchers from Blaine, the two Cree trackers and the dive team. Refusing to make camp before nightfall, Ethan and Ty had ventured far ahead. Too far, Ethan thought. This was the second search they'd done. Now winter had set in. What could they expect to find?

He wanted to give up. But giving up meant acknowledging Jack Brand wouldn't be coming back. Could he live with that? Never knowing what happened to his father?

He wouldn't get a choice. The crust of frozen snow abruptly gave way. Ethan and Tyler Rash found themselves dropped waist deep in white.

Struggling was useless. Out of breath, Ethan watched as Ty laid his poles on the snow in a cross. Placing his hands in the center of the X, Ty pressed down, leveraging himself out of the snow. Ethan did the same.

Kneeling, he stared up at the jagged mountainside looming over the frozen field. The snow was too soft. Even if they crossed the field, they'd have to climb without proper gear. And in the dark. Impossible.

There was no conquering this. No learning its mysteries. Humbled, exhausted, Ethan thought: You're greater than I am. He's yours now.

"I'm turning back," he said.

Tyler Rash made no sign he'd heard. Since Ty had moved out of the Brand house, Ethan hadn't seen much of him. The teen had grown into a wild young man. A stranger.

"Said I'm turning back."

"Go ahead."

Every vaporous breath seemed to steal more heat. Ethan gestured around them. "What do you think you're gonna find? It's almost dark."

"Go back if you want."

"We can maybe try tomorrow—"

"Go."

Ty was staring at the mountain. Ragged sobs issued from his mouth.

"He's gone," Ethan said, as gentle as he could.

In response Ty started forward again, poles stabbing the ground. His shoes sank in the snow with each step. Still he kicked on. Soon Tyler Rash was only a blot on a white landscape.

Ethan started back the way they'd come. If he followed their tracks, he reckoned, he'd reach camp in four hours. His mother would be relieved. It had been selfish to leave her to worry, especially after losing her husband.

"He was right about you," Ty shouted across the field.

Maybe so. Ethan didn't reply. It would be too much like talking to a dead man.

6

"Did you resent him?" Brenda Lee asked. They'd finished their dinner and were lingering over the empty plates. Lucky's was closed, Mei in the kitchen doing prep for tomorrow's breakfast rush.

"Not at first," Ethan said. "I was happy. We shared a bedroom, took turns sleeping on the floor. Like finding a long-lost brother."

"Where was the kid's family in all this?"

Ethan shrugged. "Ty would mention his mother once in a while. She was just a kid herself when she had him. He didn't know much about his dad."

"So he stayed with your family," Brenda Lee said.

Ethan pushed his plate away, rested his chin on his hand. Strange to have been so close to someone, then lose track of them so completely. Now Tyler Rash was dead, and finding his killer had fallen to Ethan's department.

Brenda Lee's pen had leaked ink on the counter. She blotted it with a napkin and stared at the mess on her hands. "So why did Ty leave?" she asked.

"You might not believe this, Officer Page, but the cool, handsome, and all-around exceptional man seated next to you wasn't like that at fourteen. I hated my father and wanted desperately to please him. With Ty, I thought I had an ally. Instead, he took my father's side. It was the two of them against me."

"That's got to be hard on a teenager."

"What Nettie said was true, though. Ty was more of a son—the kind of son my father wanted, anyway. My mother recognized what that was doing to me. I think she asked Ty's folks to take him back."

"What does that do to a child?" Brenda Lee asked. "I'm sure your mother thought that was the right thing, but Ty must have felt unwanted. Unloved."

"I think he did. The Sterankos took him in after that, but I don't think Ty ever trusted anyone again. And when my father died..."

He couldn't finish the sentence. An image flew to mind from Jack Brand's funeral. Two teenagers in the church vestibule nearly coming to blows. Ty had been more grief-stricken by the disappearance, but also more hopeful. He felt the search should continue indefinitely until the remains were found. A grave with no body was a joke to him. A grim irony that at the moment, Tyler Rash was a body with no grave.

"And that was the last time you saw him?" Brenda Lee asked.

Ethan nodded. "Yeah. I went to work, then college briefly, then the Marines. When I came back I joined the department, got married, had the boys... I don't know what Ty was up to during all that time." *While I was having a life,* he thought.

"Probably not a nine-to-five job, in any case. Do you think he built the tunnel himself?"

"Wouldn't surprise me."

Brenda Lee flipped back in her notebook. Behind her glasses her eyes looked red. A long day, with longer days to come.

"So as a teen, Ty lived with your family," she recited. "Then with Nettie and Mac. Ty leaves them once he's old enough, and doesn't come back until he's about thirty. He stays in their shed for a few months, slipping them some cash. Then Ty disappears. Nobody knows where he went. Nobody looks. And at some point after that, he ends up shot in a tunnel that nobody knew existed till today."

"That covers it," Ethan said.

"It doesn't cover anything."

"No, I guess it doesn't."

Brenda Lee closed the book and stood up. "I've got to wash this ink off."

Ethan paid the bill and moved his rook down the board to certain doom. He let himself out. For an evening in August, it felt cold. Food and coffee hadn't settled his stomach. The memories had only made it worse.

He owed something to Tyler Rash. Whatever sequence of events had left Ty dead in a half-finished tunnel, he deserved better.

A car sped down H Street, well over the speed limit. Ethan thought of calling it in. But the car was already looping toward the interstate. He didn't feel much like a lawman at the moment. He felt like a lost kid in a darkening wilderness.

Or a tunnel.

* * *

Portable construction lights had been set up on tripods around the shed and the opening in the ground. Between the lights, the barricade tape, and the canopy, the crime scene looked conspicuous at night.

Ethan had no particular reason to stop by. The property wasn't on his way home. But he drove the beat-up Dodge into the pasture, following the tread marks left by the vans. The rain had eased off. The pasture was still. The truck's high beams tossed more shadows over the break in the ground.

Mercy Hayes had drawn the short straw for night watch. As the junior officer, there were a lot of short straws. A former naval officer and single mother from the Lummi of Lhaq'temish Nation, Mercy had been working security at a casino before joining the department. She'd taken to the job swimmingly.

As she loped over to the truck, Ethan passed her a takeout cup. "Fast food coffee. Not good but it's hot."

She took a sip. "You're right on both counts, Boss."

"How are Nettie and Mac holding up?"

"They seem pretty shaken," Mercy said. "Were you really out here to buy a horse?"

"Wasn't buying, exactly." Ethan added, "I was looking for something that would engage my kids more than their phones."

"Davy isn't at the phone age yet, thank God." Mercy's son was three years old. "Why not a dog?"

"Didn't seem grand enough."

From the trees to the north, the high-pitched yipping of a screech owl. Mercy sipped her coffee, gripping the cup with both hands for every bit of warmth.

"Can I say something, Boss? You don't mind if I call you Boss instead of Chief, do you? Where I come from, a chief is ... well, a chief."

Ethan nodded.

"I'm not a parenting expert," Mercy said. "And I'm not saying a grand gesture like getting a horse wouldn't be nice. Just that there's other types of gestures, too."

"Worth thinking on," Ethan said. "You're all right here?"

"I'll be fine. Thanks for the coffee, Boss."

* * *

The inside of his house was dark. Ethan took a Coors out onto the porch and sat with his legs up on the rail. Like Henry Fonda in

My Darling Clementine, he thought. Did Fonda get the girl in that one?

In Boston it would be close to midnight. Too late for a call. Ben and Brad would be asleep, he hoped. He missed them.

Ethan had purchased the vacant lot next door to his house on Kickerville Drive. Occasionally, when he looked out his window, he'd see his coyote out there. Blue-eyed coyotes were a rare mutation. Last year, one had taken to frequenting the town. Now she was raising her pups. Buying the lot had been a reasonably smart investment, but part of him had done it just to give the animals a place to roam.

The grand gesture, he thought. What it amounts to is too much loneliness when the kids weren't there.

Since Jazz had left there had been one serious relationship. Steph Sinclair was everything he'd wanted—funny and cutting, sensual and strong, yet vulnerable, too. She'd also been married. When Steph had broken things off to focus on her family, she'd left a void in Ethan Brand's life. There had been dalliances since her, but nothing lasting.

He thought of the woman with the SUV. The one who hadn't needed his help. If the bikers had pushed their luck, she would have responded ferociously. Ethan didn't doubt that for a moment. It wasn't temper and it wasn't cruelty. What was it, then?

An old-fashioned sense of justice, perhaps. Or manners.

The last thing he needed right now was a federal agent in Blaine with a hair trigger. All the same, he wouldn't object to seeing her again. What was it about dangerous women?

No coyotes tonight. A strong breeze off the bay. He thought about the lost and the dead. How soon before he reached a point where the deceased people in his life outnumbered the living?

He'd lied to Brenda Lee Page in one respect. Ethan had seen Tyler Rash one final time.

7

From Blaine to Fort Lejeune to the Helmand Valley had been a series of shocks. But they were nothing compared to the trip home.

His fire team had stopped the LAV at a stretch of highway a few miles from the Forward Operating Base. The spot had been swept only two days ago. To Ethan those were the most dangerous areas. Familiarity and repetition could make even the sharpest person careless.

He'd been zero-five-twentying a short distance from the detonation. Shrapnel had torn into his knee, buttocks, and thigh but hadn't done lasting damage. His left foot had taken the brunt. All things considered, Ethan had been lucky. His teammates, Corporal Benjamin Henriques and PFC Bradley Dobbs, hadn't survived.

He remembered a screaming pain, crawling to check on Ben and Brad. Passing out and being dragged by the rest of the 2nd Light Armored to the FOB, then choppered to Bagram, to Frankfurt, and then on to Bethesda, Maryland.

In the hospital he'd processed the news of the loss. His body healed. He learned to function with his injury. A doctor prescribed him oxycontin for the pain.

The numbing feeling of the drug came to order his days. It wasn't the way it deadened the pain in his leg so much as how it deadened everything else. The pills made memory and emotions hazy. They set up a barrier between present and past, between Ethan and the world. That distance allowed him to sleep and not to think.

Out of the hospital, hobbling with a cane, rehabilitating a body that would never be exactly as it was. The heel plate and prosthetic allowed him to move, but the ankle ached if he exerted himself too much.

His physician had wanted to wean him off. Ethan had doubled the dosage. He'd come to rely on the feeling, the comfort, of nothingness.

Who knew better than him what dosage he needed? Who could say he didn't deserve to go to hell exactly as he pleased?

Instead of hell, he ended up back in Blaine for his mother's funeral. At twenty-six, with no direction or prospects and a gallery of memories of fallen friends, Ethan had needed that nothing feeling. Enough to head down to the Blue Duck Saloon and ask around to see if he could score. Sure enough, a low-level dealer connected to the McCandless family had sold him two vials. Ethan would have paid any price.

An abyss had opened up inside of him. He was smart enough to know the pills wouldn't close it. But they pushed the question of *why them and not me?* from his mind.

The next time he'd gone to the Blue Duck, the dealer was nowhere around. Ethan's supply was dwindling. He'd gone home and chased one of his remaining pills with a bottle of Crown Royal.

The next day Tyler Rash came to see him.

Still woozy and fighting a protracted engagement with nausea, Ethan had sat on his porch with his head hung over the rail.

When he looked up, a man was standing in the driveway. Ethan didn't recognize him at first.

Ty had let his hair grow to his shoulders. His beard was darker than his hair. He wore camo-patterned fatigues and a padded camo vest over his shirt. His belt had a sheath for a knife, and a hatchet hung from a leather thong. Ty took a tin of snuff from a pouch on his belt and pinched some.

"Saw you at the Duck," Ty said. "When'd you get back in town?"

He couldn't remember. A week ago? Two? Nausea assailed him and he bent over the rail to spit.

Ty crossed to the porch. He parked himself on the railing, staring at Ethan for a long moment.

"Your folks were good to me. Figure I owed it to them to see if there's something I can do for you." Ty watched him wipe his chin on his T-shirt. "You're a damn mess, Ethan."

All he managed in reply was a mumbled, "No idea what I been through."

"Probably not," Ty said. "Probably you got plenty of reasons for hanging around the Duck asking for what you're asking for."

How did he know?

"When you see a guy circling the drain, you ought to say something. This is a bad fit, Ethan. It's not what Jack would have wanted for you."

"I stopped caring what he wanted a long time ago."

"Sure. 'Cept your mother wouldn't like it any better. Would she?"

"Go to hell."

"Once I've said my piece."

Another bout of nausea doubled him over. When he looked up Tyler Rash had gone inside the house. He returned with a towel, holding it out for Ethan to take.

Ethan ignored it. He looked for his cane and saw it had fallen into the flowerbed below the porch. He'd spat up on it.

"Say what you've gotta say."

"You won't find any more of that junk in town," Ty said. "Won't stop you from getting it elsewhere, if you're really committed to washing out. My guess, though, this is more a case of self-pity. Feeling sorry for yourself."

His words seemed both unfair and accurate. They hurt. Furious, Ethan pushed up and rushed at Ty, determined to beat the man's head in. Ty didn't even have to block. Woozy from drink and unsure on his feet, Ethan had fallen forward, crashing against the boards of the porch. He found himself staring at the worn hiking boots on his mother's welcome mat.

"You only think you're lost. Remember what your father said? No such thing as being lost."

"Didn't save him, did it?"

"No, it didn't. Doesn't mean he was wrong."

Strong hands lifted Ethan and deposited him in his mother's chair. Ty looked down at him with a mixture of wistfulness and sorrow.

"You're not much like him, Ethan. So why share the same fate? See if you can do a bit better."

Ethan had dismissed Ty's words, watching the man drive off in the dirty white Mustang. But as the days wore on and his supply kept dwindling, Ethan comprehended the wisdom in what Ty had said. Jack Brand had rejected society. Ethan had only found himself outside it for the moment.

One morning he'd woken up and flushed the remainder of the pills. The withdrawal had been ugly, but he'd gutted through it. Each night was an endurance test. The next morning was never easier.

Weeks passed. Months passed. He didn't see Tyler Rash again.

One day, Chief of Police Frank Keogh knocked on his door and told him of an opening in the department. Frank wanted someone who had been up close with violence and wouldn't rush to perpetuate it. Before he left, Frank had given Ethan advice that would change his life. "You want to find anything worth looking for, son, you need to look beyond yourself."

Words to live and die by. And a debt Ethan owed, both to Frank Keogh, and to the dead man in the tunnel.

8

"I've seen some appalling things in my time." Gus Murphy stood over the side table in the department's muster room, shaking his head in dismay. "This, though. This, Ethan, is worse than a crime. It's a humanitarian crisis."

The deputy sheriff picked up one of the single-serving boxes of cereal laid out for the meeting. He held it up accusingly.

"Corn flakes, Ethan? Really?"

"You should have sprung for donuts," Moira Sutcliffe agreed. The State Patrol commander helped herself to milk, an orange, and a yogurt. "If we'd held this meeting at my office, there'd be donuts."

"Not even Raisin Bran," Gus muttered.

"We're saving those," Ethan said.

"And skim milk." Gus nudged Brenda Lee Page's shoulder. "Does your chief really think we can fight crime on this gruel?"

Ethan drank coffee, used to the teasing. Gus and Moira had been commanders in their respective departments for years. He was junior to them, with a smaller force and only a year of being in charge. Gus was large and boisterous, Moira sharp-featured and acerbic. Despite the banter, both were competent professionals.

Also present were Jaspreet Gill from the Border Patrol, who'd brought his own breakfast in Tupperware, Assistant District Attorney Hayley Hokuto, and at the end of the table, across from Ethan, the woman with the SUV. Moira introduced her as Agent Vonetta Briggs of the DEA.

"If you're done critiquing the fare, we can get started," Ethan said.

Brenda Lee Page had prepared a slideshow, leading them through the discovery of the body in the tunnel. Images from the scene appeared on the overhead projector, dissolving into the next slide with a sound effect like wind chimes.

"The body hasn't been positively identified as of yet," Brenda Lee said. "Personal effects found on the corpse and in its proximity include Timberline boots in men's size 11, a man's leather belt, a tin of Copenhagen tobacco, and a wallet carrying a driver's license in the name of Tyler Rash."

"Anyone know him?" Moira asked.

Ethan nodded. "Not for years, though."

"This Mr. Rash have a sheet?"

Brenda Lee read from the charges. "Trespassing. Hunting out of season. Nothing for the past decade, which is the very rough estimate we have on the timeline of our murder."

"Arrived at how?" Gill asked.

"A combination of factors including condition of the body, expiration date on the license, plus Mr. and Mrs. Steranko's testimony."

"What did the old couple tell you about the tunnel?" Vonetta Briggs asked. This morning she was dressed in a tailored gray suit with a black and gray tie. Aside from a nod, she hadn't looked in Ethan's direction.

"The Sterankos know nothing of the tunnel," Brenda Lee said. "Fourteen years ago Rash lived in the shed for a period of a few months. Stands to reason he constructed the tunnel in that time."

"And then four years went by before he died there?"

"We're still putting it together, but that seems like how it happened."

"They're probably holding something back," the DEA agent said. "If they saw him as a son, it's unlikely they'd tell you all of his secrets right away."

Ethan hid his irritation behind a sip of coffee. It went without saying that people didn't always tell the truth, especially when their friends and family were concerned. Another interview with Nettie and Mac was a certainty.

"What can *you* tell us about the tunnel?" Ethan asked her.

Vonetta Briggs didn't answer right away. Taking my measure, Ethan thought. He smiled at the agent. Measure away.

"A small time operation," she finally said. "Amateur, but a skilled amateur. From a design point of view, the construction was sound but the materials relatively primitive. Not much more sophisticated than Tom, Dick, and Harry from *The Great Escape*."

"World War Two prisoner movie," Hokuto whispered, in answer to Gill's quizzical look. The attorney asked, "Is it even possible one person built it alone?"

"Mr. Rash would've had to have been a very skilled, resourceful sort of person."

"He was," Ethan said.

"Even if the digging was accomplished by him alone, the tunnel was leading across the border. That almost makes it a certainty there was someone on the other side working with him."

"How can you be sure of that, if the tunnel wasn't completed?" Brenda Lee asked.

"Experience, Officer Page."

A tense few seconds passed, broken up by Gill dropping his spoon in the container. "A cross-border operation seems likely," he agreed. "We've seen partners on either side, digging to meet in the middle. Or one digs and the other sets up a hand-off on the other side. We're talking with the Mounties and checking real estate along Zero Avenue. We'll have to go back fourteen years to see who owned nearby property back then. That requires some digging—pardon the pun. Anything you can do to narrow down the time frame would be appreciated."

"So not cartel," Gus Murphy said.

"Not impossible but not likely."

Moira's empty yogurt container rolled on its side. "It's about time for one of us to speak the name of our favorite family of troublemakers. I'll bite. Does this have the McCandless brand on it, or what?"

"They haven't been charged in relation to tunnels," the ADA said.

Moira looked at Ethan. "What does the recognized expert on the McCandless family think?"

Before he could answer, Vonetta Briggs asked, "What makes Chief Brand the expert?"

"He's put two of them in jail."

Ethan's arrest and testimony had put the oldest, Seth McCandless, away for assault and trafficking. Jody, the youngest, was serving time for accessory to murder and attempted murder, Ethan being the target of Jody's attempt. Of the two, Seth was the more brutal, Jody the more cunning.

That left the middle child running things. On the surface, Sissy McCandless was as different from Seth and Jody as a dolphin from a school of sharks. Sissy wore granny glasses and hand-me-down sweaters. She ran a travel agency in Blaine, and had a degree in graphic design. Sissy had also sold the portion of the family homestead that was part of the township, meaning Blaine PD no longer had jurisdiction there. Ethan suspected Sissy McCandless had masterminded the crimes that had put Jody away, giving her control of the family business. Suspected, but couldn't prove.

Despite that, and for reasons he didn't quite understand, Ethan was fond of Sissy. Growing up the only sister of Seth and Jody had been rough. She'd found a way to distinguish herself. Sissy McCandless was smart and resourceful, subtle, and all the more dangerous for it.

"Too early to say if they're involved," Ethan said. "If they were, it would be Seth. He was running things fourteen years ago. It's a possibility we'll look into."

"No relationship between Rash and the family?" Moira asked.

"Not that I know of."

"Which doesn't mean there isn't one."

"No, it doesn't," Ethan admitted.

"You seem to know Rash pretty well," she observed. Again that cool stare. Challenging him.

"Knew," he corrected. "A long time ago my parents took him in for a while."

"That presents something of a conflict of interest, doesn't it?"

For a moment the only sound was Gus struggling to open the plastic liner of a small box of Frosted Flakes.

"Officer Page is in charge of the investigation," Ethan said. "Authority in the case rests with her."

"Doesn't answer my question," Vonetta Briggs said.

Brenda Lee spoke up, stating the obvious for the DEA agent. "In a town as small as Blaine, ma'am, *everything* is a conflict of interest."

9

After the meeting, with Gus Murphy's last gripes about the lack of donuts fading away, Ethan returned to his office. He forced himself to attack the growing mountain of paperwork. If it grew any larger, he could start selling lift tickets.

No sooner had he written the first email, though, came a triple knock on the glass. DEA Agent Briggs opened the door before he could ask her in.

"Hope I wasn't too rough on you," she said. "Is this your first homicide?"

Ethan shook his head.

"But they're not all that common here, are they?"

"Thankfully not."

She sat down, crossing her legs and tugging the tail of her blazer smooth. "Chief Brand," she said.

"Ethan, if you like."

A smile. "Von, then. In my job, Ethan, homicide is all too common. Trafficking and diversion is a multinational business on a grand scale. The people involved treat human life as a relatively minor expense."

Ethan nodded.

"It seems likely to me," Von said, "that your Mr. Rash was in business for himself. The bigger operators likely got wind of this and took care of him, sealing him up in his own tunnel."

He considered the facts. It seemed to fit. Ty wasn't the kind of person to accept a boss, or ask for permission. "Why not say so during the meeting?"

"No offense, but I've dealt with a lot of small agencies."

"We've dealt with our share of larges ones," he said. "Again, no offense."

"I have a rule for myself. No conjecture during these multi-agency deals. It bogs things down and can lead to groupthink. And in the extremely rare cases where I'm wrong, it doesn't reflect well on the DEA."

"Good rule," Ethan said. "So why tell me now?"

The agent's expression remained cool. "Some things are better said one on one. Which brings me to my other point. Does Officer Page know?"

"Know what?"

"Whatever it is you're holding back," Von said. "As I said, I've dealt with a lot of small agencies."

He supposed he should take offense. Vonetta Briggs had gone from accusing him of incompetence to accusing him of tanking the investigation. She didn't seem to mean it as an insult. And she wasn't entirely off-base.

Von slid one of her cards onto the corner of Ethan's desk. He took the occasion to admire her nails once more. "My advice, Ethan, is to tell Officer Page everything, even if it's unflattering. She'll appreciate it in the long term. She's too smart not to."

Ethan looked at the card, embossed with the logo of the Drug Enforcement Agency. *Agent Vonetta Briggs, San Diego Division.*

She'd struck a line through San Diego and printed *Seattle* in tight purple script.

"I get the sense this one-on-one is less about advice than sizing me up," Ethan said. "The hired gun checking out the locals."

Von smiled. "You're not terribly hard to size up, Chief Brand."

"And how am I supposed to take that, Agent Briggs?"

"As a compliment," she said.

* * *

The fitness reports didn't seem to be writing themselves. Ethan was tempted to scrawl SATISFACTORY across all of them and kick any potential problems down the road. Next year might be better. Or it might not. But at least the reports wouldn't be cluttering his desk.

He liked his people. They'd been coworkers longer than subordinates, and he knew them, their families and their personal histories. That made it hard to judge their actions.

Hard, but necessary. Otherwise you ended up with a Cliff Mooney on your hands. Frank Keogh had cut Cliff slack, since Cliff was the mayor's nephew. The result had been disastrous. But then, Frank had cut Ethan himself slack on one or two occasions. The injury to his foot might have disqualified him for service. Frank had known about it, and simply looked the other way. How did a person know where to draw the line?

Maybe what mattered was that you drew it and held to it.

Brenda Lee knocked. Ethan was so grateful for the interruption he stood and ushered her in.

"Tyler's mother is still alive," Brenda Lee said. "Married and divorced twice, last known address in Snohomish. Heck and I were going to head over there to canvass."

"Only what," Ethan said, guessing there was a hitch.

"Only I won't make it back in time for the autopsy. Would you have time?"

"I'll make time," he said. Before she could leave, he added, "There's something I should have told you before. About Ty."

He drew the blinds, waited until Brenda Lee was seated. Telling his most trusted officer about the lowest point in his life wasn't something he enjoyed. At one point, Brenda Lee Page had been a rival for the job of chief. As he told her about his last meeting with Ty, he could see Brenda Lee's mind flitting back over their shared history. If this had been common knowledge, would Frank Keogh have chosen him as a successor for the job?

Brenda Lee didn't interrupt the story. When he was finished, she said, "I don't know whether to be thankful for your confidence or pissed you didn't tell me before."

Before he could reply, she struck a fist into the opposing palm.

"That's not true," Brenda Lee said. "Damnit, Ethan, you should have told me."

"I'm not proud of it," he said.

"And I'm not judging you. Hell, you'd just lost two friends, you were injured. I can't imagine what that was like. But Ethan, I'm working on a decade-old homicide. We need every bit of information we can get our hands on. The little things matter. You said it yourself yesterday, remember? For want of a nail?"

"I think Ben Franklin said that."

"Doesn't matter," Brenda Lee said. "If we can't trust each other, what do we have?"

* * *

At noon he headed to Lucky's to meet Arlene Six Crows and discuss her campaign for mayor. With an autopsy in the late afternoon, the last thing on his mind was politics. Arlene was already in the restaurant, holding court at the counter, a short and boisterous woman with a voice like a cannon fusillade. She was addressing a small crowd of truck drivers and locals.

"Fact is, our esteemed mayor dragged his feet over funding for the Indigenous Youth Center, but we got it passed. He dragged his feet on cleaning up the bay, but we did it anyway. Fact is, Eldon Mooney sees this place as suiting him and his rich friends to a T. I believe there's a wee bit of room for improvement."

"You have to admit, that Mooney's one hell of a sailboat captain," one of the regulars said.

"And that would be a boon to his campaign," Arlene said, "if he were running for mayor of Sea World."

Amid the laughter, she broke away and snagged Ethan by the arm, directing him toward the door.

"'Scuse me, ladies and gents," Arlene said. "I require a word with our illustrious chief of police."

On the street they kept walking, past the station, in the direction of the waterfront. The day was humid, almost cloudless. The last weeks of August in the Pacific Northwest could seesaw between summer and fall.

"Skipping lunch today?" Ethan asked.

"Some things are bigger than lunch. How's your speech coming along?"

He'd forgotten he was introducing Arlene at an event for—what was it for?

"Don't take this the wrong way, Ethan, but you're not exactly silver-tongued. Just a few remarks about our vision for the town."

"What exactly is our vision for the town?"

They passed the Drayton Harbor Oyster Company. Further down was the Ocean Beach Hotel, which had a very good and very pricey supper club attached. Both the hotel and supper club were owned by Wynn Sinclair, whose support and money were firmly behind Eldon Mooney.

"I know you've got a lot on your plate," Arlene said. "But this matters to me. I'm not white, not rich and not a man, which means I'm a long shot, even against a crumb-bum like Mooney. I need as much support as you can swing."

"The department can't take sides," he said.

"Not asking the department, I'm asking you."

"What exactly do you need from me?" Ethan asked.

"A few appearances here and there. The pancake breakfast with the Legion, I'd like you to introduce me."

"Sure."

"There's also a rumor you're a member of the Blaine Women's Book Club."

"Can't confirm nor deny," he said.

In fact, his ex had been a member. When Jazz moved out, she'd forgotten to cancel her membership. The books still arrived, once a month. Though he hadn't attended the discussions, Ethan had taken to reading the books when he had the time. It was good to have new things to think about. After a few months, and without his say-so, someone at the club had switched Jazz's name on the mailing label for his own.

"Well, if you *are* a member, I'd like you to bring me as a guest to the next meeting. What's the selection this month?"

Ceremony by Leslie Marmon Silko. The book had arrived two weeks ago. He was making slow progress, but enjoyed what he'd read.

"I can do that," he said. "What else?"

"Someone's been pulling up my yard signs," Arlene said.

"I'll look into that, but it's not exactly a hanging offense."

"More than the signs, Ethan."

She had led him down to the boarded-up old train station, covered with graffiti and littered with cigarette butts. A secluded spot with a view of Semiahmoo Bay over the tracks.

"I've been hearing people drive past my place late at night," Arlene said. "Gunning the engine, you know? Couldn't see the vehicle on account of the high beams were on."

"What happened?"

"Nothing 'happened.' They woke up half the damn block. Drove off after a while."

"Has anyone threatened you recently?" he asked.

"Nothing out of the usual. A few cranks that are pissed I'm running for mayor."

"You think the engine noise could be connected with Mooney's campaign?"

"Not officially," Arlene said. "Someone associated with him, though. Like that nephew of his."

"Cliff?" Ethan hadn't heard anything about Cliff Mooney for the better part of a year. "I doubt it, though he's dumb enough. You asked Cliff Mooney to change a bulb, he'd reach for the garlic."

Despite the joke, the city councilor's expression remained tense. Arlene hugged her arms around herself

"Maybe it's all in my head, Ethan, but I think there's someone out there who doesn't want me to win."

"I can assign a car to swing by your place," he said. "Maybe a protection detail, if you want."

"In a close race like this? I can't be showing up to peoples' houses with a bodyguard." Arlene managed a grin. "'Less it's Kevin Costner."

"I'll find time to speak to Cliff."

If Arlene Six Crows was refusing protection, there wasn't much he could do. Hopefully these were isolated incidents. The murder of Tyler Rash was enough to deal with without someone trying to interfere with the election by terrorizing one of the candidates. Or worse.

One more thing to worry about.

10

Unflappable was the word he would choose to subscribe Dr. Sandra Jacinto. Over the years, Ethan had watched the Whatcom County Medical Examiner handle a dozen death scenes and as many autopsies. The fifty-something Filipina was usually unbothered by the corpse, directing her team of assistants with good-natured efficiency, often bantering with Ethan in her casually flirtatious way. In the autopsy room in the basement of Bellingham General, Sandra was at home. Normally.

Today, however, there were no assistants in sight. He listened as Sandra dictated her notes, cataloging the remains of the body from the tunnel, weighing and measuring, taking samples for laboratory analysis. The remains had been peeled out of the clothing, leaving something that looked less like a corpse than a diagram of the human body with different sections missing. The skull and collected fragments were relatively clean. The hands, too. Sections of the torso were withered and shrunken, what remained of the skin like leather. Below the waist was a yellow, waxy section of hip and thigh. The body's faint smell reminded him of the tunnel.

Ethan was known to have a strong stomach. In Helmand, he'd seen bodies in worse condition, some of them people he'd known. No way to truly get used to it, but death no longer surprised him, either. The human form could be broken and torn apart in a multiplicity of ways.

But the remains on the slightly tilted autopsy table, laid out on that stainless steel, affected him more than he'd thought. Part of it was the decomposition, the mixture of wax and leather, bone and parchment. Partly it was thinking this was what remained of Tyler Rash. The kid he'd met in the forest, who'd come to live with him for a time. The man who'd intervened and tried to help him.

Something else, too. Ethan had been down in that tunnel. He'd seen the dead man's resting place, shared it for a brief while. Their lives had intersected over the years—in a way it was like viewing one possible outcome of his own life. *If Ty hadn't come to him that last time . . .*

Ethan left the room.

* * *

Out of her hospital smock, Dr. Sandra Jacinto dressed fashionably, in high waisted slacks and a crimson blouse. Her neckline plunged as far as she allowed it. The doctor placed two mugs of chamomile tea on her desk, slipping her shoes off and leaning back in her chair. She'd done her toenails in black.

"Did you know I'm psychic, Ethan?" Sandra said.

"When did this happen?" His stomach still hadn't settled, and he could only fake his end of the banter.

"The moment I got the call about the body in the tunnel. I knew you were going to ask me for two things: a name and a timeline."

"It's nice to be understood," Ethan said.

"Well, I hope you don't mind waiting. The body is an adult Caucasian male with no broken bones or distinguishing features. None left by the ravages of time, at least. No fingerprints. Shot twice from behind, in the head, with a .45 ACP round. Part of the lower palate is missing, but a good forensic dentist might be able to match an X-ray."

"DNA?"

"Amid the mummified and adipocere sections, I have several promising samples."

"In layman's terms, doc?"

"Find me a comparison, and I can match it."

Now that they were a room away from the body, the scientist in Sandra Jacinto came out. She explained how several of the factors of decomposition—moisture and heat and time and exposure—had contributed to the condition of the corpse.

"The tunnel acted as something of a coffin," the medical examiner said. "Did you know, in rural parts of Brazil where refrigeration isn't possible, they bury bodies to preserve them before autopsies can be performed?"

Ethan wasn't a fan of herbal tea, but took a sip to be polite. "So why isn't he just a skeleton?"

"All the above reasons plus his clothing. That soapy, waxy part, that's called saponification. Deposits of saturated fat. Other parts were mummified. The plastic at the bottom of the tunnel slowed decomposition as well. All of which makes for a very interesting specimen."

"And probably plays hell with our timeline," Ethan said.

Sandra nodded. She blew across the top of her mug before taking a sip.

"Ten years is as close as I'm willing to guesstimate," she said. "And I won't commit that to paper until soil samples and the lab results can be compared to the biomarkers. A year, either way. Maybe more. In cases like this, PMI, or post-modern index, is very troubling."

"The body was found with ID belonging to Tyler Rash," Ethan stated. "Rash hasn't been seen for about that long."

"That's probably him, then. Bring me dental charts and a DNA sample, and I'll confirm it."

He nodded, hesitated. "This might be a dumb question."

"I tell my students there are no dumb questions. It's a lie, of course, but it makes them feel better."

"The way he died," Ethan said. "There are no signs he suffered, are there?"

"Not a dumb question but an odd one," Sandra said. "The deceased was shot from behind, twice, at close range with a large caliber round. I imagine death would have been instantaneous. No disruption to the plastic other than a few fragments of skull, which indicates the body wasn't moving."

"Or moved?" Ethan asked.

"Every indication points to the tunnel being the site of death. Quick and painless."

Ethan thought of Tyler Rash being marched into the tunnel by an unknown assailant. Or leading his killer along willingly, never suspecting what was to come. Would that make it somehow better?

A question too philosophical for the morgue.

The department would get the lab results as soon as the tests were run. As the two of them were finishing up, Sandra's phone blared with music. "Dreams" by Fleetwood Mac. Her ring tone. She looked at the number and grinned.

"New boyfriend," Sandra said, hand over the mouthpiece. "He's twenty-eight and insatiable."

"Congratulations. I'll let myself out."

As he reached the door of her office, the doctor called his name. Ethan turned.

Sandra flashed him that grin again. "You wouldn't by any chance have a spare set of handcuffs you could loan me?"

11

A hunch can be a dangerous thing. Ethan ignored the one forming out of the background noise of his mind. Instead, he concentrated on the task at hand. Which right now happened to be teeth.

Thirty years ago the residents of Blaine had few options for dental work. A retired dentist had turned the main floor of his house into a part-time clinic. Dr. Lowry's niece worked as his receptionist. Ethan remembered the waiting room being full of antiques that children weren't allowed to touch, and the niece being kind and pretty. Cooking smells of fish or frying onions would waft down from the living quarters on the second floor.

Dr. Lowry himself had been gruff, a touch absent-minded, and smelled of a cloying aftershave. He didn't like kids. His scraping and prodding had always seemed a little vindictive.

Now the house was gone, the clinic relocated to a professional building around the corner from City Hall. Dr. Lowry had been retired for decades. His business had been taken over by Dr. Adichie, a trim Black man from Senegal, now approaching retirement age himself. Ethan wondered what happened to Lowry's niece.

Dental charts alone couldn't prove identification. They could only confirm an ID. X-rays and charts, even old ones, could be compared by a forensic odontologist to the teeth of skeletal remains.

Ethan didn't know if the adult Tyler Rash had ever visited a dentist. But in the year Ty lived with Ethan's family, his mother had made Ty accompany him to Dr. Lowry's office. Somewhere in the late dentist's records might be a file containing Ty's charts.

The clinic's receptionist didn't have a Tyler Rash in her computer. She explained that only the records of those patients who'd continued on with Dr. Adichie had been digitized. The hard copies weren't in the filing room. Maybe the dentist knew where they'd gone. Could Ethan please wait?

He could. Ethan browsed the magazines in the reception area. World affairs, fashion. A perfume advertisement caught his eye, a black and white image of a famous actress astride a horse. The animal had a black coat and looked nothing like his horse, but had a white blaze on its face.

Ethan caught himself. When had he started thinking of Trim Reckoning as *his* horse?

"A pleasant afternoon, Chief Brand. This way." Dr. Adichie spoke with a faint French accent. They passed a row of alcoves, each containing a dentist's chair and a young technician cleaning or flossing a patient. The clinic was busy.

In his office, the dentist slipped on a pair of nitrile gloves. "Open, please."

"This is more of a business visit," Ethan said. "I need the charts of an old patient of Dr. Lowry's."

"Ah." The dentist seemed curious. "Is this connected to that tunnel business? I heard someone in the waiting room mention you had found a body."

Ethan didn't deny it.

"Unfortunately, Chief, the older records were stored for a time in my garage. My daughter was performing an experiment for her science project. It involved magnesium."

He could see where this was going. "They burned up?"

"Worse," the dentist said. "The sprinkler was set off. Damp paper and film. We had to dispose of them."

"Worth a try," Ethan said.

"I wish I could be of help. If it's any consolation, my daughter's now on the faculty of WSU."

Dr. Adichie showed him out, adding a gentle reminder. It had been a few months since his last cleaning.

* * *

The hunch kept nagging at him. Ethan phoned every dental office in Blaine and Bellingham. Still no luck. Had the times his mother dragged Ty to the dentist been the only visits of the teen's life? There was something sad about that.

He drove to the Steranko property, taking the long way so he could drive past the scene. The tent and cordon were still in place. Heck Ruiz waved as he approached. The young officer looked like he had something to say.

Hector Ruiz had earned his nickname from his aversion to swearing. A family man and a good all-around officer, Heck was especially gifted at talking to kids. Not everyone in the department was—Ethan remembered Brenda Lee Page once asking a thirteen-year-old why he wasn't familiar with the town bylaws. Mal Keogh would treat juveniles as babies who could talk but couldn't reason. In contrast, Heck listened to kids. He spoke to them with respect for the complexities of their young lives. An admirable skill to have.

"Aren't you supposed to be canvassing with Brenda Lee?" Ethan asked.

"Mal asked me to cover for him. Says he can't make it in today." Heck pointed at the sky. "Least the weather's not as cruddy as it was yesterday."

Not coming in on a day off was one thing. "Did Mal say why?"

"Not to me, Chief."

Troubling. With a decade-old murder to solve and an election coming up, this wasn't the time for the department to be short-staffed. "If you need someone to spell you for a washroom break," he told his officer.

"Thanks. Hey Chief?"

Heck dug something out of his back pocket and handed it over. A business card. Ethan recognized the purple slash through *San Diego*. Vonetta Briggs.

"Where'd you get this?" he asked.

"The lady herself. She stopped by about half an hour ago. Asked me a whole crap-ton of questions."

"Did Agent Briggs happen to mention why she's taken such an interest in our case?"

Heck shook his head. "Actually, Chief, most of her questions were about you."

12

Heck had thought the agent was making small talk. At least at first. "She asked did I like working here, what you were like as a boss. How you got along with the rank and file."

"I hope you lied convincingly," Ethan said.

"Then she got personal. Did Chief Brand handle a lot of calls himself? Did personal relationships ever make that tough?"

He had an idea what Vonetta Briggs was up to. Questioning his officers behind his back went beyond sussing out the capabilities of the local department. The agent suspected him—of what, he didn't know.

"And what did you say?"

Heck scratched the back of his neck. Conflict wasn't something the young officer enjoyed.

"I said it's tough, a small town, everyone knows each other, but you usually do a pretty good job. She asked about this fella in the tunnel, if it concerned me that you and him were friends. I didn't answer. Figured I'd said too much already."

"*Does* it concern you?" Ethan asked.

"I dunno, Chief. You grew up here. I guess it'd be weird if you *didn't* know the guy."

He suspected Heck Ruiz wasn't giving him a full answer. But why should he expect one? Who shares their full opinion about their boss with the boss himself?

"It's good you told me," Ethan said. "And if you think I'm overstepping, let me know."

"What are you going to do about Agent Briggs?" Heck asked.

A good question.

* * *

The inside of the Steranko home was a tribute to their long personal and professional relationships, which were as entwined as Nettie and Mac themselves. Rodeo buckles gleamed on the walls next to Nettie's silver spoons. Photos of derby winners, of the couple with friends and the odd celebrity. Ethan recognized Tammy Wynette and Chris LeDoux.

Mac was asleep on the living room couch, an old Hudson's Bay blanket over his knees. Ethan followed Nettie silently through the kitchen to the screened-in back porch. He could see the doors of the stable from here, the hilly pasture behind it.

"Mac wasn't sleeping all that well before this foofaraw," Nettie said. "He blames himself."

"For Ty, you mean?"

She eased onto a swinging bench moored to the ceiling with chains. Ethan pulled an old deck chair in front of her.

"Mac wanted kids more than I did. Broke his heart when the doc said I wasn't built for it. We discussed adoption once or twice. The business and travel just took so damn much out of us."

After gazing at the field for a moment, Nettie seemed to remember he was there. She summoned a smile.

"You have kids," she recalled.

"Two boys. They live with their mom. I get them in the summer and every other Christmas."

"How do you deal with not seeing them all the time?"

"Not as well as I should," Ethan admitted. He steered the conversation back to business. "When Ty wasn't living with you, did he keep in touch?"

"How would he? The boy never owned a telephone in his life. Didn't have a fixed address half the time."

"Ty left your place in his late teens, then came back for a few months when he was thirty. In between, any idea what he was up to?"

Nettie watched a fly settle on the mesh of the screen door. She didn't answer until it had flitted off.

"I know he spent some time across the border," she said. "Up in that same wilderness where your father . . ."

He nodded to show that it was all right to mention Jack Brand.

"Ty never got over Jack being gone," she said. "He told us he'd gone up a few times to look, but didn't find any trace."

"After our search party, you mean."

Nettie nodded. "Years after. I don't mean he loved Jack more than you did. But you had your mother, friends, girls. All Ty felt he had was the outdoors, and Jack was the one that showed him how to thrive out there."

"He must have had a passport, then," Ethan said.

"Well, you didn't need one back in the day. Might've got one later."

"Your address was on his driver's license. Did you get mail for him? Packages?"

"Sometimes."

"Any of it still around?"

"Wouldn't think so. I'll root around after Mac's done his nap."

Nettie Steranko was looking tired herself. Ethan still had questions, but tried to prioritize them. "The second time he stayed in your shed. Did you get the sense Ty was in some sort of trouble?"

"'Fraid I did." Nettie pushed one foot along the porch, swinging the bench listlessly back and forth.

"Criminal?" he asked. "Financial? Drugs?"

"I wouldn't know. Just got the sense Ty didn't want to see anybody."

Ethan suspected there was more to that. "Did anybody want to see him? Come by the house?"

"Can't recall."

"Did Ty ever mention the McCandless family?"

She shook her head. "I'm sorry, Ethan. It was ages ago."

He stood up. "I better get out of your hair pretty soon. The reason I came over was to see if you had anything of Ty's. Anything personal, like an old comb with his hair on it."

"Looking for DNA?" Noticing his surprise, Nettie said, "I'm old, not dumb, Chief. I know from the TV that DNA's how they identify folks."

"Even an old envelope he licked," Ethan said.

"Like I told you, Ty wasn't much for writing letters. But I'll have a look."

She insisted on walking him out. They left through the back so as not to disturb her husband. As they passed the barn, Nettie's mood brightened. "Good news about your horse. The doc says it's only a sprain. No lasting damage to the suspensory ligament. Once she's her old self again, you and me can knock out a fair price."

"To be honest, I'm not sure I'm still in the market," he said.

The old woman didn't reply, but her expression told him that his ownership of Trim Reckoning was a foregone conclusion.

They said their goodbyes. Before he drove away, Ethan watched her climb the steps of the front porch. One at a time, dragging up the left leg to join the right. On the second step from the top Nettie paused.

"You all right?" he called through the window of the truck.

"Fine and dandy," Nettie said. "Just had a thought. You're looking for things of Ty's right? I'm surprised you didn't find any up at the house."

"Whose house?" he asked, tumbling to the answer even as Nettie confirmed it.

"Yours," she said. "'Tween your mom and dad, they must have kept something of his."

13

Brenda Lee Page was at her desk, eating a cold shrimp stir-fry and typing reports. Still no location for Tyler Rash's mother. Heck Ruiz was in the field, following up on leads from Rash's spotty employment history. Ty hadn't stayed at any one job too long, and most of the employers didn't remember him.

One did. Fifteen years ago, Ty had worked as a dishwasher at a diner outside Spokane. The owner had remembered him, only because Ty had insisted on payment in cash, and had parked his Mustang in the owner's backyard. A good employee, a quiet man, who was simply gone one morning.

If Ty had been alive he would be forty-five. Middle-aged. Ethan's memories of him were of a teenager or a man in his twenties. A thirty-five-year-old Ty had been shot twice, and they were no closer to getting a sense of who that man was, let alone finding his killer. Did Ty have a love life, a circle of friends? Or was he as alone he seemed?

"I'm going to send his DNA sample in," Brenda Lee said. She was using her chopsticks to spear the shrimp, popping them in her mouth as if on a shish kabob. "Maybe Rash was using an alias, and got picked up and typed in some other state."

"Anything you need?" Ethan asked.

"A good night's sleep, a raise in pay . . ." Brenda Lee brought up an email on her desktop. "Jaspreet Gill from the Border Patrol might have something on the tunnel. He wants to meet tomorrow afternoon."

Ethan volunteered to go, and she didn't argue. "How's your horse?" she asked.

"Banged up but still standing."

"Her and me both," Brenda Lee said.

* * *

Unsure what to do with himself, Ethan headed back to Lucky's. Sometimes after a day spent in the company of death, his stomach would surprise him with a fierce hunger. A rejection of mortality, perhaps. Food and company, familiar surroundings. None of that today. He needed coffee and a momentary distraction, and above all, time to process what he'd learned.

Mei Sum had the chessboard in front of him before he'd settled onto the stool. The café had emptied out after the lunch hour rush. Mei had her own meal sitting behind the register.

He stared at the board, trying to remember the strategy he'd started the game with. Strategy and tactics were different, he reminded himself. Strategy was the big picture, tactics how you dealt with the roadblocks in front of you. If you could master both skills and somehow knit them together . . .

But all he saw today was a slog of pawns up the board. He moved one. Mei flitted over and slid her bishop into check.

"Toldja it was useless," she said.

"There's no trash talking in chess."

"Course there is," Mei said. "There's trash talking in everything."

Mei, now eighteen, was a prodigy who had finished her first year of college over the summer. Bound for university in the fall,

Mei possessed an analytical mind that Ethan envied. Maybe she'd get tired of Stanford and join the department—unlikely, but then so was victory.

And then there it was. Her bishop move had been meant to push Ethan's king into a trap. But a jump of the knight not only blocked the bishop but revealed a check of his own. Ethan examined it a second and third time. He could find no fault with the move.

Had Ty felt the same, just as sure of himself, as he led his killer along the tunnel? Or had he crawled forward in the dark, knowing that the end was approaching? Ethan couldn't picture Tyler Rash in either scenario. Too close to the victim, he thought. How many times had he heard the same lines from friends of family of the deceased? *Not like him. She wouldn't do that. Not the person we knew.*

The fact was, he didn't know Ty well enough to rule out smuggling or drugs or any number of illicit activities. Ty might have been executed by the McCandless family, or been double-crossed by a partner. Or killed to cover up another crime.

And yet something didn't fit. The hunch, which he couldn't even bring himself to name, kept surging through his thoughts.

Ethan watched as Mei returned to the board. Her expression changed to a frown. He'd seen something she hadn't, and her response was to get her king out of the fray. On the next move he captured her bishop.

"Nice skewer, Chief," Mei said. "Had me there for a moment. Must be I was distracted."

"Or maybe I'm gaining on you."

She laughed at that.

"I been distracted a lot this week," Mei said. "Can I tell you something, Chief? I think I'm in love."

Ethan looked up. Mei didn't often confide in him. "That's a nice feeling," he said. "First time?"

Mei nodded. "I really like her. You know Jess, right?"

"Jessica Sinclair?"

Ethan frowned at the board, trying not to give anything away. Jess was the oldest child of Wynn and Steph Sinclair. For a while, after Ethan's wife had left for Boston, he and Steph had seen each other.

The affair had begun quietly and slowly. It had deepened during midnight walks, the odd rendezvous at the Orca Fin Motel. Later, when Steph was thinking of leaving her husband, they'd met at Ethan's home.

Steph had opted to stay with her husband. The decision hadn't been easy. Both Jess and her brother, Wynn Junior, had learned of their mother's affair. Between love and family, family had won. The Sinclairs renewed their vows in a ceremony on the beach that had cracked Ethan's heart even further.

"I didn't realize the family was back in town," he said, as casually as he could manage. After the ceremony, the Sinclairs had gone on an extended vacation to their vacation residence in Hawaii.

"Her mom and brother are still on the big island. Just Jess and her dad at home now."

"What happens when college starts?" he asked.

"No big deal, Chief. Jess and I text every day. Send each other videos. You really sure you want to move there?"

Three moves later he was staring at checkmate.

Ethan began resetting the pieces, thinking that everyone seemed to be in love these days except him.

* * *

Home. The last place he'd expected to look for evidence.

Ethan opened a Coors and pulled up a Randy Travis playlist. Was there ever another voice like his? Agnes Brand hadn't thought so. The first song was her favorite. "Diggin' Up Bones." A fitting choice given his current chore.

His mother hadn't been much of a pack rat. After she died, Ethan had sorted through her possessions. Anything relating to Tyler Rash was either long gone, or boxed up at the back of the storage closet.

To get at the boxes meant moving his kids' bikes and sporting equipment, then the Christmas stuff, and finally the crates of household things Jazz hadn't taken with her. Place settings and cutlery they'd been given for their wedding. Some multi-attachment food processor Ethan couldn't figure out. Part of him always believed Jazz would come back. Maybe it was time to admit that if his ex wanted this stuff, she would have taken it? The life she'd made for herself in Boston didn't include any of it. Or him.

After two more beers he'd dug his way to the back of the closet. The sun had set and he was working by the hallway light. Another confined space, he thought. Another set of remains.

Three boxes. One held his mother's wedding dress, a copy of a poetry book from her childhood. Binders of photographs of her side of the family. The second was full of old clothes. Ethan dragged it out and rummaged through, seeing nothing he could pinpoint as Ty's.

That left only one box, the smallest. His mother's printing on the top flap told him what to expect inside. *Jack*, it read.

Death certificate. Condolence cards. Newspaper clippings about the disappearance. Agnes Brand had saved all of it—for him, Ethan realized.

He brought the box to the kitchen but found he didn't have the energy to sort through it tonight. What would he find among a box of old papers, anyway? Nothing that would have Ty's DNA. The box would have to wait for the morning.

The toolshed was the only other spot where a trace of the dead man might be found. Ethan turned on the porch light. He moved to the small structure to the left of the house and found the key for the padlock. The garden tools lurked in the shadows, as if shunning him for a summer's worth of neglect.

Past the tools he saw an old Radio Flyer sled, a car seat both boys had long since grown out of. An unstrung bow, a slug sticker, his father's old tool chest. Bits and pieces of lives, but not the ones he was looking for.

As he gave up, he heard coyote song from the property next door. One voice and then a second in response. Sounding mournful tonight, he thought, but at least you're not alone.

14

His dreams were often of shipwrecks. A midnight squall, bells clanging, lifeboats being lowered by desperate hands. And Ethan Brand at the center, amid the noise and panic, rain-lashed and unmoving.

The deck rose and tilted beneath him in the dark. Foam spilled over the sides. In the dream, his left foot was intact. He felt the cold briny water sweep over it, up to his ankle.

He needed to call for someone. It was his duty to call. Yet he was silent.

Ethan could never decipher his own motives in the dream. Was he frozen in panic? Or the only one *not* panicking? Or a ghost, simply watching the storm unfold? Usually the dream would simply end, but this morning there were new sensations. Hoofbeats. A glimpse of a large and terrified animal charging about on deck.

The storm dissipated. He was in his bed, but not alone. The woman in his arms ran her hands over his chest, kissing his throat, raising herself above him.

"What took you so long, Chief?" Sissy McCandless said.

The dream grew more explicit.

Loud persistent knocking drew him back to the world. Alone in his bedroom, Ethan Brand rubbed his face. The dream mystified him, but also left him feeling guilty. Sissy McCandless was a criminal. What did that portend?

The knocking grew louder as he dressed in trousers and his round-the-house shoes, making sure the heel plate was snug. Trudging down the hall, he saw Brenda Lee Page through the front door's window. She stood on the doorstep, holding a white paper bag.

"I found Tyler Rash's mother," she said. "Buy me breakfast, and I'll tell you about her."

She was already past him, heading for the kitchen. Ethan closed the door.

"I don't have much in the fridge," he said.

Brenda Lee held up the bag. "I stopped at Bordertown Grill. You can pay me back. No delivery fee."

"You're all heart."

He filled the coffee maker and they sat at the table. Brenda Lee laid out tamales and breakfast burritos and an army of sour cream and picante sauce. She eyed the box with his father's name perched on the table's end.

"Memory Lane?" she asked.

"Might be something in there related to Ty. They were close."

"So I keep hearing." Brenda Lee unwrapped a tamale and stabbed it into the sour cream. Noticing he wasn't digging in, she paused. "You OK?"

"Strange dream, that's all. Nothing coffee can't cure."

When they each had a cup before them, Brenda Lee told him what she'd learned.

"His mother was born Emily Maynard. Married at seventeen and became Emily Rash. Divorced, remarried, became Emilia Lazzaro."

"Emilia."

"Nice touch, isn't it? She never officially divorced that one, but when they separated, she changed her name to Emily Heller. She and Mr. Heller have since split, but she hasn't updated her nomenclature."

"I hope there won't be a quiz this morning."

"Tracking her, Ethan, was like traveling around one of those big cul-de-sacs that's made up of little cul-de-sacs. Dead ends all around."

"But you found her."

Brenda Lee unwrapped another tamale. "She has a house in Olympia. I was going to send Heck down there yesterday, but—"

"I know," he said, preempting her criticism of Mal Keogh. "I'll deal with it today. Do you think her switching names is deliberate? Trying to escape from someone, or part of a scam?"

Brenda Lee chewed, swallowed, sipped and pressed a napkin to her mouth. "What I think is that Emily Maynard-Rash-Lazzaro-Heller-Whoever got married far too young. Her ideals got crushed. Crushed but not destroyed. Worked down into a diamond-hard substance, an unattainable idea of domestic bliss. Each name is another attempt at that. This time will be different. *I'll* be different."

"Maybe it finally worked," Ethan said. "So what about Ty?"

"He dips in and out of her life. Rash doesn't seem to be the father. I think when the boy was an inconvenience to her marriage, Emily farmed him out. One of her cousins remembers Emily dropping off a baby with the family for months at a time."

"For someone you haven't spoken to, you seem to understand her," Ethan said.

"I understand her fantasy. You want the last one?"

"Yours."

Brenda Lee dipped the tamale in hot sauce. In between bites, she said, "I waited for Terry. Didn't want to settle. And when we got married, I thought that was it. Perfection attained, achievement unlocked."

"Sure."

"I love my husband. But it's not white picket fences, you know? It's bad breath and cellulite, burned spaghetti sauce and movie nights where he gets to pick. Do you know how many Jean-Claude Van Damme movies I've sat through?"

Ethan smiled. "Domestic bliss."

"You either accept what the world offers or chase after something that doesn't exist. Emily chose the latter. Maybe Tyler Rash did, too."

That seemed too romantic for what he remembered of Ty. But there were different types of romantic. Some had nothing at all to do with love.

"Any luck finding Ty's dental charts or a DNA sample?"

"None at all," Ethan said.

"Great. So we know who the dead man is but can't prove it. Unless Emily Heller gives us a saliva sample or can somehow ID a body that's been in the ground for ten years."

"I don't know that anymore," Ethan said.

Brenda Lee paused with the mug halfway to her mouth. "Beg your pardon?"

"I don't think the body is his."

Voicing his long-simmering hunch was the moment he knew it had to be true. How to explain that logically, though?

"How long would you say the tunnel was?" he asked. "A hundred yards give or take?"

Brenda Lee nodded and swallowed. "About that. That part that caved in was roughly at the midpoint."

"And the body was only a few feet from the end. At the autopsy, Sandra said Ty was found where he was killed. Facing away from the entrance and shot twice from behind."

Repeating this brought back the dank smell of the tunnel, the sound of rain on grass. In his periphery he could almost see the nervous movement of the injured horse.

"Someone else had to know about the tunnel," Ethan said. "Not just that it existed, but that it didn't go anywhere. Either they marched Tyler at gunpoint into the tunnel—"

"—which they wouldn't do if they knew it had an exit," Brenda Lee interjected.

"Right. Or Tyler took them down to show off the progress and the killer surprised him."

"OK."

"Either way implies a high level of trust, something Ty never had, and a lack of situational awareness, which he had in spades."

"What are you angling at?" Brenda Lee asked.

"If there was even a chance he would have been ambushed, Ty would have designed a way out for himself. Maybe he'd leave a gun down there. Or build an escape into the tunnel. Something."

"No one can think of everything, Ethan," Brenda Lee said. "Not even Ben Franklin. You know he didn't even coin that phrase?"

Ethan gathered the corn husks and garbage and tossed them, refilling their cups. He poured milk for Brenda Lee and leaned back in his chair.

"Who knew that the tunnel was one way?" he asked. "The only person we know for sure who had that knowledge was—"

"—the builder," Brenda Lee finished.

"Which makes it an advantage. The more I run through the scenarios of what happened, the harder it is to picture Ty as the victim."

"But he fits, Ethan. Body, clothes, wallet, shed, tunnel. Plus he's been missing the same time the body's been down there."

"Every indication," Ethan agreed. "What if that's the point? Someone was trying to kill him. What if, instead of building an escape route into the tunnel, the tunnel itself was his escape?"

For a moment each of them contemplated their coffee mug, thinking through the possibilities. Brenda Lee spoke first.

"It's conceivable, I have to admit. At the same time I can only follow the evidence. Which right now is taking me to Olympia."

Ethan nodded.

"I can't stop you from following up on this hunch, and I really don't want to. But if it turns out you're wrong, Ethan, will you consider stepping back from the investigation? That maybe it's proof you're too close to this?"

"Sounds fair," he said. "And for the record, I know I'm too close." Not adding *and I know I'm right.*

15

On a scale of 1 to 10, 10 being highly satisfactory and 1 being not satisfactory at all, rate the officer's performance in the following areas:

APPEARANCE. The officer meets the standards of the department's dress code. The officer's uniform is clean and well-maintained. The officer's hygiene, hair, and/or facial hair are maintained within acceptable boundaries.
ATTENDANCE. The officer is punctual and well-prepared at the start of shift. Equipment, including but not limited to department vehicles, are returned promptly and in working condition.

Ethan Brand paused at INITIATIVE and set the report aside. He wondered how anyone filled out a document like that without wanting to set it on fire. What exactly did "highly satisfactory" mean? Wasn't satisfactory another way of saying good enough? So what did "highly good enough" entail? And how was he supposed to chart this level of satisfactoriness on a scale?

He'd wasted an hour deciding the forms should be filled out in pencil first, then tracking down a box of Ticonderogas and sharpening them. Next he'd browsed Frank Keogh's old forms, looking for inspiration. Frank had given Ethan almost all 8s and 9s, a few rare 10s and a 7 the year he'd dinged up a brand-new cruiser during a chase. The 7 rankled. He'd caught the fleeing felon, hadn't he? And wasn't 7 out of 10 still highly satisfactory?

One of the 10s had been from the time he and Brenda Lee Page prevented a riot at the Black Rock construction site. They'd walked a suspect out through a mob of the victim's coworkers. A trailer had been smashed but no one had been hurt. That had been good policework.

Looking through the reports on the others, he estimated that ninety percent of Frank's marks had been 8s. A safe number to assign. Very good, but with room for improvement. No one would be too upset about receiving an 8, nor would they get too cocky. Frank Keogh was a very smart man.

Ethan worked at the reports until his eyes were beginning to swim. He left his office for water and found Mal Keogh heading to his desk.

"Morning, Ethan," Mal said. "I mean, Chief."

"We need to talk. My office."

Mal had his father's heavy build, though the rigors of the job kept him active. He wore wire-rim glasses and kept his hair cut short. Ethan hid the reports beneath a pile of bulletins from other departments. They took their seats.

"The other day when we asked you to come in," Ethan began.

"Yeah. I was in Portland for the weekend. Commitment I couldn't get out of."

"I appreciate you have a life outside the department, Mal."

"Not like it was a fresh homicide," the officer said. "The body's been in that tunnel for years, right?"

Ethan nodded, thinking how to proceed. Mal Keogh was young, Black, forensically inclined, and the son of the former chief. A highly satisfactory officer in most regards. Yet there was an aloofness, a sense that the job was his to do in his way. That didn't always jibe with his fellow officers. Or with Ethan himself, for that matter.

"Whether the body's been there ten years or ten minutes isn't the point," he finally said. "We're a very small department."

"I know that."

"And you're an important part."

Mal nodded.

"A red-ball case like this demands everything we can give until there's a suspect in cuffs. You not showing up yesterday when you were scheduled meant Heck had to cover, which meant Brenda Lee had to canvass alone. If something happened to them because of that, could you live with it?"

Mal's response was genuine but cool. "Understood. Won't happen again."

"Anything going on I should know about?"

The officer hesitated. He wasn't given to confiding in Ethan. His leg pumped in the chair, and he fidgeted with the armrest.

"I was in Portland for an interview," Mal said. "I might not get the job, but I think I impressed them."

Ethan's turn to nod. "Here's hoping," he said.

"Chief, look—it's not—you're not—"

He waited and let the young officer collect the proper words. Mal applying to another department wasn't a shock. Still, losing a capable officer would present problems.

"Can I speak freely, Chief—Ethan?"

"I'd be hurt if you didn't."

"This isn't about you or about my dad. OK, maybe in a way it is. You both love it here in Blaine. But you both *left*. Hell, you were in Afghanistan."

"For a time," Ethan said.

"You know what the world has to offer. You choose to be here. That's cool, but I didn't choose. Other than college, I haven't really been anywhere. Passing out tickets to Canadians, rousting drunks at the Blue Duck, that's all I see on the horizon if I stay here."

"Portland has its share of drunks," Ethan said. "Probably of Canadians, too."

"You get what I mean, right?"

He did. Before joining the department, Ethan had worked a variety of jobs, from day labor to trucking to logging camps. Plus college, and then the Corps. That was one definition of a life. By contrast, Mal Keogh had followed his father into the job after a brief stint at college for forensic science. Perhaps that choice hadn't been entirely his. People did an awful lot of things to please their fathers.

"Are you giving your notice today?" he asked.

Mal shook his head. "Not today."

"All right. Head down to the Six Crows campaign headquarters. Find out who's been harassing Arlene."

"I can do that, no problem," Mal said. "Ethan—I mean, Chief? Portland PD might contact you. I mean, for a reference."

"Happy to write one for you, long as there are no more absences."

"From here on out, I'm Cal Ripken Jr., Chief. Thanks."

Mal deserved his shot, same as anyone else. He doubted the officer would find Portland any more amenable. Ethan turned back to the evaluations. That was the problem with forms like these, he thought. Life itself was highly satisfactory—and at the same time, not satisfactory at all.

16

Jaspreet Gill of the Border Patrol and his RCMP counterpart, Sergeant Monica Yan, led Ethan along Zero Avenue. The Canadian side of the 49th Parallel looked no different to him. Same blackberry and laurel bushes dotting the road. Same second growth Douglas fir. If he dug his hands into the earth, they would touch the same soil that Tyler Rash had tunneled through. Somehow an invisible line drawn between countries was more significant than the land they shared.

On the north side of the road were three beige McMansions with long sloping driveways. Slender yards with chain link fences ran back to the next street. Sergeant Yan paused on the driveway of the middle house.

"Fifteen years ago this was all farmland. We were sure the owner was a front for some big-time operation, but we couldn't find out who. Bikers, most likely."

The RCMP officer didn't look like Ethan's idea of a Mountie. Instead of red serge and a peaked hat, Yan wore the dark military-style fatigues of a big city cop. She seemed grateful to be out of the office for the afternoon.

"The owner sold off parts of the property and turned the rest into this subdivision. We think the construction was supposed to coincide with the digging of a tunnel."

"Why's that?" Ethan asked.

Yan pointed at a standalone garage to the left of the building. About twenty feet of gravel yard separated it from the house.

"There was a basement passage built between the house and that garage. We've seen this before with high-level gangsters or foreign officials under suspicion. A car with tinted windows pulls into the garage. A few minutes later it leaves, seemingly without dropping anything off."

"Or picking up," Gill said.

Ethan took a few steps up the drive and turned. Through the trees and across the road he could see the green swath of Mac and Nettie Steranko's pasture.

"Not too far to dig," he said.

"Not as the crow flies, no." Yan directed his attention back to the house. "When this address was raided twelve years ago, we found that one wall in the basement had been left unfinished. We also recovered tools and lumber that would likely have been used for the digging. Even a ventilation system."

"What happened to the owner?" Gill asked. The Border Patrol agent wore small mirrored shades. He seemed irritated with his Canadian counterpart. Ethan barely understood the squabbles involving his own department, let alone those of others.

"The owner is currently residing in Thailand," Sergeant Yan said. "The property was forfeited and resold. The new owners bricked up the basement."

"So the builders were long gone by the time Ethan's friend was shot?"

"That's correct."

"Not quite a friend," Ethan said.

"Whatever he was." Gill shrugged. "Any thoughts?"

Too few and too many. Ethan pointed at the road. "What about Zero Avenue? Would the tunnel go beneath it?"

"Tunnels usually do," Yan said. "I see your point, though. Cables, sewer lines—it would have to be deeper and a lot more sophisticated than the relatively crude tunnel you discovered."

"Actually a horse discovered it," Ethan said.

"Chief Brand doesn't like to take credit for the work of his officers," Gill said, earning a laugh from the Mountie.

At least he'd given them something to bond over.

When they finished, Yan and Gill headed for separate cruisers parked on the shoulder. Ethan strolled through the forest and boosted himself over the Sterankos' fence, dropping back into America. Crossing this way allowed him to survey the tunnel's path. It also amused him, simply walking across the world's longest undefended border. A tunnel hardly seemed necessary.

As he tramped across the field, Ethan wondered if Tyler Rash's tunnel had really been meant to line up with the one beneath the house. What if Ty just aimed to get over the border and not the road? The forest would offer cover, especially at night. Someone could park a car on Zero Avenue and meet up with him. A quick stop, a transfer of goods with a minimum of risk. If Ty was working independently, that scenario would be more likely.

The perimeter tape around the opening in the ground was undisturbed. As he angled around the crime scene, though, he saw a familiar vehicle parked behind the shed. The tail gate of the dark SUV was open. Vonetta Briggs had a foot on the bumper. She was pulling a pair of coveralls over her slacks, trading her stylish boots for the rubber kind.

Mercy Hayes was on guard duty that afternoon. Ethan couldn't see her. He quick-stepped across the field, closing the distance between himself and the DEA agent.

"Did you order my officer to leave?" he asked.

Von didn't look up. "If you're having issues with chain of command—"

"Where is she?"

"A coffee shop. Officer Hayes had to make a feminine adjustment. And pick up a drink order."

"On your suggestion? While you hold down the fort?"

Von rolled the cuff of the coveralls over the top of the boot. "Don't be too hard on her, Ethan. It took me a while to earn her trust. And there aren't exactly bathroom facilities out here."

"I'm not upset at her." Mercy had made a rookie mistake. Under the same circumstances, he probably would have done the same.

"You're upset at me, then? Or yourself?"

"Both of us. You slightly more."

Von nodded and adjusted the straps. "Sorry if that means we can't be friends. Unfortunately, making friends isn't a high priority of my job."

"What exactly is your job?"

"Curtail the trafficking of contraband substances and disrupt the networks that profit from said trafficking." Her recitation was glib, but when she finally looked up from her wardrobe change, he saw she meant the words.

"How does misleading my officers curtail anything, Agent Briggs?"

"I thought we were on a first name basis. It's Von, remember?"

"Von. Why the hell are you in my crime scene?"

The agent had traded her shoulder holster for a smaller belt-clip model. He watched her cinch a nylon utility belt and attach the holster, squaring it on her hips for a smooth draw.

"I'm a sharpshooter, Ethan. I ride into a place and size up the players. Figure out who's trustworthy and who's not. My agency hears of a body in a tunnel. The investigation's being handled by a six-person department. And oh, by the way, the dead guy is an old pal of the Chief's. That's not supposed to raise a few eyebrows?"

"Eyebrows I don't care about. Finding who did this is all that matters."

"To you," Von said. "What matters to me is much more complicated. I'm in a battle with an industry that operates on a scale you can't imagine. And I can't even begin to do my job if I have doubts about the department I'm working with."

"So did we pass your integrity test?" Ethan asked. "Or should I set aside the afternoon for polygraphs?"

"Don't be snippy," Von said. "Right now I'd like to take a look at the tunnel for myself. Then we can talk. Maybe you can buy me lunch."

"With my cartel millions, you mean?"

As miffed as he was, he had to admit that Vonetta Briggs had a great laugh.

17

The contents of the shed had been catalogued and inventoried. Since the department didn't have a place to store the tools and bags of seed, they'd simply been shoved back inside. Ethan and Von began unpacking them again.

"Amazing how much of this job turns out to be yard work," Ethan muttered.

"That's the truth." Von walked a wheelbarrow backward out of the shed. They used it to hold the smaller tools. The square of flooring that covered the tunnel's entrance had been replaced at an angle. All they had to do was shift it over.

As Von strapped on a headlamp, Mercy Hayes returned with a coffee tray. The officer saw Ethan's expression and instantly comprehended the mistake. To her credit, she didn't offer an excuse for leaving her post.

The coveralls swished as Von moved toward the tunnel's entrance. She held her hands out to Ethan, who took them and lowered her into the square in the floor. He saw that the tarp had been dirtied and ripped by the technicians. He let go as Von touched the bottom and had to crouch. The headlamp moved side to side, the light fading as she crawled forward. Soon he was staring down at darkness.

Ethan looked at the empty interior of the shed, with its crumbling Styrofoam insulation. He tried to imagine living in such a place. Six square feet, give or take. A cot or bedroll in the corner, a lamp, maybe a portable heater for cold nights. Of course, Ty would have spent his nights digging.

The nearby hill offered a keen advantage, he reasoned. It shielded the shed from view, and the hill itself could be built up with the excavated dirt without drawing much attention. Lonely, fervent work, Ethan thought. Desperate work. On a scale of 1 to 10, such a life would seem hardly satisfactory at all.

"Okay down there?" he called into the tunnel.

No answer. Mercy Hayes resumed sentry duty by the road.

Ethan checked his phone and found a message from Eldon Mooney. *You avoiding me?* it read, followed by a semicolon and a bracket. The mayor had attempted to send him a winking smiley face.

Before Ethan could think of a reply, a second message arrived from the same source. *A friendly chat. 4:30 at my office. See you there.*

Ethan didn't know what the mayor wanted. That wasn't exactly true—what the mayor wanted, of course, was to keep being mayor. Ethan didn't know how he fit into that plan.

Mooney had been in power a long time. He was used to wielding it. Firing his nephew had automatically made Ethan an adversary. Mooney had tried to cost him his job by leaking his medical records to city council. Since Ethan had never disclosed the extent of his injuries, Mooney claimed, he wasn't fit to be an officer. Whether that was true or not, the council had voted and decided he was fit to serve as Chief.

Since then, Eldon Mooney had been civil to Ethan. Perhaps he was biding his time.

"Almost finished," Von called.

When he heard the rustle of knees on tarp, he reached his arms down. Soon muddy hands took his. He braced her as Von walked up the sides. The agent took a deep breath, then inspected her face in the side mirror of the SUV. She scowled.

"Learn anything?" he asked.

"Confirmed a few suspicions."

Von's hands were dirty, and she'd transferred some of that to his own. He brushed his palms on the grass.

"I need to wash up before we have our talk," Von said. "Does the shower at your place work any better than the one in my motel room?"

"Can almost guarantee it," he said.

"Then lead on. I'll drive."

As he opened the passenger door of the SUV, Mercy Hayes gave him a look that was easy to interpret. *I hope you know what you're doing.*

* * *

Steam issued from the gap at the bottom of the washroom door. Ethan made coffee. As it percolated, he thought of the woman currently occupying his shower stall. An hour ago he'd been furious with her. Very few women inspired such a ricochet of strong emotions. His ex, of course. And Steph Sinclair. Vonetta Briggs made three.

Four, he corrected himself, remembering his dream about Sissy McCandless. Danger was as strong an emotion as any.

Von called through the door, "Could you grab my overnight bag from the Explorer? Keys are in my pants."

Cracking the door and averting his eyes from the shower, he dug the key ring out of the heap of dirty clothing on the floor. Outside, Ethan dropped the gate of the SUV and rummaged until he found the small Fossil valise. A rifle case, a flak vest, a flat of

Kirkland bottled water, and two pairs of sneakers were jammed into the trunk space. Agent Briggs prepared for every eventuality.

Placing the bag near the door, he knocked, and turned around while she retrieved it. Von emerged with her hair in a towel, wearing leggings and a gray off-the-shoulder sweater.

"Not my dressiest ensemble," she said. "If you want to save those cartel millions, you could cook us a couple of eight-minute eggs."

He put a pot of water on, prepared a bowl with ice cubes. Von's exposed collarbone had a small star-shaped mark on the skin. She noticed him looking.

"I was shot once," Von said. "Well, twice, one incident but I took two rounds. Ever heard of a sucking chest wound? Well, it lives up to its name. Really sucks. Second worst moment of my life."

"And the first?" he asked.

"A 365-way tie for every day I was married." Von smiled. "He wasn't all that bad. I was just young and thought marriage would be something else."

Ethan thought of Tyler Rash's mother, farming out her child to chase after her ideal of a happy union.

"The real answer," Von said, watching as he lowered the eggs into the boiling water, "I served a warrant on this spread out in the Mojave. Chemical warehouse. The cartel had cleared out, but they'd booby-trapped the front door. We had the bomb unit come in, disarm it with that little robot they use. If it had gone off, given the chemicals we found inside, the whole block would've gone up, us included."

"But you came through it OK," he said. "That's worse than being shot?"

"Dumb as it sounds, I never really believed I would die. Not till that day in the desert." She took a sobering breath and sipped her coffee. "I'd ask about your worst day, but I think I have an idea."

He made toast. They ate at the table, peeling the shells onto a paper napkin. Von sliced hers neatly, adding pepper but no salt, same as him.

"Perfect, not runny, just jammy enough."

"One more test passed?" he said.

"Hey, if I'd found evidence of corruption among your staff, wouldn't you want to know?"

"Of course."

Von nodded, chewing. "You can rest easy. Aside from a lapse in procedure here and there, you run a tight ship."

"And I can cook an egg," he said. "Tell me about the tunnel."

"If it had been completed, I'm sure it would have been used more than once. Possibly by multiple persons. Care was taken to shore up the sides. Modest means but ambitious intent."

"Sounds like Ty," he said.

Von cut the toast into triangles. "Do you believe the dead body is Mr. Rash?"

"You first," Ethan said.

"The person who designed that tunnel strikes me as organized. Thorough. Someone who'd be very hard to ambush."

"For those reasons, I don't believe it's him," Ethan said. "Only one person could out-maneuver Ty in a survival situation, and he's dead."

"Your father, you mean," Von said. "I read up on his disappearance. That would be tough for a person to get over."

"I don't think Ty ever did." He remembered Nettie telling him about Ty's trips to the Canadian wilderness.

"I meant for you," Von said.

His meal finished, Ethan set his elbows on the table. He stared at the box holding the papers relating to Jack Brand's disappearance.

"Maybe I haven't at that," he said. "My father pushed his family away. He wanted his son to be able to meet the world on its own terms, and I guess part of me wants that for my kids. I don't like the similarities between us. The differences, either. But they're there."

"And between you and Ty?"

"Similar. And different."

"You want him to be alive, don't you?" Von's voice was soft. He couldn't argue the point. "You realize, Ethan, if he is, he'll have to answer for the body in the tunnel."

"Someone does," he said. "When we find who, we'll arrest them."

"Even if it's Tyler Rash?"

"Even if."

Von placed a hand on his, her fingers pressing into his knuckles.

"I like you, Ethan, I like your town. A word of professional advice, though. Don't underestimate the person who built that tunnel. And don't expect him to underestimate you."

She kissed his cheek, lips cool. Ethan walked her out. He watched as the SUV receded down the road. An exceptional woman, he thought. One that knew more than she'd told him.

Yes, danger was as strong an emotion as any.

18

Eldon Mooney was a boating enthusiast. His office reflected that. Aside from the usual trappings of a small town mayor, flags and framed certificates from the Rotary and Elks, the wall behind Mooney's desk showcased a large lacquered ship's wheel, and a shelf of sailing trophies Mooney and his yacht, the *Sassy Bess*, had won over the years. His speeches often included nautical terminology, long metaphors about rocky seas and all hands rowing in the same direction. When he was nervous, the mayor practiced his knots.

He was doing this now, tying a phone charge cable into what looked to Ethan like a reef knot. Mooney nodded at him to take a seat. Though shorter than most of his guests, the mayor's chair was double cushioned, giving him the advantage of height.

Ethan watched as Mooney tied, untied, and retied the knot. The mayor slid the cable into a drawer of his desk.

"Terrible," he said.

"Looks OK to me. Right over left, left over right."

"Terrible about us. You and me, all this unnecessary grief. When it comes down to it, Chief Brand, don't we all want the same things?"

Ethan knew better than to answer a rhetorical question. Mooney squared his shoulders, sitting up in his chair. Ethan wondered if it made him feel mayoral. "Where are we at with this tunnel situation?"

"We're still investigating," Ethan said, trying not to be insolent. "Officer Page is confirming the identity of the remains."

"I gather you knew the victim. What's his name? Lash?"

"Tyler Rash, Your Honor."

"Homeless, wasn't he?"

"I doubt he'd describe himself that way."

"Well, he's not here to quibble," the mayor said. "Does your department have the resources to resolve this?"

Ethan recognized the political significance of his answer. If he said yes, he'd be expected to deliver results. If no, he was admitting to a political foe that his department wasn't capable of handling a major homicide case.

"We're working with other agencies," he said. "If we need help, we'll ask."

"Good. I'll expect a report to council as soon as you can."

"Anything else, Your Honor?"

Mooney's expression softened, the fearless leader now becoming everybody's best pal. "We've had our differences, Chief Brand, but I think you'd agree we work effectively together."

He didn't answer, waiting to see what the mayor was getting at.

"You and I have kept this little vessel from capsizing. No mean feat, wouldn't you say?"

Ethan gave the smallest of nods.

"I'll admit when I found out about your foot injury, how you'd hidden it, I was more than a little concerned. But you've proved to me you can overcome your handicap. No limits to what a person can do. You're quite inspiring, Chief."

"All right," Ethan said.

"Naturally we each have our own beliefs and goals, your office and mine."

"Naturally."

"Wouldn't it be something for the citizens to read a statement from your department, acknowledging the terrific work we've done together, and will continue to do in the future?"

"I'll be happy to write that the department is committed to working with the mayor," Ethan said.

"Excellent."

"Whoever the mayor happens to be."

Mooney kept nodding, but his hands took up the cable again, winding it around his fingers.

"You annoy me sometimes, Ethan."

"I thought I inspired you?"

Mooney pointed across the desk with the cable still in hand. "I don't want to see your office playing partisan politics. No signs at the station or on department vehicles. No appearance in uniform to support certain candidates. Neutrality."

"Not a problem, Your Honor."

"Good. Let's keep it from becoming one."

"How's your nephew these days?"

Eldon Mooney stood and loomed over his desk. This had the opposite of the desired effect, making him seem shorter, more comical. The mayor's voice filled with thunder and tarnation.

"Cliff has a good job now. Don't you dare harass him any further. Frankly you should consider yourself lucky he opted not to file for wrongful dismissal."

"I do consider myself lucky," Ethan said. "Lucky and inspiring. Anything else, Your Honor?"

Mooney would have the last word.

"Stick your oar in where it doesn't belong, and I will blast you out of the water," the mayor said. "There'll be no safe harbor for you, Chief Brand. Good day."

Ethan left, fighting the urge to answer with *aye, aye, skipper*. Mooney was ridiculous, but a ridiculous man was a tough enemy to have. If a person wasn't careful, they'd laugh their way right into his crosshairs.

* * *

Blaine's City Hall occupied a floor in the Banner Bank building on Martin Street. A short walk along Fourth back to the station. Ethan cut across the parking lot of the post office, hanging a left onto H Street. Small businesses filled the block: jeweler, hair stylist, masseuse. And in the midst of these, Breakwater Travel.

He found himself slowing as he neared Sissy McCandless's place of business. Then lingering on the opposite side of the street. Sissy had lived in Blaine her whole life. Odds were she knew Tyler Rash. If Ty was involved in smuggling, he was involved with her family. Closing time might be the ideal opportunity to brace her.

So why was he nervous?

He told himself there were good reasons. No doubt Sissy was dangerous. Clever, too. Ethan had only tumbled to her plan to replace her brothers after she had succeeded. Sissy was also friendly and unassuming, all the while likely thinking ten moves ahead.

His dream hadn't helped. Why had she appeared in his fantasy—because she was a criminal, and as such taboo? Or was there something between them he didn't want to acknowledge?

Ethan pushed the eternal mysteries of his subconscious out of his mind. It was nearly five o'clock. The lights were already off in the travel agency. The venetian blinds were closed. Ethan watched as the OPEN sign turned to CLOSED as Sissy finished locking up.

Only the person locking up wasn't Sissy. A palm like a side of bacon nudged the door open. A pair of overdeveloped shoulders stooped to fit through the frame. Ethan recognized the man's crewcut and build. His former colleague wore a burgundy polo with the travel agency's name stitched on the breast. This was the "good job" the mayor's nephew had found.

Cliff Mooney, the disgraced cop Ethan had fired last year, was now taking orders from Sissy McCandless. Ethan didn't know what to make of that. He considered stopping Cliff and asking, knowing even if the man lied, he'd give away more than he intended. But Ethan's phone was buzzing with a text.

Brenda Lee Page had written: *Tyler's mother wants to see you.*

19

"I can't tell which of us had the crappier day." Brenda Lee merged into the left lane of I-5. Like a bad joke, all forward movement in that lane immediately halted. She beat her fist on the steering wheel of the cruiser.

"You, I'd wager," Ethan said.

They were stuck on the S-curves south of Seattle, almost at their destination. The trip from Blaine to Olympia took three hours when traffic was running. But between rush hour, construction, and late summer vacationers, movement on the highway was reduced to a crawl.

Brenda Lee had already made the trip once. That morning she arrived in Olympia at the house of Emily Heller, explained she was an officer from Blaine here to talk about Emily's son. The woman asked if Brenda Lee knew an officer named Ethan Brand.

"I'll talk to him and him alone," Ty's mother said.

To her credit, Brenda Lee didn't show her frustration. She simply about-faced, collected Ethan, and headed back south, only stopping for a chicken sandwich and an extra-large iced latte. The department vehicles didn't have cup holders that fit the giant beverage, so Ethan held it for her as she drove.

"Any idea why she insisted on you?" Brenda Lee asked.

"Either she feels more comfortable talking to someone who knew her son—"

"Or?"

"She just wants to spit in my face."

"Worth the trip either way."

The right lane began to move now. Brenda Lee sighed and put her indicator on.

"Cliff Mooney is working for Sissy McCandless," Ethan said, passing her the beverage and taking it back as their own lane picked up speed.

"In what capacity, a leg breaker?"

"Worse. Travel agent."

"Just when you have people figured out, huh?"

Ethan doubted he'd ever have people figured out. Himself least of all. "Maybe they both went legit," he said.

"Sure. I'd believe that about Cliff before Sissy. You forget what her last name is?"

"Family doesn't determine everything."

"Killing people does." Brenda Lee glanced over at him. "You don't actually believe she's mended her ways?"

"Just stating it's a possibility."

They crept along a few miles in silence.

"I've been wondering something, Ethan. If I'm overstepping, let me know. But it seems relevant to our case."

"Shoot," he said.

"Your mom and dad, they didn't seem to have much in common. Why did she put up with him?"

"Love," Ethan said.

"Sure. I guess what I mean . . ."

Ethan knew what she meant.

"My mother paid the mortgage and the taxes and taught me to read and drive. She held a steady job her whole life, sometimes more than one. Jack contributed when he could. I think his time away made her forgive him more than she should. She used to say he reminded her of Thoreau."

"Thoreau as in Henry David?" Brenda Lee asked. "As in 'two roads in a forest?'"

"That's Frost. Thoreau was 'lives of quiet desperation.'"

"Why him, though?"

"Thoreau preached self-reliance, living in the woods on his friend's land. Not exactly the wilderness he wrote about. But my mom liked what he wrote just the same."

"A romantic," Brenda Lee said.

Ethan nodded. "A disappointed one. But I guess there are worse things to be."

"You know that's the most you've ever talked about your parents?"

"As you said, it seems relevant to our case."

As both lanes jolted to a stop again, Brenda Lee said, "My mom and dad both worked for Boeing."

* * *

When they reached Olympia, they turned off Sleater-Kinney Road onto a boulevard of close-set, one-story houses. Former military quarters, from the look of them. Emily Heller lived in a faded yellow corner house with a collection of paint cans and propane tanks stacked in the carport. They parked across the street.

"How do you want to handle this?" Ethan asked.

"If she likes you so much, I'm fine with you taking the lead."

"She did say me alone."

Brenda Lee worked the straw around the slushy remnants of her drink. "I just fought I-5 traffic twice. She's not undercutting my authority by making me wait in the car. Plus I need to pee."

Motion lights caught them as they started up the drive. The windows of Emily Heller's house were grubby, but Ethan could see a light on inside. It turned out to be the television, frozen on an ad for dishwasher pods. The screen door had fist-sized rips in the wire mesh. Banging on the door itself didn't yield an answer.

"Ungoddamnbelieveable," Brenda Lee said. "Not home. She knew I was coming back with you."

"How did you find her in the first place?"

"Brilliant detective work."

"Went without saying."

"Not mine, alas. One of her aunts left Emily a small inheritance. The executors put an ad in the local papers. Emily contacted them to claim her share."

"Did they happen to tell you where she worked?"

Brenda Lee shook her head. "I assume if she works at all, it's under the table. Her tax returns aren't exactly detailed." She beat on the door one last time, hard enough to rattle the windowpanes. "You're so close to the family, why don't you make an educated guess where she went?"

There was humor in her tone, as well as exasperation, but buried beneath was a note of bitterness. Brenda Lee Page was more intelligent than he was, a fact his ego had found hard to accept the first few years they'd worked together. But it was true. She picked up on things he didn't, was more systematic in her work, more rigorous in the way she approached a case. That often meant proceeding slower, but moving in the right direction.

But Brenda Lee wasn't especially good with people. She struggled to make them comfortable, to earn their confidence. Part of that was the unease they felt, being interviewed by someone smarter than they were, and a woman at that. But Brenda Lee's approach could be too frank, too subtle, or too clever, and Ethan could see that even when she couldn't. So much of the job was putting people at ease, a great variety of individuals wrestling with emotional extremes, fear or grief or anger. The wrong approach could make someone flee, or turn them fighting mad.

"Let's check the nearest bar," Ethan suggested. "If I'm wrong, at least you can use the restroom."

The nearest bar turned out to be Ernie's, a low-lit tavern a few blocks over. It reminded Ethan a little of the Blue Duck, only smaller and punkier. Same gravel parking lot, same neon signs in the grimy windows. Miller and Michelob and Molson Export. At night, after a few cold ones, those signs took on the holiness of stained glass. A perfect place to hide.

The bar was three quarters full, a good crowd for a weekday. Joan Jett blared from the sound system, competing with three televisions, each turned to a different recap of the day's sports. A pool game went on in the corner, a pitcher of beer resting in the center of the green felt.

Ethan recognized Emily Heller immediately. Her hair was the same dirty gold as Ty's, but teased up in an Eightiess 'do. Short and hippy, snapping gum, Emily waited for the bartender to add lemon wedges to the Collins glasses on her tray.

The woman saw him, too. Ethan watched recognition settle over her.

"Your show, Chief," Brenda Lee said.

Emily Heller weaved across the room, depositing her tray in a booth. As she did she spat her gum out and jabbed it beneath the table. When she was standing squarely in front of Ethan, she cocked her head back and spat in his face.

20

The music from the bar was loud enough that Dire Straits carried to the edge of the parking lot. Emily Heller smoked. Under the fluorescent street lights, her thick layer of foundation looked like the skin on wax fruit. Her eyeliner had run, creating dark crescents under her eyes. She seemed out of place and time, stranded in the wrong decade.

"I was a kid myself when Ty was born," Emily said. "His daddy wasn't in the picture. Could barely get close to my own folks 'thout getting the death stare of disapproval, y'know?"

"When did you see your son last?" Brenda Lee handled the interview with no objection from Emily. It seemed she only wanted Ethan present so she could hurl abuse at him. And spittle. Brenda Lee kept a good poker face, but Ethan thought she was amused by this.

"Ages and ages," Emily admitted. "We weren't all that close."

"Can you tell us about the last time you spoke with Tyler?"

She coughed, squinting at the ground while she considered the question. Dire Straits faded and Heart replaced them with "Barracuda." Emily Heller nodded in time to the drums.

"Woulda been back when I was living in Spokane. Twelve, thirteen years ago. Ty showed up, asked could he borrow my car for a couple hours. I told him I'd need bus fare, and he had to gas it up when he was done. Plus a little something for my inconvenience. When I came home that night, the car was back where it should be. A few tins of Cope and the money he owed were beneath the passenger seat. He was a good boy. Always paid his way."

"You said was."

A gold fingernail flicked away ash. "A cop asks when's the last time I saw somebody, there's only two possibilities. He's dead or in trouble."

Brenda Lee nodded coolly. "Any idea why he borrowed the car?"

"Drive somewhere, haul something, pick somebody up. I didn't ask. Only made him swear he wasn't carrying anything that stunk too bad. One time a friend leant her Jeep to a guy to haul a load of mushroom manure. Took her ages to bleach out the smell."

"Do you know anything about a tunnel in Blaine?" Brenda Lee asked.

"What kind? Railroad?"

"Dug in the ground, close to the border."

Emily smoked and didn't speak.

"What do you think happened to your son, ma'am?"

She turned from Brenda Lee and pointed the butt of her cigarette at Ethan.

"Tell you exactly what happened. This man's daddy put all sorts of notions in Ty's head. They cost Jack Brand his own life, and prob'ly did the same to my boy."

There was nothing Ethan could counter that with. A mother was entitled to her feelings. Even if he didn't trust her answers, her hatred was genuine.

Brenda Lee tried to angle for specifics. "Who was your son hanging out with? What was he up to?"

"His life was his life. Kept himself mostly off the grid." She pointed at Ethan once more. "Learned that from his old man. Rather be outdoors than a contributing member of society."

"We recovered a body from the tunnel," Brenda Lee said.

"So?"

Ethan watched the woman's reaction. She chained another cigarette, flicking the butt in his direction. He sidestepped, and it landed on the asphalt with the others.

Abuse was part of the job. An officer couldn't afford to take it personally. Under duress, a person reacted to authority in all sorts of ways. Yet this was personal. Generational, in fact. Emily Heller despised him because he was his father's.

What he'd tried to communicate to Brenda Lee was that Jack Brand's beliefs were absolute. Hypocritical, yes, and ultimately impossible to sustain. But beautiful in their simplicity. A person walked out into nature with nothing and lived there, disturbing as little as possible. Even his mother, as practical and community-minded as anyone he knew, could see the appeal of that.

Tyler Rash had absorbed those beliefs. In a way, his father had cursed Ty with an ideal no one could live up to. Ethan wondered if Ty secretly felt hatred for his father along with love. Like he did himself, he thought, but without someone like Agnes Brand to model a different way of living.

"Had Tyler ever been in trouble with the law?" Brenda Lee asked.

"Depends whose law, I suppose."

"Was he ever involved in trafficking, smuggling, anything like that?"

"Wants me to blacken my own son's name," Emily muttered.

Brenda Lee let out a sigh. She stooped and retrieved the cigarette butts. "I can't abide litter," she said. "Ethan, want to jump in?"

"Why are you lying to us?" he asked.

It was the first question he'd addressed to her. Emily Heller erupted with a litany of four- and twelve-letter words. When the cursing was done, she fired up another cigarette, ignoring the one still burning in her hand. The music had changed to something with a disco beat, rattling the windows of Ernie's Tavern.

"You know it was your mom brought him back to me," she told Ethan, gloating a little. "Agnes was a beauty and from good people. A Devereux, if I remember. Must've stuck in her craw that her man preferred being alone to being with her so much of the time."

"Wasn't easy on her," Ethan said.

"She was a polite woman, but the day she dropped him off, she let me know Ty wasn't welcome around her place. Said I wasn't a good mother. Know what I told her?"

He could imagine, and began to say so, but Emily cut him off.

"I told her I'd rather be a bad mother than a bad wife. Couldn't give her man what he wanted. Your saint of a mother tried to slap me. Called me all sorts of names." Emily expelled her smoke with a mean satisfaction. "Fact is, Jack didn't want much to do with her. Or you, I guess. Wonder why."

The icy wall of his professional demeanor was melting thin. He knew Emily Heller was trying to goad him, and hated that it was working. He mentally pulled back, trying to view her objectively. A sad woman in a parking lot trying to derail their line of questioning.

"Chief Brand's many deficiencies of character aside," Brenda Lee said, "do you know anything pertinent about your son that would help us?"

"She knows he's still alive," Ethan said.

The words cut through Emily Heller's disdain. She started, looked nervously at the bar. After a moment she composed herself and shook her head in denial.

"Know nothing of the sort," she said.
"Where is your son, Mrs. Heller?"
"Where's your father?" she countered.

Before he could steer the questioning back to Tyler Rash, the door of Ernie's slammed open. Two couples spilled out, lighting smokes and pulling on vape pens. They spotted Emily and headed over, slowing when they noticed her questioners were in uniform.

"Pigs bothering you, Em?" one called.

"Matter of fact, yeah." Ty's mother backed up, fitting herself into the crowd. They closed ranks around her. "These two aren't even from town."

The two men were roughneck types. One wore a denim vest, the other an oversized hoodie that hung to his knees. The women were older than their dates, dressed in blouses with plunging necklines, one in red vinyl pants and the other in a black vinyl skirt. Maybe thirty bracelets and bangles between them.

"You could take him, Miles," the woman in red vinyl said. "He didn't have that gun, you could take him easy."

"No doubt." Miles was the man in the hoodie. Unshaven except for his head, with a slightly upturned nose.

"Miles taught karate back in high school," Red Vinyl boasted.

"I'd like you all to step back, please," Brenda Lee said. "We've just about finished our talk with Mrs. Heller."

"Em's our favorite waitress," Black Vinyl said. "You don't even have distinction here."

"Jurisdiction," Red Vinyl clarified.

"Yeah. And where's your warrantee?"

Emily was enjoying this. She spoke to Miles over the gabble of voices. "I was telling Ethan here that his mother was trash."

"That true?" Miles spoke with the deadpan grin of a bully. Warm whiskey breath struck Ethan's face. "If it's true, think I could get her number?"

A nose was easy to break. Lucky for Miles, the baton only glanced off the bridge, swiping down his cheek. Blood spouted and Miles grabbed his face, the violence so instantaneous the others didn't realize until their friend was reeling backward.

Brenda Lee Page pointed the baton in the group's direction.

"I spent ten hours in traffic today. I have no tolerance left for drunken nonsense. Understand? Clear out."

They did, hurling insults and tossing their smokes. Emily Heller left with them. As the door swung shut, Ethan caught the opening riff of a ZZ Top shuffle.

He helped Miles to a standing position, keeping his grip tight until he was sure Miles wasn't going to try anything.

"She's the nice one," Ethan told him. "You're lucky she didn't break it."

"Yes, sir."

"You can go."

As they walked back to the cruiser, Brenda Lee said, "Perfect end to the day. Use of force in front of my supervisor."

"They brought up a good point, though," Ethan said. "Technically we're out of our distinction."

In place of a laugh, Brenda Lee tilted her head in a tired nod. She retracted the baton and replaced it on her belt, then brought a small evidence bag from her pocket. Inside were two cigarette butts. Emily Heller's DNA. The forensic lab in Bellingham was on their way home.

21

A warm and promising morning at Blaine Marine Park, where the ocean breeze met the smell of frying bacon. Perfect weather for the Legion's pancake breakfast. A pair of picnic benches had been set up near the food tent. Veterans and their families worked the griddle or tonged sausages onto paper plates. Ethan had been roped into manning the coffee station.

He had dressed casually for the event, in a snap button shirt and old cardigan. There was a small hole in one armpit that he'd noticed too late. His wardrobe hadn't grown much since Jazz left, with the exception of a brick of athletic socks from Costco.

He spelled the cooks when they needed it, turned sausages, and beat batter. Maxine Duke and her husband, Teddy Vance, greeted guests. Both had served during Operation Desert Storm. Roth and Orr, a pair of Korean War veterans who'd lied about their age to enlist, held court at one of the tables.

There were younger vets, too, including a woman named Shields. She had been involved in an altercation in the parking lot of the Blue Duck. Ethan nodded at her. Shields returned the gesture warily, and didn't take her eyes off him until her husband handed her a plate of eggs. The couple found a spot to sit away from the others.

"Heya, Chief. Nice to be served by you for a change." Away from Lucky's Café, Mei Sum wore a windbreaker and flared pants. He handed her a cup of decaf, and they chatted for a moment. Behind Mei trotted Jessica Sinclair.

"Hi, I guess." Jess's greeting was delivered with an awkward smirk.

"How's your family doing?" he asked the teen.

"Fine. Dad's fine. My brother's fine, too." Mischievously, Jess waited to see if Ethan would ask after her mother.

"Are you all back from Hawaii now?"

"Mom is taking some time there. You probably won't see her for a while." Jess eyed the milk and sugar on the table. "You don't have any blue agave syrup, do you?"

"Disappointments abound," Ethan said.

The two teens shared one plate, strolling off together.

He saw other people he knew. Sally Bishop from the Super Value. A couple who ran a gallery of Indigenous art. Workers for Black Rock Gas and Pipeline and their children. There were also people he didn't know, more than he expected.

And there was Eldon Mooney, trailed by an entourage of assistants and business owners. The mayor was attired in a navy blue blazer and a stars and stripes captain's hat. Each lapel sported a Support the Troops ribbon. Ethan watched Mooney press the flesh, circling each table and touching elbows and shoulders, careful not to disturb their eating. A consummate politician, you had to give him that.

Ethan looked for Arlene Six Crows but the councilwoman wasn't around. He sent her a text. By the time Maxine relieved him from the beverage station, Arlene still hadn't answered.

Equal parts concerned and relieved he didn't have to give a speech, Ethan considered what he owed Arlene. She would want him to get the word out about her campaign. To mingle. An unpleasant task, but he could give it a shot.

"How are you folks doing?" he asked a group of Black Rock employees.

"Could use a short stack and another glass of juice," one said, assuming he was taking orders.

"Large stack with bacon."

"Coffee with cream for me."

At another table, he was drawn into a debate over the best Jimmy Stewart western—a conversation he would have been glad to linger over if he hadn't promised Arlene. Someone asked if they could see his gun. Ethan said no and withdrew, thinking he would probably do less harm representing himself as working *against* Arlene than for her.

Despite this, he pressed on, and found occasion to mention his choice for mayor. People listened politely, some nodding in agreement. Mooney was familiar, and they were comfortable with him, but Ethan detected dissatisfaction.

"I'd like to see Blaine get a train station again," Mr. Roth said. "It would be nice to take 'er down to Portland for the weekend."

"The councilwoman wants that, too," Ethan said.

"Also pretty tired of these kids skateboarding around. Oughta lock a few in jail to send a message."

Ethan gave up.

Before he left, he paid his respects to the mayor. Mooney insisted on a handshake, and turned this into a photo op, his assistants snapping away. With an arm around Ethan's shoulder, Mooney held him in place.

"Law and order," Mooney said. "It's a proven fact that people feel safer now thanks to the work of Chief Brand and my office. And we're just getting started, aren't we, Ethan?"

Caught off-guard by the question, Ethan's answer came out stilted, sounding silly to his ears. "We've done work." He tried to add something about Arlene, but Mooney steamrolled him, laying out a plan to clean up the parks for the hard-working citizens to enjoy.

He pried off the mayor's arm and broke away, but soon found Jay Swan walking alongside him. The journalist brandished their recorder at him.

"What do you think of the job the mayor's done, Chief?"

"The department will work with whoever," Ethan said.

"And personally?"

Jay was giving him a chance. He composed what was left of his wits and cleared his throat.

"Personally I think Arlene Six Crows is the right person for the job. Her priorities are more in line with people than business. She cares and she puts in the work. Arlene has my vote and my confidence."

"Do you feel she'll be tough on crime?" Jay asked.

"I don't even know what that means," Ethan admitted, done with politics for the day.

* * *

Arlene wasn't in her office or campaign headquarters. She wasn't at City Hall. Ethan checked at the station to see if she'd left a message. There was no word from the councilwoman.

Yet another thing to worry about, he thought.

The evaluations were still on his desk. If he had to write one for himself at that moment, his score would have been less than satisfactory. A decade-old murder, a tunnel that went nowhere, a DEA agent who treated him more like a suspect than a colleague, and now a missing candidate. And that wasn't even counting the injured horse.

Ethan stepped outside and looked down the street. Almost nine. Breakwater Travel would be opening about now.

Ethan approached from the alley. Sure enough, Cliff Mooney's Range Rover was parked behind the agency. Dents and scrapes aplenty on its hood. MOONEY FOR MAYOR bumper stickers covered the back window.

The agency's door chimed as he entered. Cliff Mooney leaned over the desk, reading a catalog of firearms. "One sec," he called without looking up.

Ethan reached the desk and slid the bell closer to Cliff's ear. The mackerel tabby curled on a customer chair ignored him. He struck the bell hard. The heads of both Cliff and the cat shot up in surprise.

"Toldja I'd be a sec—" Cliff started, seeing who was waiting. "The hell are you doing here?"

"How's the new job?" Ethan asked.

"What do you care?"

"Sooner or later one of us has to answer a question 'stead of ask it. I'm here, Cliff, because someone's been bothering Arlene Six Crows."

"And you think it's me?"

Ethan waited.

"Well, it's not." Cliff shifted the gun book out of the way. "That's my uncle's fight, not mine."

"Any recent interactions with Arlene?"

"Yeah, we're getting married in the fall." Cliff grunted in appreciation at his own joke.

"Know of anyone with a grudge against her?"

"Lots," he said, but didn't elaborate.

"Do you know anything about a tunnel?" he asked. "A guy named Tyler Rash?"

"Like I'm gonna do your policework for you."

"Fair enough," Ethan said. "Somehow I never pictured you in customer service."

"Not like there's a whole lotta choice for me. Thrown off the force and all. People assume I'm corrupt."

"Well, you are."

Cliff gripped the counter, the veins in his forearms going taut. Whatever supplement he was taking had done its job too well. Ethan wasn't afraid. He'd bested Cliff in unarmed combat before. The mayor's nephew was still formidable, though. If those arms snagged him, he'd be hard-pressed to break free without resorting to lethal options. Cliff was dumb and volatile, but those weren't problems that needed a bullet to sort out.

The chime on the door rang again. Ethan stepped beyond Cliff's reach before pivoting to see who it was.

"Hello there, Chief," Sissy McCandless said. "What kind of vacation are you in the market for?"

22

They ended up walking down by the old train station. The same walk Ethan had taken with Arlene when she'd told him someone was harassing her. As he strolled along with Sissy McCandless, the irony wasn't lost on him.

Sissy wore a coarse sweater, faded blue and the texture of an old washcloth. Her auburn hair was clipped up in an efficient but messy knot, and her oversized glasses hung on a red nylon cord. Hardly the image of a crime boss. Which Ethan knew was exactly the point.

Thinking he was staring at her sweater, Sissy explained, "I spilled tea on my work shirt this morning. If I knew I was going to see you, I would have aimed to be a bit more presentable."

"You look fine," Ethan said.

"So do you, though that cardigan could use a stitch or two."

Talking with Sissy made him feel like he was treading on loose sand. And yet it felt natural, too. Easy. That worried him.

"Why hire Cliff Mooney?" Ethan asked.

"He has potential."

"To give you inside dope on the mayor?"

"Why would I need that?"

A pair of cyclists in spandex outfits rode past them. Sissy took his arm and stepped closer to give them room.

"Is he hired muscle, then?"

"Cliff? He's a junior sales associate."

Ethan thought about it carefully as they walked.

"Cliff's a former officer," he said. "If it's not the mayor's office you want info on, it's mine."

"He certainly holds strong opinions about you." Sissy halted their steps and guided him to a bench. They sat, looking at the boats riding the gentle morning tide.

"I'll tell you why I hired Cliff," Sissy said. "Whether you believe me is another question."

"I might."

"The secret to business is spotting value where others don't. Cliff isn't quite a model employee, but he shows up on time and does his best. Plus the Mooneys are a well-known family. Having one work at the agency adds familiarity."

"Smart," Ethan said.

"I also believe Cliff deserves a second chance. Even if others don't."

"As long as he's not breaking the law or trying to enforce it, I'm happy for him."

"Then you came to see me?"

Despite every instinct to fear and mistrust her, Ethan had to admit he admired Sissy McCandless. She seemed sincerely pleased to talk with him. He knew psychopaths could appear that way, but he didn't think Sissy belonged in that category. Rather she seemed able to inhabit different roles completely. A prosperous and casually dressed businesswoman, fond of animals and walks along the train tracks. At the same time, whatever else she did.

"Does the name Tyler Rash mean anything to you?" he asked.

"It used to," Sissy said. "Is that who you found in the tunnel on Nettie and Mac's land?"

Not wanting to share his suspicions, Ethan said nothing. A heron lighted on a boulder near the shore. The bird seemed to stare at them for a moment. Then it set off, its blue-gray wings pumping to gain altitude.

"You must get an awful lot of confessions this way," Sissy said. "Remaining silent. Patiently letting other people fill the space with their chatter."

"Maybe I'm naturally laconic."

She smiled. "I imagine that makes relationships quite tough."

"Easier," he said. "Less to argue about."

"But more difficult to articulate the arguments you do have."

Ethan shrugged. "I suppose that's true. Jazz and I had good conversations. But we could also just sit by a fire, or listen to music and be content."

"I'm sorry it didn't work out, then."

"Our kids are healthy, which is all that matters. And I don't know the last word has been written on the subject."

"Meaning reconciliation?" Sissy asked. "Or the possibility of another marriage?"

Ethan realized she'd turned the tables on him. Now he was the one filling the conversational space. "Tell me what you remember about Ty."

"You'll laugh at me," Sissy said. "He would have been in his mid or late twenties. I was thirteen. The perfect age for a crush. With that hair, Ty looked like a Viking—like a Viking from a movie, if you know what I mean."

He nodded. "What was the purpose of his visit?"

"Oh, something to do with my dad. Seth brought him around, I think."

"Was Ty working for them?"

"Believe it or not, Chief, Big Joe McCandless didn't share his business dealings with his teenage daughter."

"All the same, I bet you know."

Sissy didn't answer right away. The burden of discussing her family was a heavy one. He could relate to that. "No one saw Big Joe who didn't want something. There were always deals being made."

"Legal or otherwise," Ethan said.

"Ty may have been buying a used car, for all I know. Why assume the worst of him?"

"The tunnel makes it hard to do otherwise," he said. "I recall digging up an old van in your family's backyard that had been converted into an underground safe."

"Then you should remember who told you where to dig," Sissy said. "Your father was a survivalist, what might today be called a prepper. I don't assume you share his beliefs. Yet you think I'm guilty of everything my family has done."

"You're right, Sissy. I apologize."

"I don't know anything about the tunnel," she said. "What I remember is taking snuff after seeing Ty take snuff. Thinking he'd like me if I did. Getting sick to my stomach afterward."

"Ten years ago, Seth would have been running the family business, right?"

Sissy didn't dispute it.

"Would your brother know more about what Ty was mixed up in?"

"Possibly," she said. "Would you like me to ask him?"

Seth McCandless was in Clallam Bay, with two years left on his sentence. Ethan remembered Seth's face in the courtroom, clouding with rage as the judge read out the verdict of guilty. His anger directed at Ethan, focused on the man who'd put him away.

"I'd appreciate that very much," Ethan said.

Sissy nodded and patted his knee. Her touch reminded him of the dream. Ethan looked down the tracks, hoping his face didn't betray anything.

"I like talking with you, Ethan," Sissy said. "Outside of work, I mean. We should do this again. Do you know what a repositioning cruise is?"

"All I know is they're cheap."

"Free, in my case. Sometimes I take one and spend a few nights in Seattle or L.A. You should come with me sometime. You'd find I'm a different person down there."

They stood and Ethan found himself offering his hand. An odd, self-conscious thing to do. Before he could retract it, Sissy took it in both of hers.

"Forgot to ask your thoughts on the election," Ethan said.

"I'm not particular, Chief. I'll be in touch after I speak to my brother."

Sissy started back toward her business. Ethan reminded himself that the pretty and unassuming woman walking away from him had killed at least one person. Her family many more. Tyler Rash might turn out to be among them.

23

Ethan Brand yawned. Slouched over his desk with the sun beating through his window, he considered breaking his "no coffee after noon" rule for the third day in a row. Caffeine kept him up nights, but he wasn't sleeping much anyway. Some rule, he thought.

He'd completed the evaluations an hour ago, but went over the numbers again, adjusting them here and there. On the whole, he was about as generous as Frank Keogh had been, though his grades had a larger spread. More nines and tens, the occasional five or six. He wondered if Frank had agonized over the process as much. Probably not. One thing his former boss had mastered was leaving the job at work.

The DNA comparison between the remains in the tunnel and Emily Heller's cigarette butts was being fast-tracked. Moira Sutcliffe had promised him results by the end of the day. A vague term—was "end of the day" 5 PM? Midnight? In return, Ethan had promised Moira a favor to be named later.

The tunnel sample was also being checked against DNA collected from offenders around the country. CODIS testing could take even longer. Same with the ballistic tests run on the shells and slug fragments. If the murder weapon had been used before or since, that could tell them a lot.

In the meantime, Ethan read through missing persons reports dating from ten years ago: twenty-five to fifty-year-old white males of average height, starting with Washington and radiating out to the rest of North America. The odds that someone involved in cross-border smuggling would be reported as missing were slim.

But you never knew.

The day seemed destined never to end. Fatigued, Ethan leaned back and surveyed his surroundings. In the year and change that he'd been Chief, he hadn't done much to make the office his own. A photo of his kids had hung behind the desk, but his chair kept scraping against the frame. Now the photo rested on the floor against the wall, waiting for him to rehang it in a better spot.

For want of a nail, he thought. Or a hammer, in this case. No better time for it.

The evening shift had started. Heck Ruiz was on patrol. Passing Heck's desk, Ethan saw a box on the floor, its flaps open. Pamphlets inside. *Eldon Mooney for Mayor—The Proper Choice. Proper* was underlined in red, white and blue.

Heck had never voiced much in the way of political opinion. Of course he was entitled to vote his conscience, but if an officer was using department time for pamphleting, or showing up in uniform on a candidate's behalf, that could present a problem.

But then Ethan was one to talk. His comments about Arlene were already on the home page of the *Northern Light*. "Chief Says Time for Change." An understatement.

And still no word from Arlene.

He texted Mal to see if the officer had heard from her. Mal phoned back as he was replacing the tack hammer in the utility room.

"I'm just leaving Bellingham, Ethan. I mean Chief."

"On department business?" Portland, now Bellingham. If Mal was blowing off work again—

"I've been looking at security footage," Mal said. "Arlene's OK, but there was another incident."

Arlene had spent the morning checking bookstores for a copy of *Ceremony*. She'd parked near the water in Bellingham's Fairhaven District, and been in the bookshop about twenty minutes. She bought a latte at a nearby café. When she came out, Arlene found her tires had been slashed, a window broken, and her phone ripped out of its holder on the dash.

Witnesses had seen a man jogging away from the scene. "Dressed for winter," one described. Watch cap, thick down jacket, boots and gloves. The colors of the garments ranged from brown to green.

Arlene had reported it, mentioning the other incidents. Bellingham PD had contacted Mal. He helped them review footage from an ATM and the seafood restaurant across the street.

"The tires were punctured with a hunting knife, and the guy swung what looked like a tire iron at the window," Mal said. "None of the footage is great, but he's over six feet, medium build, and white. He moved pretty fast, too. The whole thing only took about twenty seconds."

"Is Arlene all right?"

"A bit shaken up. I just drove her home."

Ethan looked at the hammer in his hand, feeling the urge to plant it in the nearest computer. Thankfully the councilwoman wasn't physically hurt, but even nonviolent crime left its mark. This was clearly more than a prank. Someone was out to intimidate Arlene Six Crows.

"She didn't recognize the man, did she? No leads?"

"No, but if she quits the race, we all know who benefits."

A direct action like this didn't seem like Eldon Mooney's style. Even if the mayor was more desperate than he let on. Ethan thought of the vandal reading the messages of concern he'd sent to Arlene's phone.

"Find who did this," he told Mal.

"Nothing's gonna stop me, Chief."

"Good man."

Give Mal Keogh a task and it would be done competently. But give him a goal and some discretion, and he'd outperform damn near anyone. That kind of difference was what made evaluations so difficult. Hard to shove all that data into a single digit.

Mercy Hayes could be freed up to watch Arlene. The crime scene didn't need to be guarded any longer. He'd stop by the Steranko place on his way home and deliver the assignment to her in person.

Ethan was leaving the station to do just that when Jon Gutierrez intercepted him. "Call for you, Chief. Want to take it in your office?"

"Here's fine." Ethan reached across the front desk and took the receiver. "What?" he said, more curt than he meant to.

"Nice manners for someone doing you the mother of all favors." Moira Sutcliffe chuckled. "Bad day, huh?"

"Not the best."

"Well, maybe this will cheer you up. Results are in. Less than five centimorgans shared between your sample and the deceased. Know what that means?"

He did. The dead man in the tunnel wasn't Tyler Rash.

24

"Don't you dare say I told you so," Brenda Lee said.

Since a biological parent and child shared fifty percent of their DNA, and that wasn't the case with Emily Heller and the body in the tunnel, they now had two separate but connected problems. The first was finding Tyler Rash, who had gone from likely victim to possible suspect. The second problem involved finding a name to put with the body.

Ty's circle of acquaintance was a small one. Nettie and Mac would have to be interviewed again. Seth McCandless, if his sister could convince him to talk. Ty's mother had lied to them; they would need a new approach, something to make her confide.

The only other people who might fit in that circle were dead. Not counting Ethan himself.

Brenda Lee Page had taken over searching through the missing persons reports. She seemed determined to finish the task before calling it a night. A mug of tea, a Coke Zero, and a bag of Tim's salt and vinegar chips surrounded her keyboard. As Ethan squeezed past, Brenda Lee didn't look away from her monitor.

At another desk sat Mal Keogh. His screen was frozen on a frame from the security footage, a blurry figure swinging a weapon at Arlene's car. Mal was reviewing the minutes from city council meetings, adding names to a list of people with a grudge against Arlene.

This was what policework looked like sometimes. Long hours of steady concentration, working into the night, with no solution in view. Ethan looked at the two officers hunched over their desks and wished a silent goodnight to them both.

* * *

Arlene wouldn't want round-the-clock surveillance or a police car parked in her driveway. Instead, Mercy Hayes would use the department's unmarked cruiser to make sure the councilwoman got to work without incident. She'd check in during the day, then escort Arlene home in the evening. A candidate for mayor worked long hours, which meant Mercy would be on the same schedule. She didn't mind. Mercy admired Arlene, and was thrilled to be done with guarding the crime scene.

Ethan threaded a plastic tie through the door handles of the shed. He affixed an evidence seal. In lieu of an officer, this would have to do for a deterrent. The gap in the fence would need to be repaired, and eventually a backhoe would be required to fill in the tunnel. Life would move on.

At home, he parked and collected his mail. Two bills, two flyers, a large kraft envelope with no return address. He paused on the porch, feeling he'd missed something. A difference in the landscape. But what? Exhaustion was no excuse for carelessness. He scanned the driveway, the front yard, the shed, and the fence. What was off?

The signs. He'd put up two election signs for Arlene, one in his yard and one in the vacant lot next door. The yard sign was gone. He walked to the fence and saw the one in the lot was missing as well. Stolen.

A crime he was too tired to solve. Ethan left the mail by the door, sat at the table, and opened the box with his father's name on it.

He read through the news clippings, not to learn but to remember. The local papers had followed the story as it developed. The disappearance, the official and unofficial searches, the funeral with no body. A magazine had profiled Jack Brand, calling him "a throwback to the adventurer-heroes of Jack London and James Fenimore Cooper." His disappearance was a "tragedy," an "unexplained phenomenon," or "a curious riddle of the natural world." The story had made the Associated Press, and there were smaller clippings from Chicago, Toronto, New York.

No mention of Tyler Rash in any of the articles. When they bothered to write about Jack Brand's family, it was the stoic wife and child he'd left behind. No mention of the arguments between father and son, or how diligent and clear-eyed Agnes Brand had worked to organize, hire, and pay for the searches they conducted. Grief and mourning were all the stories focused on. Yet they ignored the one person who'd mourned Jack most deeply.

Ethan set the clippings aside. His mother had put together an album of photos. Sometimes grinning, often holding a beer, Jack Brand always seemed to be gazing somewhere to the left of the camera lens, as if the end of his life was just out of frame.

Wedding photos, Polaroids of the Brands with their baby son. One of Jack with his arm around Tyler Rash. The teen's mouth attempted a smile, though his eyes carried a frightened and far-off look. A mistrusting look. As if any happy occasion might be ripped apart at the last second.

Once, during his courtship of Jazz, Ethan had taken her to a dance club. The music had been thunderous, the lights both too low and too strobing. He found himself disoriented, his attention slipping from the enchanting woman in his arms to the exits, or the stream of strange bodies being wanded by the bouncers. Easy enough to sneak a gun inside. Or a knife.

They left early.

As he drove her home, Jazz had told him to pull over, to turn the engine off, to talk with her.

"You're not present tonight," she told him. "You know that, don't you?"

"I'm sorry," he said.

"Don't be sorry. I understand after seeing what you've seen there's a mechanism you can't just turn off. I will never discount that or hold it against you. But you *must* talk to me. Be present when we're together. Or else let me out now and keep driving. Deal?"

He'd done his best. At first it had felt unnatural, confiding doubts and fears he'd never shared before, things he'd witnessed and could neither comprehend nor forget. And in the end all that openness hadn't kept them together. But maybe it had given him the tools to find his way back. To be present and accountable.

Looking at the photo of his father and Ty, with their expressions that didn't quite match their eyes, Ethan wondered if that was the difference between him and them. In the woods they could quiet the part of themselves that saw danger around every corner. In society, that part ran their lives.

Or maybe the difference was imaginary.

He flipped the pages and found empty leaves in the album. No more photos of his father. At the bottom of the box was the memory book from the funeral. Ty had printed his name inside, the letters large and childish. That was the last trace of Tyler Rash in the box.

Ethan felt deflated. He had hoped he'd find something that would make sense of it all. Foolish, he realized. Not every question has an answer. He went to bed.

The plain brown envelope with no return address sat among the flyers and the bills until the morning, when he almost opened it.

25

The tape was the first clue. The gummy glue of the envelope flap hadn't been licked. Instead, a double strip of silver electricians tape held the flap closed in the middle. To open the package there was only one place to rip.

There were runs in the surface of the tape as well, which contrasted with the unwrinkled envelope and typewritten address. An air pocket could cause a run like that. Or it could conceal a wire.

Ethan studied the envelope while sipping his morning coffee.

For years after Helmand, he'd seen bombs everywhere. The desert had been littered with trash, some of it dating back to the Soviets. The enemy had been very good at disguising death as something ordinary and innocuous.

But this wasn't the desert, it was his kitchen, on a morning with no shortage of claims on his time. He simply didn't have the bandwidth for this.

Funny how that didn't make the problem go away.

The wrongness of the envelope was apparent. Why take the time to type the address and then sloppily attach the tape? Why not lick the glue? And where was the return address?

The contents were heavier than expected, too. Thinner than a book, larger than a deck of cards, yet weighing more than a pound. Ethan's mind went to one of those awards made of engraved Lucite. But what award would he be up for, and who would send it in such an envelope?

Faint red ink had been applied over the address in a roughly stamp-like shape. At first glance it seemed an official-looking postmark. Under scrutiny, though, he saw the marks were approximations. The postage was inadequate—he had mailed enough presents to his sons in the last two years to know how expensive shipping was. The envelope hadn't arrived here by courier. It had been placed in his mail slot amid enough other mail to seem innocuous.

Ethan backed away from the table, took his phone and coffee mug out to the porch. He sat on the steps and phoned Jon Gutierrez's home number.

Jon's husband, Warren, picked up and said a testy "Yes?" into the phone. "May I ask who's calling?"

Ethan told him.

A moment later Jon's sleep-slurred voice said, "Something the matter, Chief?"

"Hate to bother you on your day off, Jon, but I have kind of a situation here," Ethan said. "Can you borrow Warren's phone and call the station without hanging up on me?"

"Sure, OK. Can I ask what's going on?"

"Nope. First call work and tell whoever's on the desk to look through the mail. To do this very carefully, touching none of it. If there's an envelope or package in there—am I going too fast?"

"No, I got it," Jon said.

"Any sort of parcel. Tell them not to touch it. Repeat that part to them, all right?"

"Copy."

"Get everybody to clear out of the station. Everybody. And clear the buildings on either side."

"Are you saying there's a—"

"Even if there is no package, someone needs to do a sweep of the office anyway, just to make sure. And yes, this is real. Convey that without starting a discussion with them."

He listened as Jon made the call, hearing the administrator's voice relay the instructions in a clear yet urgent tone. The sun was beginning to backlight the horizon. He could see the lawn needed cutting.

Texts began arriving from Brenda Lee asking what was happening. She must have worked through the night.

"All right, everyone's clear of the building," Jon told him.

"Good work. Now please call WSP and ask them to send the bomb squad. You have my home address?"

"Are you—" Jon broke off. It wasn't the time for questions. "Calling right now, Chief."

Up the block, an automatic sprinkler kicked on. Stripes of white clouds overhead. It was fixing to be a beautiful morning.

* * *

Moira Sutcliffe arrived herself, riding in an armored truck with two troopers from the bomb disposal unit. All three wore vests over their fatigues, and the technicians had helmets and masks. Rolling down the residential streets of Blaine, they cut an ominous figure.

There had been no suspicious envelope in the department's mail. That meant a personal motive, a grudge. As glad as he was that the threat was centered on one person, he wished that person wasn't himself.

Normally Moira took a lighthearted approach. She saw Ethan and his department as punching far above their weight class. This morning her expression was all business. She waited with him in the yard as Trooper Sanchez and Trooper D'Addario, the two bomb techs, entered the house.

Ethan noticed a curtain move in one of his neighbors' windows. He waved.

"You seem awfully cavalier," Moira said.

Across the street, Mrs. Higashino opened the door, cinching her robe. Ethan responded to her look of concern by raising his palm, showing her everything was fine.

"I'm scared out of my wits," he said to Moira, still grinning at his neighbor. "She doesn't need to know that."

"Just when I think I have you figured. Any idea who sent the package?"

"A good idea, yeah. I'll show you when we go inside."

It was another forty minutes, and even then Moira insisted he wear a spare vest and helmet. Odd to walk through a house that had once been his mother's, where his children slept when they visited, viewing the rooms like a crime scene. Trooper D'Addario was inspecting the house while Trooper Sanchez examined the contents of the envelope.

"Sheet explosive," Sanchez said. She pointed at a piece of cardboard on which had been placed a thin square of rubbery material the color of milk. Small strips of the same silver electricians tape held batteries, a blasting cap, and two loops of wire to the sheet. Under the envelope's flap was a piece of fishing line.

Sanchez explained how opening the envelop would tug the line, in turn causing the two loops to touch and complete the circuit. Ethan understood the design. In fact he'd seen a diagram of the bomb before.

The sheet explosive and the blasting cap were common enough in construction, but could possibly be traced. The rest would be dusted for fingerprints. He doubted very much they'd find any.

In the living room he crouched and pushed aside a double stack of paperbacks, most of them old romance novels. Jazz had read one a week, even while in grad school. Like his mother, Ethan was loath to get rid of any book he hadn't at least tried to read. He shifted the paperbacks and pulled out a slim bundle of old manuals, held together with a frayed elastic.

These had been his father's. Training manuals printed by different military branches, copied and distributed on the black market. Field medicine, improvised munitions, hand-to-hand combat. Ethan found the book he wanted, a pamphlet the army had issued in 1965, simply titled *Boobytraps*. He flipped through the pages. Bombs in canteens, land mines buried in rice paddies. There it was, a diagram of a very similar device. Step-by-step instructions below it.

"Old-fashioned design, but that's pretty close," Trooper Sanchez said.

Ethan recalled how Vonetta Briggs had described the tunnel. *Modest means but ambitious intent.* The same could apply to the envelope bomb. Not only was Tyler Rash alive, but he knew Ethan was looking for him.

26

There was a chaotic bent to the afternoon. More foot traffic in and out of the station than usual, and the phones rang incessantly. That couldn't be helped. Although Ethan had told the staff not to comment on the bomb recovered from his house, rumors circulated. People in town wanted to know.

He handled most of these inquiries himself—after all, it was his bomb, and everyone else had assignments. He confirmed to Jay Swan that there'd been a suspicious package delivered to his place of residence, but shared no other details. The threat to civilians was nonexistent.

"Why target you?" the reporter asked, leaning forward in the chair so Ethan could speak into their recorder.

"Can't comment, but it's being looked into," he said.

"Can you confirm whether this is somehow connected to your investigation of the body recovered from the Steranko property?"

"That's Officer Page's investigation."

The journalist didn't seem satisfied with his answers. "What about the incident involving Councilwoman Six Crows? Is there a connection there?"

"We don't know yet," Ethan said.

"What can you tell my readers about Tyler Rash?"

Jay was a tenacious reporter, well-informed, and had lived in Blaine their whole life. They'd piece things together sooner or later. All the same, Ethan didn't want Jay to write something that his suspect might read. Ty would learn soon enough that the bomb hadn't worked.

"Tell you what," Ethan said, making a motion to switch the recorder off. "If you leave Ty out of this for now, I'll answer any question you have about him at a later date."

"Including about your father?" Jay asked.

Ethan nodded. "The whole story."

The reporter found that acceptable. On their way out, Jay hesitated. Ethan had seen that look before, a person vacillating between whether or not to share some piece of information.

"The mayor heard about the bomb," Jay said at last. "I don't know what His Honor is planning, but he's called a press conference for later today. I think he's going to use it somehow to hurt the councilwoman—and you."

"Thanks for telling me," Ethan said. Political harm was a low priority today.

"Any other exclusives you can throw my way?" the journalist asked.

"Matter of fact there is," he said. "Someone's stealing election signs from peoples' lawns. Might be worth looking into."

* * *

At three o'clock Brenda Lee Page shot out of her desk, rushed to the door, then backtracked to collect her phone and keys. Palpably excited. A lead, Ethan thought. She'd been working hard enough to deserve one. Brenda Lee was gone for the next two hours.

After a brush with danger it was good to get back out and reassert yourself. Show the world you hadn't been cowed. But each time Ethan thought to leave, some new piece of business came up.

The most interesting development was the arrival of Cliff Mooney. The former officer walked past the front desk, and made it halfway to Ethan's office before Mal Keogh intercepted him.

Words were exchanged. Fists clenched. Ethan didn't catch the first volley, but heard Cliff say, "Your daddy's not here to back you up anymore."

Leave it to the mayor's nephew to throw around charges of nepotism.

Mal held his ground. "This area is for personnel only. Which you're not anymore, Cliff. Thank God."

Ethan interposed himself before tempers escalated. "What are you doing here?" he asked Cliff. "If you don't have business—"

"I'm here to cooperate. About Arlene." Cliff Mooney spoke reluctantly, eyes on his feet. "I'm s'posed to answer any questions you got."

Ethan and Mal exchanged a look. The officer shrugged. Cliff had made Mal's suspect list, though Mal hadn't requested an interview.

Sissy McCandless, Ethan thought. She'd heard of the incident with Arlene, knew Cliff would be a suspect, and sent her employee in with orders to cooperate. Once again, Sissy was thinking several steps ahead of anyone else.

They spoke in Ethan's office, though part of him felt Cliff deserved the "hard" interview room, an uncomfortable seat and no windows. Mal stood on Ethan's side of the desk, arms crossed.

"I get down to Bellingham pretty regular," Cliff said. "Yesterday, though, I was at work all day. You can check with my boss if you want."

"And before work?" Mal asked.

"Home. Asleep. I closed down the Duck the night before."

"And after the bar closed, you went straight home to bed?"

Cliff sighed. "I bought a few road pops and went driving around. I do that sometimes when I get bored. Helps clear my head."

"Road pops?" Mal asked.

"Beers, OK? I had four or five at the bar, then bought a sixer for the drive. Like you never done that."

"I don't drink and drive, no," Mal said.

Cliff snarled, rose an inch off his chair. Ethan readied for a charge. But instead of following through, Cliff sank down and counted silently back from five. His lips moved. Cliff's nostrils took in a long breath.

"Anyhow," Cliff said, calmer than before, "that's the whole story. I drove around a bit on the backroads, then went home around two. Didn't have nothing to do with Arlene's car. You can check."

Ethan studied Cliff's face. The former officer seemed sincere. "Did Sissy tell you why she asked you to share this with us?"

"Just told me I had to cooperate a hundred percent. Said she didn't want her employee refusing to help the authorities."

"Nice of her," Ethan said. "Sissy teach you that counting trick?"

Cliff nodded. "I get angry real easy. 'Specially when ignorant people piss me off. It helps keep me in control. She said it worked for her brothers."

Not well enough to keep them out of prison, he thought. "Give your boss my thanks."

As Cliff left and Mal went back to his desk, Ethan considered what Sissy's strategy might be. Perhaps ordering Cliff to speak with him was meant to curry favor, or keep her legitimate business free of suspicion. Or maybe Sissy thought it was the right thing to do. Stranger things had already occurred today.

* * *

The initial inspection of the explosive found no prints or DNA. The lab technicians would keep him apprised. Ethan had written up his statement of events, and sent copies to the bomb squad and the other authorities. He mentioned there was a possible connection to the homicide, but didn't go into detail.

Vonetta Briggs phoned him at five. She was back in Seattle and had just received the report.

"Must have been terrifying," she said. "And at your home. How are you feeling?"

"Not sure yet. Curious coincidence, though."

"What do you mean?"

"The other day you told me that story about the bomb in the desert. And today I find one."

"Ethan, you're not by any chance suggesting..." Von didn't finish.

"I have some other news, too," he said. "The body in the tunnel isn't Ty's."

"Do you think Rash mailed the letter bomb?"

"I think he placed it in my mail box himself. Or paid someone too."

"You mean he's in town?" Excitement in her voice. "I'll meet you at your place later."

"And you'll tell me what you know? The whole story?"

"As much of it as I can."

Which could amount to nothing at all. But he didn't argue. "I'll pick up something for dinner," he told the DEA agent.

"Stay safe till then."

Hard to do that when people kept holding out on him.

Ethan stood and stretched. He stared at the photo of his sons. In a crisis everything extraneous dropped away. It was only later, when the facts had sunk in and he had time to consider them, that his feelings came out. And what he felt right now was cold and ugly. A man he knew had tried to kill him in his home. The man had used a design from a book Ethan's father had shown them. If the kids had been staying with him—

There wasn't time to finish the thought. Brenda Lee Page had returned. Judging from the way she was grinning, she'd found something.

27

The last days of Archibald Gatlin had been well-documented.

Gatlin was a lifelong resident of Tacoma. A thirty-four-year-old unmarried plumber, Archie had no children, no living mother or father. No rap sheet, though his juvenile record was sealed. After a less-than-honorable discharge from the army, Archie had gone into business for himself. He earned a living and kept simple tax records.

Ten years and two months ago, Archie Gatlin seemingly ceased to exist.

On June 13th and 14th, Gatlin dealt with a septic tank issue for a Tacoma resident. He was paid $475 for the call-out, including parts and labor. He deposited the check the afternoon of the 14th.

Gatlin had been planning a fishing trip for the 16th with his cousin Miles, who lived on Anderson Island. Emails between them showed that Archie's plan was to finish work early on the 15th and catch the ferry at Steilacoom. He had purchased a ticket ahead of time for the 5:35 PM crossing. He would drive to Miles's property, they would drink and catch up, then get an early start the next morning.

At 3:13 PM, Archie gassed up his Jeep Wrangler at a Texaco station in a town called Castle Rock, near Longview. He paid

$60.42 at the till. Miles called Archie while he was gassing up, asking if his cousin was going to make the ferry. According to his cousin's statement, Archie said he was on track.

There was no record of whether or not Gatlin made his ferry. He never arrived at his cousin's home. Miles Gatlin was used to Archie changing his mind last-minute, "flaking out" as he called it. At the time, Miles had been too annoyed to worry.

Four years later, a Jeep Wrangler was found in the forest near Tukwila. The receipt from the gas station was still in the glove box. No sign of violence, and no sign of Archie Gatlin.

The missing plumber wasn't especially missed by anybody. The case file included bank records, cell phone data, statements from his cousin and client, as well as reports on the search of Archie's apartment. Miles stressed that Archie was a rambling sort of person. He carried cash and tended to rub people the wrong way. Archie never told his cousin why he'd left the army, but he hated discipline of any kind. He worked on his own schedule, at the pace he set for himself. His clients either accepted that or found someone else to fix their toilets.

The parallels with Tyler Rash stuck out to Ethan as he read over the file. Both had almost no family to speak of, and few close friends. Both were antisocial, and both had carved out lives that suited their nature. And both had gone missing with hardly anybody taking notice. Physically, Archie Gatlin was heavier than Ty, a year older, and balding. In death he'd been a near match.

Brenda Lee Page had read the case file and noticed the similarities. She'd located Gatlin's dentist and asked for his charts to compare against the teeth of the dead man. A forensic dentist offered her a preliminary opinion. Gatlin had a chipped lower left incisor. So did the corpse.

"Gatlin's DNA was collected from his apartment when he was declared missing," Brenda Lee said. "We'll know for sure soon, but it's him. And not only do we know who, now we know when. June 15th."

Ethan flipped to the report on the recovered Jeep. "Did anyone search around the vehicle for Gatlin's personal items, the fishing gear?"

"Not immediately. The Wrangler was impounded before anybody ran the plate. Afterward a search was conducted. They didn't find anything."

Ethan nodded. He was seated next to Brenda Lee at Heck's desk. The box of pamphlets had disappeared.

"So Gatlin leaves Tacoma on the 15th," Ethan said, trying to fix the chronology in his mind. "He gasses up in Castle Rock, intending to make the ferry to Anderson Island. Instead he drives up to Blaine, where someone shoots him in a half-finished tunnel. That someone then abandons Gatlin's Jeep an hour and a half south of town."

"Closer to two hours," Brenda Lee said.

Ethan studied the two photos included with the file. The first showed Archibald Gatlin at twenty-three, dressed in military fatigues. Small eyes, weak chin. Something furtive and dangerous about him, like a nocturnal animal that would leave you alone unless it was cornered, at which point it became ferocious. Another picture showed Archie a year before the disappearance, standing with his cousin Miles in a river. Both were bald and bearded, Archie taller and paunchier. They wore hip waders and carried freshwater rods.

"So what's the connection between Gatlin and Ty?" he said, more to himself than his senior officer.

"To state the obvious, it seems highly likely that Tyler Rash killed Archie Gatlin."

"But why? To what end?"

"Do people even need an end to do bad things, Ethan?"

It was the type of fatalistic comment Brenda Lee only made when tired. And she looked tired. Sifting the information out had cost her.

"No one else would have found this," Ethan said. "It's exceptional work."

"And if I want to take a few days off, I can. Right?"

"Terry probably hasn't seen much of you since we found the tunnel. Why not take your husband and the dogs and go camping for a few days?"

She shook her head emphatically. "Since when do you know me to camp, Ethan?"

"Jet skiing, then. Whatever."

"Someone is trying to kill you." Brenda Lee said this as if emphasizing a point in a debate. "Now, despite the matter-of-fact way you're acting, we both know you can't afford having me on leave right now."

"It hasn't been the easiest year for you," Ethan countered.

That was true. From losing the job of Chief to being shot in the line of duty, Brenda Lee Page had gone from the hospital to rehab to her first days back on the job in short time. Her toughness and dedication weren't in question.

"Do me a favor, Chief Brand," she said. "Hold me to the same standard you hold yourself. No way in hell you'd take off right now. Would you?"

"I wouldn't mind," he admitted. "But no."

Brenda Lee folded her hands in her lap, the matter settled.

"All right, so how did these two end up together in the tunnel?" Ethan asked.

"Maybe a dispute over a plumbing bill."

"Not much plumbing in the places Ty lived."

"Romantic dispute," Brenda Lee suggested. "Or some sort of scam one was running on the other?"

How had Archie Gatlin learned about the tunnel? And why, after killing Archie, had Ty attached his wallet to the dead man's belt?

They threw suggestions back and forth, covering the common and uncommon motives for murder. Rage. Greed. To cover up another crime. A case of mistaken identity. An altered mental state. Assassination at someone else's behest. None seemed to fit.

"Maybe," Brenda Lee said, exhaustion flooding her voice, "it was simply too much trouble *not* to kill him."

28

The bomb squad troopers had tracked dirt throughout his house. A small price to pay for disabling the explosive, but unsightly just the same. Ethan changed out of his uniform and ran a broom and mop over the floorboards. He dusted and tidied the living room. The Blaine Women's Book Club had twelve regular members, plus Arlene and himself. He'd need to improvise a few chairs.

Was it a smart idea to go ahead with the meeting? If Ty was trying to kill him, he might be attracting danger to those around him. On the other hand, the house had been examined thoroughly. If he posted an officer on the street during the meeting, it would likely be the most secure spot in town.

Wise decision or not, Arlene was intent on going through with it. She had phoned twice to make sure the meeting was on, and to ask whether she should bring baked goods or a vegetable tray. She had found out about the suspicious envelope later in the day, and texted him *OMG I hope ur ok,* followed by *I'm leaning toward bringing brownies.*

After cleaning up, his shirt was grubby and stained with sweat. Ethan sat with a High Life, working up the energy to shower. A tentative rap on the door. Vonetta Briggs was early.

Only it wasn't Von. On the doorstep stood the woman named Shields he'd seen at the Legion breakfast. She was wearing a ratty blue hoodie, both hands shoved into the pouch.

"Uh, hi, Chief," Shields said.

Her eyes were very blue, eyebrows so pale as to almost be invisible. She wasn't looking at him but past him, eyes never lingering in one spot. Under the porch light, with the hood up, Shields resembled half the robbery suspects caught on surveillance footage. Instinct told him there was something in the pouch besides her hands.

"Beg your pardon but I don't know your first name," Ethan said.

"Zelda. Like the video game."

"Or the writer. What's going on, Zelda?"

As casually as he could, he shifted his weight so his shoulder braced the door. If her hands swept out with a weapon, he could slam the door and free his pistol in one move. But Shields hesitated. Her boots scraped the boards of the porch.

"I heard about the bomb threat today. And I was just sort of thinking. Maybe you, I dunno, need me to keep watch or something."

The toe of her boot circled a knothole. She looked down, almost embarrassed by her own words. Ethan thought he understood. For someone so recently out of service, feeling adrift in the world, this was a chance for Zelda Shields to feel valuable again. To put the skills she had mastered to use.

"I'm OK right this minute, thanks," he said.

"Sure. Yeah, of course."

"Are you busy tomorrow night?"

He explained about the book club meeting. Another set of eyes on the property wouldn't be the worst idea, and the department was already spread thin. If Zelda Shields wanted to attend, unofficially of course, that would be one more trained body should something happen.

She brightened at the offer. "Sure, I can totally do that—I have kind of a dinner plan, but I'll move it."

"How are things at home?" he asked.

"Good. Totally fine." Zelda smiled, not entirely convincing.

"You want to come in and talk?"

"No, I mean no thanks, my husband will be worried. Not worried, but—you know what I mean."

He nodded. "Till tomorrow, then, Zelda."

"Right. Till tomorrow."

As she stepped off the porch, he called out, "This is a no firearms meeting, by the way. I don't need to tell you that, I'm sure."

Zelda nodded, hands still in the pouch of her sweater, and dissolved into the darkness of the street.

* * *

When Vonetta Briggs arrived, the table was set for the first time in months. He'd even found a pair of emergency candles and mounted them in mason jars. He wasn't sure what kind of music Von liked, but it was hard to argue with George Strait—at least it was for Ethan Brand.

Von wore a sleeveless gray silk blouse with high waisted slacks. A carved piece of ivory hung from a braided gold necklace, and her earrings were simple gold hoops. She smelled good. Ethan had changed into clean jeans and a comfortable shirt, and felt severely underdressed.

He'd been given a bottle of good red wine for Christmas and hadn't had occasion to uncork it. Von accepted a glass. "What's on the menu?" she said.

"Eggs and brown toast and a few mildly wilted green onions."

"Breakfast for dinner? I'm into that."

They split an omelet, eating and talking about the single life. Von was in the field more than her last boyfriend had liked. He wanted a stable domestic situation. A routine. That clashed with Von's job and her expectations for life.

"I love seeing different places," she said. "Love hotel rooms, and I *really* love expense accounts. I love going where the job takes me. Maybe one day I won't feel that way, but I haven't hit it yet. Pass the hot sauce?"

He slid the bottle of Cholula across to her, their fingers touching. Her red hair looked rich and gold-tinged in the candlelight.

"You never feel like up and leaving?" Von asked.

"Sometimes. I'm in Boston a couple times a year. Up and down the coast."

"And that's enough for you?"

"For now."

"But you didn't always feel like that."

He folded a piece of toast around a forkful of egg, chewed and thought of how to answer.

"As a kid I couldn't wait to leave. Never thought I'd come back. There was a moment, though. I was in this village in Garmsir District, having dinner with my interpreter and his family. All of us sitting in a circle on the floor, watching as his uncle tended the stew. And I remember thinking: this old man knows every inch of this place. I could stay here years and never learn a fraction of what he does. First time I ever really felt homesick—or understood what home meant."

"And you feel that way about Blaine? That you understand it?"

"The damndest thing is, I don't," Ethan said. "Every day surprises me. Which leads me to believe it's less the place than the person."

"Nothing good or bad but thinking makes it so," Von quoted.

"I don't know I'd go that far. Can I ask you something?"

"Ask me anything," she said.

"So far there hasn't been a whiff of narcotics in this tunnel investigation."

"That's not a question," Von said.

"It implies one. What do you know about Tyler Rash that I don't?"

Von's smile turned thin and almost regretful, but it didn't disappear. "And we were having such a nice meal."

"No reason to change that," Ethan said. "Ty put a bomb in my mailbox. That entitles me to a little interagency cooperation, doesn't it?"

She refilled her glass with a flourish, taking the bottle high before swooping it back down. A perfect pour. "Two years as a bartender in college," she said. "To answer your question, I know less about Rash than you do. I'm here because of the tunnel itself. You're having dinner with the agency's expert on cross-border smuggling."

"An honor," Ethan said.

"Your town is on the world's longest undefended border, and the tunnel you found bears certain similarities to others I've seen."

"Similarities like what?"

"Built in the same manner, using the same methods. We found one in Idaho and another north of Spokane. One person had built these alone, either hired by a local outfit, or building them on spec and then selling them. The builder hasn't been operating in the last few years—or if they have, we haven't caught them."

"You didn't seem all that surprised that the body in the tunnel wasn't Tyler Rash," Ethan said. "Is he your chief suspect?"

"I'd never heard the name until you told me, Ethan. But if Rash built that explosive device, he fits our profile."

"Which is what?"

"Well-trained in wilderness survival, something of a loner, dangerous enough he can take care of himself, and proficient with explosives. That chemical warehouse in the desert I told you about? We found a tunnel below that, as well. The longest so far."

"You think Ty built all of those?"

"Or taught somebody the technique."

Ethan set his fork down, the food forgotten. "Didn't you say the warehouse was a cartel operation?"

Von nodded. "You can understand why I held back now, can't you?"

"What do you mean?"

"The profile."

"So if Ty wasn't your suspect—"

Confused, Ethan tried to think who else fit that profile. When the answer arrived, it stung.

"You were looking at me," he said.

Von stood up and let her napkin fall to her plate. She moved to the side of the table. Her hand tilted his chin and stroked his cheek.

"I can't apologize for doing my job any more than you can. If you'd like me to leave, that's all right. Or we can take this bottle of wine over to the couch and kiss a while. Your choice."

Ethan watched her walk toward the door, or maybe toward the living room, thinking this day had illustrated his point. It had definitely surprised him.

29

Funny how sex and death can change your morning outlook. Sitting in Lucky's over the chessboard and a third cup of coffee, Ethan wondered if his brush with mortality had shaded Von's attitude to him. The DEA agent seemed to move in death's shadow with familiarity—as he had, at times. Life could seem so fragile.

Their lovemaking had progressed from enthusiastic necking on the couch, to the half-shy intimacy of stripping in the hallway, to full-throated passion on top of the bed. It had been swell. And in the morning Ethan woke to the fading smell of perfume and deodorant, to a trace of violet lipstick on his chest, and to a note.

E,

You are great good fun. And possibly habit-forming. Let me take some time to see if it's a habit I can live with.
See you down the road.

Xs and Os,
—V.

He wasn't sure what to think of that. Or her. Wasn't it usually the man who left a note? But then it was his house, and Von had a long way to travel. And what about her suggestion of habits a person could live with?

All he could say for sure was that Vonetta Briggs was like no one else he'd ever met.

In the café, he'd seen a copy of the *Northern Light*. An article on the front page read, "Mayor Vows 'Tighter Ship' Next Term: 'Soft' Approach Not Working."

Eldon Mooney had pulled off an impressive logical do-si-do. He'd painted the bomb threat and Arlene's slashed tires as a crime wave that was Ethan's fault for being too lenient. If reelected, Mooney would pressure the department to crack down on Blaine's criminal element.

Ethan didn't read the entire article, but one quotation leapt out at him. "An inexperienced Chief and a councilwoman who sees crooks as victims is a recipe for choppy seas and stormy skies. I tried things their way. Now, with the help of the voters, it's time I take the helm and right the course."

Usually he could write off the words of a blowhard like Mooney as so much empty noise. The quote irked him, though. He could tolerate being called inexperienced, because it happened to be true. What bothered him was the promise of exercising power. Painting the town as overrun with criminals, implying they needed martial law to rein it in.

All things considered, Blaine was a pretty safe place to live. It was his job to remind people of that by catching those responsible. So far, he hadn't done a good job of that.

Ethan jumped a knight off the back rank. He tried to think of tactics and strategy. Mei sidestepped down the counter, filled his cup and scoffed at the move.

The envelope bomb had jarred loose a memory.

* * *

The canopy of trees darkened the trail with shadows, even at midday. As the trio hiked along the spine of the hill, they cut branches from the overhanging limbs, sharpening the ends. This afternoon his father would show them how to make a pitfall.

Fresh deer sign looked like wet black pebbles. Jack stopped them and moved a few yards off the trail. "This is the spot," he told them.

Ethan and Tyler dug, their collapsible shovels chuffing through the soil in the quiet afternoon. They dug three feet down, smoothing the floor and shoring up the sides of the pit. Jack demonstrated how to lodge the staves into the earth.

Ty worked quicker than Ethan but less precisely. "Even out your side," Jack instructed.

They cut leafy limbs from a maple tree and draped them over the pit. Jack explained that the *troup de loup*, or wolf hole, dated back to Roman times. The punji sticks could be angled downward out of the sides, to prevent prey from climbing out. He opened a beer and made small adjustments, walking the circumference.

When he was finished, the forest floor was smooth, the outline of the pit only visible if you knew what to look for.

"Should we mark it?" Ethan asked.

"What for?" His father prodded Ethan's temple. "Mark it in *here*."

"What if I don't remember?"

"Then I guess you better get used to walking with a limp."

Ty had grinned and punched Ethan's backpack.

That was the moment Ethan began to rebel. He could stand the teasing—the bullying, no sense in avoiding the term—from Ty and his father. But there was something repugnant to him about the pitfall. He had nothing against hunting, and if unarmed and starving, such a trap might prove life-saving. But the pit was large enough to trap a human, and would cause pain to anything caught in it. And Jack Brand simply didn't care.

They hiked for another hour or so, then made an early camp. In the morning before the others woke up, Ethan hiked back and filled in the pit. He worked quickly, pulling out the spears jabbed into the earth, snapping them, then covering the hole with earth. Hurrying back, he found his sleeping bag next to a cold fire. His father and Ty had struck camp.

Ethan hadn't panicked. He packed and trekked back to where they'd parked. Jack and Ty had driven home without him. Cold but happy with his decision, Ethan hitched a ride to the town limits and walked back to Blaine. That had been the last time the three of them had gone anywhere together. The last time Ethan had thought of his father as a good person.

He never told his mother what transpired, but Agnes Brand had put it together. Soon after, she brought Ty home to Emily and her boyfriend at the time. In turn, they'd sent Ty to live with the Sterankos.

If Ethan hadn't refused to accompany his father, how much more extreme would Jack's teachings have become? The manuals showed how to make complex traps and explosive devices. If Jack hadn't taught Ty how to build them, he'd certainly inspired the teen to learn for himself.

And now at least one person was dead. If Von was right, Tyler Rash was responsible for other tunnels. Other bombs. And in a way, Ethan's actions had led Ty to that.

"Something wrong with the coffee today, Chief?"

Mei Sum hovered over the table, pot in hand. Ethan hadn't touched the last cup. He pushed it away.

"Lots to think about these days."

"Like how bad you're gonna lose when I take your rook next move?"

Ethan put money on the counter, saw Mei was right. He dragged his piece to safety, losing a pawn instead. Some games were like that. Steady losses all the way.

30

Since retiring from the department, Frank Keogh's life had evolved drastically. The former Chief had downsized from a three-story house to a new condominium overlooking Birch Bay. His wife, Lena, was running for city council this year to fill Arlene's seat. And Frank's new business venture was thriving.

That business was pot. Frank and his partners operated two large hydroponic farms, stocking several of the dispensaries around the state. Ethan didn't quite know how to feel about his former mentor's new career as a cannabis impresario.

When he drove by Frank's condo, he saw both Keoghs at work in their patch of the community garden. Frank was a larger and more dynamic version of his son, sweating through a gray Huskies shirt and dockers. Lena was more compact and wore proper gardening attire. They were weeding and pruning the zucchini vines, and paused as Ethan stepped out of his truck.

"That looks suspiciously like Ethan Brand," Frank said to his wife. "Only I don't see his trusty steed anywhere in sight."

"Must be resting her for derby day," Lena said.

"I forgot about the big race. What odds are they giving you, Ethan?"

"Scant," he said, standing by the gate. The Keoghs passed a water bottle between them. "Could I talk to you a minute, Frank?"

"Long as we don't talk work."

"Yours or mine?"

Frank wiped his forehead on the cuff of his gardening glove, the leather shiny and worn. He exchanged a look with his wife of good-humored annoyance.

"We heard about your suspicious envelope," Frank said. "Never refuse a man with more problems than you. We have biscuits inside."

The Keoghs' kitchen was spotless, all stainless steel appliances and lovingly chosen tile. The dining room table was given over to Lena's campaign. Stacks of pamphlets and boxes of yard signs. Ethan agreed to take two of each, plus a poster for his front window.

Frank pulled a couple of cheese and chive biscuits from the toaster oven and set them on a plate. "Try one of these and tell me what's on your mind."

Ethan took a bite. "Delicious."

Frank was drawing espresso shots from the burbling machine on the counter. "Good, aren't they? Can't even taste the cannabis, can you?"

His second bite had been twice the size of his first. Ethan paused with his mouth open. After a serious moment, Frank exploded in laughter.

"Got you good there," he said.

"You got me," Ethan admitted.

Frank frothed a cappuccino and took the other biscuit. "So what's eating at you?"

"What do you remember about Tyler Rash?"

The former Chief stirred a teaspoon of sugar substitute into his cup. His eyes drifted to the window and the view of the water. The day was looking to be bright and warm, with just enough of a breeze to cool the skin.

"Should've guessed this visit was about the tunnel," Frank said. "Wasn't all that surprised. Tyler Rash was a guy missing a little piece of himself. When you reach my age, Ethan, one thing you gain is the ability to trace brokenness."

Ethan didn't understand, and said so.

"Shrinks call it a cycle, but I see it as a chain. Each link has something knocked out of it, and knocks something out of the next. Maybe not even knowing it's doing it."

"How does any of that relate to Ty?"

"You tell me," Frank said.

He thought about it while Frank made a latte for his wife. Lena appeared in a dazzling blue wrap dress, a crocheted cardigan in green and black. She took her coffee in a travel mug and reminded Ethan about the yard signs.

"Speaking of signs, there's a nasty rumor someone's ripping out Arlene's," she said.

"We're working on it."

"Good." Lena kissed her husband. "Don't let your crony here keep you from those zukes."

After she left, Frank asked him, "You figure it out yet?"

"Ty's family life wasn't stable. He looked up to my father. Modeled himself, in a way."

Frank nodded. "Both of them had what you might call a sideways relationship to society. When Ty lost your father, that was all she wrote."

"I lost him, too," Ethan said. "If there's this chain or cycle, how did I escape it?"

"You a hundred percent certain that you did?"

Frank said this teasingly, but it was a raw nerve. The rawest. A fear he couldn't escape, that he would do to his kids what Jack Brand had done to him—believing he was making them stronger, more prepared, yet only ensuring they were scarred.

Before he could answer, Frank, sensing the wound, waved him off. "The fact you're sitting here agonizing over this is proof you're not that broken. There are things I could've done better with Mal, but he found something that makes him happy. You'll give that to your boys, I'm sure of it."

Ethan wished he could have that in writing.

As he helped Frank fill the dishwasher, he asked if Tyler Rash had been questioned in relation to smuggling.

"Not that I recall. Only had one run-in with the boy. He'd pitched his tent on the beach. This was wintertime, and 'tween the snow and the tide, he was drenched. I bought him some McDonalds and gave him a blanket, a few clothes from the lost and found. Never saw much of him after that."

Frank set the dishwasher to the energy-conscious cycle. He stepped into his boots and picked up his gloves.

"Of course, a good investigator wouldn't ask a retired senior citizen about smuggling. A good investigator would go straight to the source."

Meaning Seth McCandless. Ethan hoped Sissy had made progress with her brother. Could he persuade her to try harder?

As Ethan followed Frank out to the garden, he asked his one-time mentor a last question. "Did you ever feel things were, I dunno, slipping out of your control?"

Frank laughed and slapped his gloves against Ethan's shoulder. "Nothing's ever really in your control. If you think it is, you must be smoking one of my inferior competitors."

The former chief walked Ethan out and closed the gate.
"Best advice I can give you," Frank said. "When you think you're drowning, don't try to swim. Don't even try to tread water."
"What do I do, then?"
"What you do is, you don't drown," Frank said.

31

Brenda Lee Page spent the morning talking with Miles Gatlin about his cousin's disappearance. From his cottage on Anderson Island, Miles recited the details over the phone for what he claimed was "the million billionth time." He and Archie had made plans to go fishing. Archie was going to catch the evening ferry. On the afternoon of July 15th, Miles phoned his cousin to see if Archie would make the 5:35 crossing. Archie said he was en route, just gassing up.

Why, Brenda Lee asked, didn't Miles call again when Archie no-showed?

Got pissed off, got drunk, Miles replied. He had waited at the ferry, and when Archie wasn't aboard, had waited for two more sailings. Miles had bought three bottles of brandy and a case of Bud Light. When it was clear his cousin had flaked out yet again, Miles uncapped one of the bottles, walked home and staggered to bed.

When Archie's truck was recovered years later, no fishing rod or tackle had been found. Miles had no explanation for that. He said Archie owned several freshwater rods and a green tacklebox, but sometimes borrowed Miles's spare.

Archie Gatlin's home had been searched by the police after he'd been declared missing. The apartment was a mess. Amid his plumbing tools and stacks of empty beer cans, they found an unregistered shotgun. No fishing gear, though—at least none that got mentioned in the reports.

Brenda Lee had dug a stress ball out of her desk. Her fist flexed as she worked the phone and her computer, often both at once.

"I'll have to swing down to Tacoma and look around myself," she said. "It wouldn't hurt to talk with Miles in person, either."

"And Emily Heller one more time," Ethan said.

The ball rolled from left hand to right. "And Emily. Although it's a wasted effort if she's as obstreperous as last time."

"Good word." Rush hour was over. If he left now, he'd be in Olympia by noon. "How about I take a run at her alone," he said. "I can be a little obstreperous myself."

"Have at 'er," Brenda Lee said.

* * *

The drive was easy. By the time side A of his Merle Haggard tape had played for the third time, he was taking the exit for Olympia. His knocking woke up Emily Heller.

"Nothing to say to you," she called through the screen door.

Ethan walked to his truck and leaned on the warm hood. The morning had been clear, but clouds were scudding in from the south, carrying with them the smell of wildfire smoke. California was burning.

He waited, sensing Emily stare at him through the screen. He didn't have to wait long. The screen door banged. Ty's mother marched down the short driveway in flip flops and a burgundy robe.

"Why're you still here?" she asked. "Told you to leave."

"Your son is still alive," Ethan said.

"Even if he is, he ain't inside."

Ethan studied her. "I can't tell if you genuinely don't care about him, or if this is an act to protect him."

"Difference between caring and knowing where he is."
"Then please help me find him," he said.
"So you can toss him in jail? Or shoot him?"
"Yesterday he sent me a bomb," Ethan said.
Emily Heller meant to breeze off the comment. Something stopped her. Whatever insult she meant to hurl at him was abandoned for the moment. Her tongue licked over her top lip.
"We're talking off the record?" she asked.
"I'm not a journalist."
"You know what I mean. I tell you something, you won't use it against me?"
"Not unless you're party to murder."
Emily sighed and looked at her home. "Didn't have a chance to tidy up, so don't expect the red carpet."

* * *

The inside of the small yellow house was actually quite tidy, though a film of old cigarette smoke hung in the air. They sat on battered recliners that faced a large TV. Ethan swiveled his chair to look Emily in the face.
"I could use a cuppa joe," she said. "Instant OK?"
As she filled the kettle, Ethan examined the room. A framed photo collage hung behind the chairs. Every photo featured Emily herself, as a girl, a young woman. In several pictures someone had been cut out, leaving unknown arms draped over her shoulders. In one picture a teenage Emily held a baby.
Her shelves held romance novels, books on fad diets and home remedies. Rusty tins lined the top of the bookcase, their labels advertising tobacco and cookie companies long out of business. Statuettes of animals served as bookends. A crystal horse and jockey reminded him of Trim Reckoning and the decision he still had to make.

Emily Heller came back with two steaming mugs. She opened a pouch of tobacco and began rolling a cigarette.

"'Fore we get to Ty," she said, "I need to know I'm protected from getting in any trouble."

"You did spit on an officer, which wasn't very nice. But I'm taking a bygones-be-bygones approach to anybody who helps find your son."

"Told you I don't know where he is."

"But you know he's alive."

A small, quick tilt of the head.

"You've been covering for him," Ethan guessed.

"All I did was lend Ty my credit card, let him ship a few things to me."

"What kind of things?"

A shrug. She licked along the seam of the rolling paper. "I don't go through his belongings. We worked out a deal when he was in his twenties. I let him use my Visa and he sends me the cash plus ten percent. Usually he leaves it under my mat. I stash his stuff in my crawlspace, and he picks 'er up when he can."

"Did any of these packages seem like construction materials? Anything hazardous?"

"Already told you I don't go through his things. A person's entitled to privacy."

"Is anything of his still in that crawlspace?"

Emily Heller lit her cigarette. A phlegmy cough issued from her throat. "Probably. 'Less the raccoons got to it."

Ethan felt the same pressure in his stomach as he had seeing the photo in Ty's wallet. He bounded out of the chair, through the kitchen and outside, ignoring Emily's calls.

Below the back deck was a latticed crawlspace with a rusty gate. He crouched, not caring that the movement sent a tremor of pain through his ankle. He slid out the bolt, opened the latch carefully to make sure there was no wire attached.

Inside the crawlspace were scraps of leaves and animal droppings, along with two cardboard boxes and a long wooden crate. Stenciled on the side of the crate was the word *CAUTION*. Ethan dragged it out and used his pocket knife to pry the lid off.

Inside, wrapped in water-resistant paper, were sheets of the same milk-colored explosive used in the envelope bomb. One of the boxes held blasting caps. In the other were reprints of the same military manuals Ethan's father had left. Mildewed and rain-damaged, but still legible.

Tyler Rash had stashed these boxes. He'd been here recently, perhaps only a day or two ago. Standing there, Ethan could feel the distance between them closing.

32

The discovery of explosives under her back deck had rendered Emily mute. Shock, Ethan guessed. He conducted Emily out of the house, into the cab of his truck. She was still in her robe, still carrying the pouch of loose tobacco. He watched as her fingers tried to construct another cigarette. After three attempts, he took the pouch from her.

"Haven't done this since high school," he said. Fold the paper, distribute a pinch of the tobacco flakes evenly along the seam.

Her hand took the slightly conical cigarette he'd rolled and set fire to it. Ethan cranked down the windows.

"The whole block," she finally said. "Sitting right beneath me. Could've taken out the whole damn block."

An exaggeration, but one Ethan could use.

"It's important we locate Ty," he said. "Is there anything you can tell me about your son? His habits? Other friends of his?"

Emily gazed at her nicotine-yellowed fingers, the cigarette burning between them. "I don't suppose I know my son all that well."

"Ever heard of Archie Gatlin?"

"No."

"Has anyone ever come to you looking for Ty?"

A faraway smile formed on her face. Emily sucked quickly on her cigarette, spilling ash and flakes of tobacco on the passenger's door.

"Jack did once," she said.

"Jack Brand? My father?"

She nodded. "We had a nice afternoon."

Ethan fought back an urge to change the subject. He suspected his father had been unfaithful. Now he was hearing proof of it. "What did Jack want?" he asked.

"Talk about some trip he and Ty were planning. Parental consent and all." Emily looked over at him, her expression showing damaged pride. "He told me Ty was a natural outdoorsman and that I should be proud. Most guys see someone else's kid as a hassle. Not Jack."

"What happened between you?"

Her laughter stirred a cough in her lungs. She tapped ash out the window. "We found we understood each other. He got who I was, and I got him. Maybe more than your mother could. If the world had given Jack and me a bit more time..."

Only days ago, Emily Heller spat at him because he was Jack's son. Ethan had assumed she felt his father had turned Ty away from her, maybe got her son killed. Now he understood. Jack Brand had been one more romantic disappointment in her life. She hated him for dying, and hated his family for keeping them apart.

"Did my father speak with Ty before his last trip?" he asked.

"Not sure, but Jack and I..." Emily's smile tightened. "Anyway, it's all ancient history."

"What about recent history?" Ethan said. "Has anyone come looking for Ty? Anyone suspicious showed up at your house, your work?"

With every question, her head titled in the negative. The cigarette had sputtered and come loose at the seam. She dumped the remains out the window.

"You're not much good at rolling," she said.

"Out of practice. How do you get in touch with Ty?"

"I don't. Once in a blue moon he calls. From a bar, payphone, something like that. Leaves the money, and I put his stuff in the crawlspace."

"So you don't see him," Ethan said. "What about messages? Anybody ever try getting in touch through you?"

Emily blinked and rubbed at her eyes. He waited as she stitched together a memory.

"A fellow came in the bar one time," she said. "I've seen a lotta shady guys. I can usually spot the rough ones. They're half-cut when they get there. Too loud, too happy, or too grouchy in that big showy way. This guy was not like that at all. He was big and looked made out of brick, but he dressed nice, y'know? Silk shirt with an open collar and some sort of jewelry. I remember thinking he prob'ly had money."

"And this well-dressed brick left a message for Ty?"

"Puts a Ben Franklin on the bar, asks to speak with me in private. We move to a booth, and he says he's got a message for my son. Doesn't use Ty's name."

"What was the message?"

"He didn't tell me. First I said I didn't have a son. Back then I didn't want to complicate my work life. This guy says he knows that's not true. He takes my hand. I remember thinking for his size he had dainty little hands."

Emily interlaced her fingers, thumbs on the wrists, demonstrating.

"He gave my hand a squeeze, just one, and I don't even think he put much behind it. I never felt such pain. All the while he's smiling. He asks again about my son, and I tell him the same I told you."

"How did the brick respond?" Ethan asked.

"Wasn't happy, but he knew I wasn't lying. Told me not to say anything."

"How long ago? Ten years?"

"About that, yeah." She flexed her hands as if still feeling the man's grip.

Ethan used his phone to call up a picture of Archie Gatlin. He held it out for Tyler Rash's mother to see. "Is this the brick in question?"

"Nah."

He showed her the picture of Archie with Miles, the cousins fishing. He enlarged Miles's face. "What about him?"

"Bigger and meaner than them," Emily said.

Ethan thought it over and retrieved another photo. A long shot. "How about this fellow?" he said.

A sharp intake of breath told him this was the person. "Yeah," Emily said in a smaller voice. "That's the brick."

* * *

Ethan watched the forensic technicians carry the crate across the yard. The techs hadn't found anything else in the crawlspace, or in the rest of the house. The explosives were old, but Trooper Sanchez told him it was the same material as the envelope bomb. Ethan dialed Brenda Lee's number to tell her the news.

A tech with a camcorder started up the driveway and began a walk-through of the house. If Emily Heller was concerned at the intrusion, she didn't say so. Ty's mother sat in the truck silently, rolling herself another smoke. Ethan wondered what she was thinking.

Brenda Lee had learned quite a bit about the dead man and insisted on sharing her news first. DNA and dental records had confirmed the remains were Archibald Gatlin of Tacoma.

"I spoke to a cop in Tacoma who remembered Gatlin," Brenda Lee said. "He was questioned once about an aggravated assault. The victim couldn't make a positive ID, never saw the face of his attacker. Gatlin was a suspect. Offered no alibi and immediately lawyered up."

"Not his first at bat," Ethan said.

"There was no history between Gatlin and the victim," Brenda Lee continued. "That led Tacoma PD to believe it was a contract job. That Gatlin did strongarm work here and there."

"Anything to confirm that?"

"Income discrepancy. Gatlin's tax returns showed a yearly income that would cover his rent and truck payments and leave just about nothing left. Yet his apartment was full of expensive gewgaws, televisions and video games."

"Wouldn't be the first person in the trades to take jobs under the table," Ethan said.

"That's true, but remember Archie had a juvenile record. Assault and extortion. The victim was a neighbor. I spoke to Archie's cousin again. Miles says Archie mended his ways after a stint in juvie. Legally that checks out. But you'll never guess who Archie did time with."

"I'll bet you ten dollars I can," Ethan said.

"No bet. You still haven't paid me back for my dry cleaning."

Ethan told her about the recovered explosive, and how around the time of Ty's disappearance, a man showed up at his mother's work looking to deliver a message. He named the man Emily Heller had identified.

"I'll be damned," Brenda Lee said. "And suddenly all roads lead to Seth McCandless."

33

White gravel pelted the windshield of Ethan's Chevy. He'd lingered too long in Olympia and been caught in northbound traffic and eastbound weather. Low clouds had swooped in from the Pacific, and now hail was clattering onto the roofs of the unmoving snake of vehicles. Like popcorn in a tin bowl, he thought. Hail in August, that was a new one.

Now matter how clever you were, how advanced your technology or how right your thinking, the universe was always one step beyond your grasp. Ethan supposed that was something to be grateful for. It kept things interesting and people humble.

With no forward movement and only the crackle of hail as a soundtrack, he tried to fit the day's discoveries into what he knew about Tyler Rash.

Born to a teenage mother, Ty had been farmed out to relatives at an early age. As a teen, he was taken in by Jack and Agnes Brand, then later by Nettie and Mac Steranko. Soon after that, Ty was on his own, living in a tent or the back seat of his Mustang. Ethan couldn't say what his former friend had done in the decade after that.

Around the age of thirty, Ty made a brief return to live with the Sterankos. He had seemed to be in trouble. While staying in

Nettie and Mac's shed, Ty constructed part of a tunnel leading toward the border.

From Vonetta Briggs, Ethan had learned that Ty was suspected of building several such tunnels. Digging as a vocation. Ty taught himself to shore up his tunnels with lumber, to work fast and trust as few people as possible. He used his mother's credit card to buy materials. He also learned how to build bombs.

A decade ago, on June 15th, Archie Gatlin left Tacoma, planning to catch a ferry to Anderson Island. Instead he drove to Blaine. Archie's and Ty's lives had collided there. Archie was left in the tunnel, shot twice, with Ty's chain wallet attached to his belt. Ty probably took Archie's Jeep, abandoning it in the wild. Then Tyler Rash disappeared.

Ten years later, Archie and the tunnel were discovered. A bomb ended up in Ethan's mail, manufactured according to a manual that Ty possessed, using materials found in the crawlspace of Ty's mother's house.

All of this was built on a pile of suppositions. Someone else could have killed Gatlin and built the bomb. For all Ethan knew, Ty could be dead himself. Possible, but he didn't think so.

The photo in the wallet of Ty and Jack Brand—the case kept turning back toward Ethan's father. Tunnel building was an extension of the survival skills Jack had taught them. The diagram for the bomb was found in a manual Jack owned, which Ty no doubt had seen. Why else would Ty send him the bomb, unless he was afraid Ethan possessed the knowledge to track him down?

The irony was, if Ethan had that knowledge, he didn't know it. He was no closer to finding Tyler Rash than anyone else.

The only connection between Ty and Archie Gatlin was the McCandless family. Gatlin and Seth McCandless had been in juvenile detention together. Sissy McCandless had seen Ty meeting with her brother. Shortly after that, Seth had gone looking for

Ty. Whatever the reason, it had been urgent enough for Seth to threaten Ty's mother in a public place.

The hail stopped as abruptly as it began. Traffic, too, began to move. Ethan was home by six, with an hour to get ready for the book club meeting.

Not enough chairs. He rearranged the living room, draping an old Hudson's Bay blanket over a chest, hoping two people could share it. They'd have to be very thin people and very close friends.

At 6:30 he phoned the kids to say goodnight. Both Ben and Brad sounded glum, or maybe just tired. Ethan sympathized, happy to hear their voices.

Brad handed the phone to their mother. Three thousand miles away and her voice could still sweeten his mood. An elegant voice, sensual, and sometimes profane, and tonight slightly weary.

"You're lucky you missed out on back to school shopping," Jazz said. "I don't know who was more of a hassle, the kids or my parents. Every three-ring binder with a calculator built in, every combination pencil sharpener and flashlight, made its way into our shopping cart."

"I had a Mr. T lunchbox with a broken hinge," Ethan said.

"I bet that made you the envy of the schoolyard." Jazz's tone became serious. "Ethan, I have something to ask. I know it's your turn to have the boys at Christmas, but could I possibly implore you to come here instead? I'll cover your flight and find a place to put you up."

He didn't answer immediately. Ethan had been looking forward to two weeks with the kids. Going sledding if it snowed, showing them the horse if he committed to buying Trim Reckoning. He'd already lined up several babysitters if he was called in to work for an emergency. Christmas was a time of high emotions and high crimes. The job couldn't be put on hold, but he could manage to give the boys as good a Christmas as possible.

Taking two weeks off to fly to Boston was out of the question. That would mean a shorter visit, less time with his sons.

"A tall order," he said, knowing in the end he wouldn't refuse. The number of times he'd turned down Jasmine Soltani were few. "What do you mean 'find a place to put me up?' Finally get rid of that futon in your office?"

"This isn't the order I wanted to tell you things," Jazz said. "Phil and I—well, he's going to be moving in."

"Ah."

"We thought at Christmas we'd tell Mom and Dad. And you, of course. The boys like Phil, but they're still getting used to the idea."

"Ah."

"Can you please say something other than 'ah?'" Jazz asked.

"Not at the moment, no."

"I recognize this is a major step. That's something else I was going to broach while you were here. You and I finalizing our divorce."

Unconsciously he'd sat down on the chest, the blanket slipping off by his feet. Barely comfortable for one person, he thought. The lawn chairs in the shed would be better.

"I know it's a lot to drop on you at once," Jazz said. He heard a snuffle over the phone. "I'm sorry."

"Don't be."

"I'm really very happy about it all."

Ethan realized what she was waiting to hear. Whether he flew out for the holidays or not, she wanted his blessing. Maybe that was too strong a word—his acknowledgment of this new reality, his acceptance of it, his solemn vow not to make things difficult.

To take the news well, in other words.

The trouble was he couldn't. A billion tiny changes would occur because of this. Sleeping in Jazz's home office, at least he'd been there Christmas morning when the kids woke up. Try that from a hotel. Last Boxing Day, he'd sat with her father over sherry, the professor insisting his daughter was on the cusp of reconciliation. Even the rare moments since their split when they'd been alone with each other—the time Jazz had been in Seattle for a conference, had called him from the hotel bar, when he'd rushed down and they'd ripped each other's shirts off in the elevator—

All done with now.

"Please say something," Jazz said.

"Yesterday someone tried to blow me up," he said.

"God. I'm so sorry, Ethan. I'm glad you're all right."

"I think today hurts worse."

A wheeze of steps on the old porch before a knock on the door. He told his ex he had to go. Ethan wanted to turn the lights off, uncork a bottle of Crown Royal and drown himself. Just sit in the dark with his heartbreak and George Jones. Blue must be the color of the blues.

But guests were arriving. The meeting was about to start.

34

A lively group, the Blaine Women's Book Club. Ethan brewed coffee and tea, and filled a salad bowl with stale pretzels. Mrs. Docherty had baked a coffee cake, and Sally Bishop brought a vegetable tray with a half-price sticker on the lid. Ethan's regret at not finishing the novel was forgiven.

The conversation ranged far from the pages, to trauma, the postwar generation, and marriage to difficult men. He'd never seen himself that way, but now wondered if his ex had. Wasn't everybody difficult? Difficulty was what made a person human.

He tried his best to keep his thoughts away from the news about his ex. Bitterness wasn't called for. Hurt, surprise, those were acceptable given the situation. Jazz hadn't set out to wound him. She was simply chasing her idea of happiness. Why not be glad for her?

Because I'm just not, Ethan thought. Not this quickly. Because I'm selfish and lowdown and mean. Because I'm a hypocrite, and because right now I'm hurting.

He scanned the group, seeing people he knew too well. Prescription forgers, suicide attempts, drunken brawlers and domestic disputes. He saw black eyes and sobbing confessions. He wondered what they saw in him.

Zelda Shields hadn't shown up, but Jay Swan did. Perhaps Arlene had invited the press, or Jay saw the meeting as a chance to get inside the home of the Chief of Police. Not a particularly happy home at present.

Arlene showed up at 7:30 on the nose, carrying a tray of home baked muffins, which were quickly scarfed up by the group. Ethan hadn't eaten since breakfast. He had two.

A magnificent performance to watch. Arlene used the book as a springboard to discuss how best to help the forgotten members of the community. Even Mrs. Docherty, who didn't seem to like much of anything, was polite.

"Too often we harden our hearts against the people who need that little bit more," Arlene said. "Why is that? Because we're selfish, we don't care? Not at all. Because there's only so much we can do."

"Compassion fatigue," Sally Bishop said, nodding. "I saw a video about that."

"Eventually we stop believing things can ever get better. And then we end up hiding at home among our gadgets and toys."

"And boats," Lorraine Rusk said to a chorus of laughs.

Arlene joined in. "You said it, not me."

At 8:40, with the meeting breaking up, Eldon Mooney strolled in. The mayor was alone, and didn't remove his overcoat. He made a light knock on the doorframe as he entered.

"How's it going, gals? Hope it's all right I drop by." Spying Arlene, Mooney's smile took on an air of concern. "So good to see you, councilwoman. Condolences about your car."

"Eldon." Arlene's tone was crisp.

"I'm sure you've already heard enough political gabble tonight," Mooney told the club. "Smart group of ladies like this, I know you won't make any decisions too hastily, not without weighing up both sides. I'm a supporter of strong women, always have been. I like to call Mrs. Mooney the real mayor of Blaine."

"Maybe she can find out who's pulling up my campaign signs," Arlene said.

Mooney's smile didn't change, but he nodded in Ethan's direction. "That's an issue for our Chief, don't you think?"

Before Ethan could respond, Lorraine spoke up. "When are you gonna fix that pothole on H Street, Your Honor?"

"Now that you've alerted me to it, I'll get right on that, ma'am."

"You weren't alerted when you drove over it this afternoon?"

"My downstairs neighbor plays music really loud," Sally Bishop said. "And it's not even Madonna or something good."

"Why's the docking fee at the marina keep going up?"

"My son was outside the post office for five minutes tops, and why's he get a parking ticket?"

Mooney parried and deflected like Errol Flynn playing Robin Hood, but the book club was too much for him.

"I will deal with *all* of your concerns, my dears, the minute this election is behind me." The mayor backed toward the door.

"Told us that two elections ago."

"Is it true Black Rock covers the cost of your entire campaign?"

"What'd you promise in return?"

Ethan looked at Jay, jotting down notes as fast as their hand could move. For a moment his own domestic problems were out of mind. He enjoyed the show.

Arlene scored the knockout by asking for a show of hands. "Raise 'em if your life is much improved since His Honor here took office."

Not an arm went up.

"Now raise 'em if you'd like to see a change in this town."

Unity, except for Jay, still writing. Mooney scanned the polite but hostile room. He noticed Ethan's hand up and made a small shake of the head.

"I can see I've got some work to do in order to win you gals over," he said. "An open mind is all I ask. Vote your conscience, and don't let yourself be swayed by the mob. G'night to one and all."

He left to silence. The meeting dissolved into recipe swapping and discussion of whether September was really the month to finally tackle *Anna Karenina*. Arlene nodded at him, shot him a thumbs up.

"Went pretty well," she said.

"You made the most of it."

"Guess we'll see come Election Day." Arlene took the empty muffin tray. He watched her head down the block to where her rental car was parked. As she drove away, he saw Mercy Hayes at the wheel of the unmarked patrol car slither down Kickerville Drive after her.

Alone.

Ethan poured a healthy shot of whiskey into a coffee mug and turned off the lights. He thought of his ex, and Vonetta Briggs, and a married woman in Hawaii he might never see again. He thought about Sissy McCandless.

"You'd think this would get easier," he said to no one in particular.

35

The department's small muster room was flooded with the sounds of cereal rattling into bowls and splashing milk. A breakfast meeting with all officers attending. Ethan hoped a crime wave wouldn't break out in the next fifteen minutes.

"This must be serious," Brenda Lee said. "You're breaking out the Raisin Bran."

Going around the table, each officer summarized where they were in their current investigation. Brenda Lee was working on the connection between Archie Gatlin and Tyler Rash. Mal Keogh had a lead on a former client of Arlene's who had once threatened her. When he asked the councilwoman why she'd refused to represent Lou Blanc, Arlene answered with, "Spend five minutes in his company and you'll know." So Mal's job for the day was to find Lou Blanc and spend five minutes in his company.

Heck Ruiz had documented three more yard sign thefts. Ethan remembered his own signs had been taken, but didn't mention it. Mercy Hayes had followed Arlene for the past day without incident.

When everyone had taken their turn, Ethan said, "I finished your evaluations. If anyone wants to discuss theirs with me one on one, I'll set time aside for that. Right now, though, I'd like you to do mine."

"Evaluate you?" Mercy asked.

"How things are going. What we can do better. What I can do."

"A raise wouldn't hurt," Brenda Lee began.

"Besides a raise."

A tentative silence descended on the room. The officers looked at each other. No one wanted to go first.

Mal cleared his throat. "A little more freedom sometimes would be nice. Especially in terms of scheduling."

"Funny, I was going to say a lack of discipline with scheduling," Brenda Lee said.

Before the officers could begin sniping, Ethan said, "I'll make a note about both. Thank you. Anybody else?"

"Better childcare would sure be nice, Boss," Mercy said.

Heck nodded vigorously. "I hear that."

"What else?"

"About the election," Heck said. "I know you're friends with, well, one of the candidates, but it makes things kind of weird. I mean, you're the Chief. It's like we all took sides already."

Ethan realized he should be writing these down. He made chicken scratches in his notebook.

"Since you asked," Brenda Lee said, "I feel there was a lack of transparency about your injury. Not so much now, but before."

"Why's that anybody's business?" Mal asked.

"Because Ethan hid it."

"'Hid' is pretty strong. He's a vet, a hero."

"He's still in the room," Ethan said. "I did keep it a secret."

"And I understand why," Brenda Lee said. "My point is, transparency matters. It's a core value of most Fortune 500 companies."

"We're not building electric cars," Mal said.

"If your coworker is hiding something—"

"You're saying you're an open book?"

Ethan rapped the table, calling for time out. "Transparency. It's on the list. If you think of anything else today, let me know. Dismissed."

As they filed out, he looked over what he'd written, dismayed at the number of deficiencies. The last one out, Mercy Hayes, caught this look.

"You did ask, Boss," she said.

* * *

Brenda Lee Page had been right: all roads ran through Seth McCandless. There'd be no meeting with Seth unless the convict's sister argued for one on their behalf. Still, bargaining with Sissy McCandless was a dangerous proposition. Owing her a favor could open up all sorts of problems down the road.

Too often the job entailed choices like this. The better of two bad options. He knew he'd deal with Sissy if there was no other way. And there wasn't.

But Sissy wasn't in Breakwater Travel this morning. Cliff Mooney was, a size twelve runner up on the counter, face buried in a dirty paperback. As the door chimed, Cliff whipped the book out of sight.

"What do you want?" Cliff asked. "Still think I'm stalking whatshername?"

"If you are, you can tell me."

"Why the hell would I do that?"

"Remorse," Ethan said.

Cliff scowled. "Not buying."

"Never hurts to ask. Where's your employer?"

"Sissy's out for the afternoon."

"The question was where," Ethan said.

Something about Cliff Mooney irritated him. A lot of things, in fact. As work colleagues they'd never so much as had a beer together. On Cliff's first day, Ethan had sized the rookie officer up as a bad fit. The kind of brute attracted to the job for the power it held. Someone aching to apply the use of force against weaker people, in order to answer questions about their own self-worth. Cliff's behavior had borne out that judgment. Even though firing him made Ethan's dealings with the mayor especially difficult, it hadn't been a tough decision.

Yet here Cliff was, by all appearances engaged in a legitimate job. Cooperating with his investigations, no less. Why did Ethan have the impulse to prod the bear, to see if Cliff would charge him? Why couldn't he help from assuming the worst?

Because there was no contrition in Cliff, he reasoned, no understanding that he'd been fired for doing wrong. And because Ethan suspected Sissy McCandless had an ulterior purpose for hiring the mayor's nephew. Assuming the worst in people was a natural hazard of the job—as was finding out how often you were right.

Often, but not always, he reminded himself.

"I don't know where Sissy is," Cliff said, mastering his anger. "She doesn't always say."

"Tell her to call me, please," Ethan said, adding the last word begrudgingly.

"Will do."

"Thank you," he said. "Look at us being civil."

In the mirror above the door he saw Cliff return to his reading. Ethan couldn't make out the title, but the cover showed a nurse stripping off her uniform, leaving only her stethoscope and cap. Probably not the book club's September selection.

* * *

Sissy wasn't in any of the neighboring shops or restaurants. He would have to drive out to the McCandless homestead. Was it possible that's what she wanted, why she hadn't been in touch?

On the other hand, she could be avoiding him. If there was this attraction between them, Sissy might feel as wary about it as he did.

Ethan took the long way back to the station, passing by the waterfront. He spotted Jess Sinclair leaving the terrace of the Ocean Beach Supper Club, heading in the direction of Lucky's. Jess and Mei Sum had both spent time working in their family restaurants. Something to bond over, Ethan thought. Jess was on foot, toting a messenger bag that seemed ready to burst its stitches. The bag didn't seem heavy, though. Something metallic stuck out of the flap.

He'd avoided the Supper Club since Steph Sinclair had left for Hawaii. Now it was under new management. The fare had been advertised as "Northwest Cuisine with a Playful Continental Twist." Whatever that meant.

As he passed the old train station, Ethan caught a glimpse of pale blonde hair swirling around the mouth of a hoodie. Zelda Shields sat on the same bench he and Sissy had occupied days ago. A tallboy beer can next to her.

He swung around, thinking he'd ask why Shields hadn't come to the meeting last night. Her focus was on the water past Jorgensen Pier. She took a sip. In her other hand Ethan noticed an automatic pistol.

36

Gravel under his boot made one step slightly more audible. Shields' head snapped around. She saw him.

Frank Keogh described moments like this as a "terrible and instant calculation." You would only really know you'd done the right thing later, if everyone survived. If not, you'd be replaying the moment for the rest of your life.

Or worse, the moment *was* the rest of your life.

He had reason enough to draw his weapon. To order Zelda Shields to disarm and prone herself on the wet ground. Depending on alcohol and mood, she might comply, or do something very damaging.

And if he didn't draw, and the former soldier's hand simply raised an inch or so off her knee and squeezed the trigger with four to five pounds of pressure—he'd seen situations go wrong as fast as that, often with no warning at all.

Zelda Shields saw him and didn't react. A good sign. Her face was puffy, dried tears on her cheeks. She set the pistol down easily on the far side, away from Ethan, and took a long pull from the beer can.

"Booze and firearms aren't a good match," he said.

"It's only light beer."

"I'm going to sit down, if you don't object."

She shrugged and inched over. Beads of rainwater clung to the seat and backrest. Ethan sat anyway.

"Am I under arrest?" Shields asked.

"Do you want to be?"

"Maybe I should."

"Doesn't answer my question," he said.

Slowly, and without putting her finger near the trigger guard, Shields passed him the gun. A Sig Sauer M17, olive colored. Loaded, from its weight. A service weapon.

"Look familiar?" Shields asked.

"In my day we used the old 1911." Ethan extracted the magazine and cleared the chamber. The 9mm casing gleamed in the morning sun.

"Jarhead, right?"

"Second Light Armored. Recon."

Pointing at her own chest, Shields said, "Gun Devils. Used to play three-on-three against some guys from the 3rd. Pretty good, at least for Marines."

"They probably felt bad and let you win," Ethan said.

Shields smiled. "I was only in the Stan a few months. Got my five jumps in, joined the 3–319, got over there just in time for the pull-out."

"You didn't miss much."

"Just so you know, I wasn't gonna do anything. With the gun, I mean. I had it out, not really sure why. I guess 'cause I heard your footsteps."

Ethan jammed the ammunition and weapon in separate pockets. "Thought I was sneaking up."

"You have a pretty particular walk, Chief. Kind of an agile lumber. Your foot bother you?"

"Some days more than others."

Shields nodded. She hadn't moved her eyes from the pier.

"Why weren't you at the meeting last night?" Ethan asked.

"You didn't really want me there."

"Because I told you not to bring a gun? You think that implies a lack of trust?"

"Doesn't it?"

"Guns aren't a trust issue to me. They're variables, and I want as few of them as possible. 'Specially when it comes to my home. Trust starts with doing what we say we will."

Ethan felt his phone buzz with a text. He ignored it. Zelda Shields's hands turned the beer can in a slow circle. Her thumbs crushed the sides.

"Can I tell you something?" she said. "I burned some toast this morning."

"Hardly a felony."

"Smoke detector went off. George—that's my husband—is scraping the thing out, saying maybe we should put it closer to the window. And I just lost it. Threw the thing at the wall and walked out."

Ethan nodded, letting her tell the story.

"I don't know why I did it. All of a sudden I had this feeling like none of this *matters*. Toaster, dishwasher, whose turn it is to take out the recycling. It's not *real*."

Her thumbs pressed against one another through the aluminum. Beer spilled onto the gravel.

"My last few weeks over there, I saw this child."

As she told the story, Shields's voice became hesitant, her words chosen carefully, then pouring out in a torrent. She became sarcastic, mocking the depth of her own feelings. Then halting midsentence to sob.

There was no advice he could give. No response that would be suitable. All Ethan could do was listen.

"Worst part is," Sheids said, wiping her nose with the cuff of her hoodie, "I know how lucky I am. Got parents and a husband and a stepdaughter I love. A support system, as they say. I made it out in one piece, too—sorry."

She looked over to see if she'd hurt his feelings. Ethan merely nodded.

"I'm drowning in my own good fortune, you know? Sorry to take so much of your time, Chief. Am I . . ."

"Free to go," he said. "Wish I had something profound to tell you. Other than turn the fan on, next time you make toast."

Shields thanked him and set the beer can on the lip of a trash can. She walked back toward civilization. He thought of what he might say next time. That the little world didn't seem like much after being out in the big world. But it was real, and worth participating in. A lesson he'd learned himself at great expense.

Ethan removed his phone, aware of the weight of the pistol. The message was from Jazz. *Should we talk?*

Not just yet, he typed. *Soon.*

When you're ready came the reply.

Ethan wondered what ready might feel like.

37

The McCandless property was beyond the town limits—teasingly so. Part of the original homestead had been located in Blaine. The family had sold that section, to Frank Keogh of all people. Long greenhouses now occupied that side of the road, fenced in with chain link and razor wire.

Ethan remembered the McCandless house looking run-down and ragged when Seth and Jody lived there. The yard had been a showcase for old cars and appliances. All gone. Now the house had a new roof of orange tile, and new purple-white paint on the sides. A paved driveway had replaced the quagmire of mud and dead grass. Bushes had been planted along the roadside, small now, but they'd grow into a privacy hedge.

Sissy's brothers had put up a crude security system on the porch above the door. She had upgraded to a less conspicuous camera with a black mirrored globe. Ethan rang the buzzer, knowing he was on camera. Brenda Lee had offered to come with him, but he'd declined. Technically they were out of their jurisdiction, and he wanted this to be informal, off the record.

No answer to his buzz. He tried knocking. Either Sissy wasn't home or she didn't want to speak to him. Ethan stepped off the porch, heard the scrape of a garden tool from around back, and headed down the path along the side.

Sissy McCandless stood next to a pile of steaming mulch. She dug out a shovelful and deposited it at the far edge of her garden, raking it smooth. Sissy had planted strawberries and runner beans. Several squat pumpkins peaked out from beneath the speckled leaves. Stalks of what looked like garlic.

Sissy noticed him and smiled, but continued her raking.

"You caught me red-handed," she said. "I just got the body covered up."

"That's a joke, isn't it?"

"Not my best." Sissy let the handle of the rake rest on the grass. "Something I can help you with, Ethan?"

"Last time we talked, you were going to ask your brother about Tyler Rash."

"I spoke with Seth. He wasn't in a very receptive mood."

"It's vital we talk to him, Sissy."

"Go right ahead."

"He's not likely to confide much, 'less you ask him to."

"You don't have siblings," Sissy said. "A sister's endorsement is almost a strike against."

"In an ordinary family that might be true, but seeing as you're the person signing the family checks, you have markers to call in."

"I passed on your request to him," Sissy said. "Are you and I bargaining now?"

"The decent thing to do would be to help."

"And if I don't, that makes me indecent?"

"Poor choice of words," Ethan said. "I'd appreciate your help."

Sissy had her hair in a kerchief. She stood and removed her gardening gloves, beating the dirt off against her thigh. She wore a man's overshirt and ratty jeans, one pale knee visible through a rip.

"Why don't you come in the house for a lemonade?" she said.

* * *

Reclamation was the word that came to mind. Like the exterior of the house, the inside was in the process of being transformed. The living room had been recently painted a bright yellow-green, and a drop cloth had been placed over the dining table. New furniture had been chosen, a lot of reclaimed wood and antique brass. What had once been the crowded and dirty domain of a family of smugglers now resembled a luxury cottage. Impressive work. There was even art on the walls. The McCandless men only valued art by how easy it was to fence.

They sat in the living room on a pair of plaid-covered accent chairs. Sissy brought a tray with two tumblers of ice, along with a pitcher of cloudy lemonade. A small bottle of Maker's Mark as well.

"I didn't know if you prefer your lemonade with a little kick," she said.

"However you take it."

"Let's live dangerously, then." She built the drinks. "You didn't answer my question, you know."

"Which was?"

"Are you and I bargaining?"

He accepted a glass, toasted her health. The drink was a tad sweet but good.

"I have nothing to bargain with, Sissy," he said. "I can't do you any favors. I can't overlook any activity that breaks the law. All I can do is prevail on you and your conscience to do what's right."

"Rightness is conditional, though, wouldn't you say?"

"I wouldn't say that, no. Right is right."

"You don't think circumstance matters? When you were in Afghanistan did you happen to shoot anyone?"

"That was war."

"And that makes it right?"

"No, just makes it war."

Sissy McCandless leaned back in her chair, staring at him over the rim of her drink.

"You do have things to offer," she said.

Ethan was conscious of the chilled glass, the unforgiving cushion of the love seat, the pinpoints of light reflected in Sissy's oversized glasses.

"Seth won't talk to you as a favor to me," she said. "He probably would, though, for an official letter of cooperation to the parole board next year. If you ask the DA to prepare something to that effect, I'm sure he would speak with you. Anything to do with my brothers has to be couched in the language of self-interest. A lesson I learned long ago."

There was irony in putting Seth McCandless behind bars only to reward him for his cooperation. But if that was the price, it was worth paying. Ethan stood and set the glass down, avoiding his reflection in the coffee table.

"I'd better ask the DA, then," he said. "Thanks for the beverage."

"I have a condition of my own," Sissy said.

He waited for her to name it. Sissy finished her drink. There was no guile in her face, perhaps a slight embarrassment. A hard person to read.

"There aren't that many people who interest me," she said. "I'd like us to put aside our occupations for an evening."

"A date?" Ethan asked.

"If it wouldn't offend your virtue, yes. I'd like to ask you out."

Flummoxed, he stood there a moment, staring at Sissy McCandless backlit by the window. Ethan felt vulnerable, challenged somehow. Sissy's expression didn't change.

Ethan tried to imagine all the ramifications of such a date, how it might color things down the road. Weighed up against locating Tyler Rash, it was no contest.

"You choose the restaurant," he said. "I'll pick where we go after."

38

When he returned to the station he found the front desk in midcommotion. A large wide man in a fringed buckskin jacket, his hair a long curly mullet, was pacing in front of the desk, yelling about having never been treated like this before. His voice was surprisingly patrician.

"After they both apologize—profusely and in front of my neighbors—I would like to lodge a formal complaint. That is in addition to any legal remedies I may pursue."

Jon Gutierrez rolled his eyes so only Ethan could see, while speaking to the giant in his mildest tone. "If you'll please lower your voice, sir."

Mal Keogh was at his desk, purposely ignoring the ruckus out front.

"What's with Buffalo Bill out there?" Ethan asked.

"That's Lou Blanc. I stopped by to ask him about smashing Arlene's car. I barely got my question out before Blanc started yelling harassment. Real persecution complex. He followed me back here."

Brenda Lee Page wasn't at her desk, so Ethan took her seat. He glanced through the door at the man still thundering away.

"How does Blanc size up as a suspect?"

"Doesn't," Mal said. "He works out of his home, selling quote-unquote authentic tribal artifacts and remedies. His own security footage shows he never left the property."

"He's Indigenous?" Ethan asked.

"Not even on his great-great-great grandmother's side. What they call a 'Pretendian.' Born in Holland to French parents, but he claims to be wise in the ways of Coast Salish medicine. Of course, the second he's pressed, he drops the act and suddenly becomes an aggrieved white man who wants to speak with my superior."

"Think Jon can handle him?" Ethan asked. So far the civilian administrator was holding his own.

"If it helps, he can tell Blanc I'm probably resigning."

"You got the job in Portland?"

Mal smiled. "Second interview next week."

"Congratulations. Fingers crossed."

He shook the officer's hand, thinking he'd hate to lose Mal. As good an investigator as Malcolm Keogh was, he was also someone Ethan had served with before becoming chief. One less person he could count on to tell him the truth.

Well, he'd have to find someone new. Zelda Shields came to mind. Could he overlook today's business with the gun? Frank Keogh had overlooked less, and ended up with Cliff Mooney. Then again, Frank had taken a chance on Ethan himself. Give Shields a few months to readjust, and just maybe . . .

A slam interrupted his train of thought. Lou Blanc was pounding on the desk now. Pointing his index finger at Jon's throat.

Enough of this. Ethan stepped into the reception area. Lou Blanc was shouting over Jon's placating words. The big man wheeled, his finger now jabbing at Ethan's chest. Ethan grabbed it and bent it toward the ceiling. Blanc yowled.

Catching the wrist and flexing the digit in ways it wasn't designed for, he made the big man trot in a circle, away from the desk. Ethan marched him at the front door and bulled him through it, walking him outside to the station's parking lot.

"I take it that's your vehicle," Ethan said.

Blanc's van was parked in the Accessible spot. Painted midnight blue, on the side panel a mural of a pack of wolves baying at a large copper moon. LOUIS GRAY WOLF AUTHENTIC MEDICINE AND CRAFTS stenciled on the hood. No wonder Arlene wanted nothing to do with Lou Blanc.

"Let me go." Chest heaving, the giant still struggled.

"What's the magic word?"

"I'm asthmatic."

"Close enough." Ethan released him. The big man staggered to his van and retrieved a puffer from the dashboard. Blanc took a long blast.

"You may have dislocated my finger," he said.

"If I did you'd hear a pop. And feel it."

Lou Blanc blanched. "The behavior of a brute. Completely and utterly unacceptable."

"We value community feedback," Ethan said. "Now go away."

Once the van was shuddering out of the parking lot, Blanc began cursing again. Ethan went back inside.

"Way to pull that guy's punk card," Jon said, handing him a message slip. Nettie Steranko wanted to see him. In the "subject" line of the note, Jon had written two words: HORSE SCHOOL.

* * *

Nettie and Mac were in the midst of lunch when Ethan arrived. He watched them sop up split pea soup with hunks of warm sourdough bread. Nettie forced a bowl and a heel of bread at him, which Ethan gratefully accepted.

The soup needed pepper but was delicious. As he ate, he noticed husband and wife exchange looks. An entire silent conversation playing out across from him. It seemed to end in agreement to tell him something.

"We fibbed a bit, Ethan." Nettie looked both guilty and apologetic. "Should've told you the whole story."

He waited for her to elaborate. Had they known about the tunnel? About Ty and Archie Gatlin?

Mac set his spoon down. "What my wife's trying to tell you, Chief, Trim Reckoning is a racer. We got her from Hastings Park during a claiming race where nobody claimed her."

"I think you mentioned that."

"A racehorse is trained differently than a trail horse. Acts differently around people. Certain habits are encouraged."

"You said she has a sweet disposition."

"And I meant it," Mac said, looking to his wife for help.

"She could use some retraining," Nettie said.

"So 'horse school' wasn't a typo on Jon's part," Ethan said.

Nettie explained. A racehorse's muscles were developed for speed, and their temperament for competition. The animal would need to be re-educated in how to act around people and other animals. The result would be a horse with less aggression, that could be safely ridden by anyone, on any terrain.

"Like obedience training for dogs?" he asked. "How much does it cost?"

"It's not cheap," Nettie said as she cleared the bowls. "But it buys you peace of mind. No biting, no kicking."

"No guarantee though, is there?"

Instead of answering, Mac started for the kitchen door. "Let's go see her again before you make a decision, Chief."

He followed the old man out to the stable, thinking this was one of the best sales pitches he'd ever been subjected to. The affable husband and wife had sized him up and planned this. Your kids will love this one, Chief. There's just one catch.

The Sterankos should have raised sheep, he though. They certainly knew how to fleece somebody.

"This horse school," he asked, "how long does it take?"

"Couple months of intense work, and then we keep at her for a year to make sure it takes."

"And you run the program?"

"I help out some," Mac said. He hauled out a sack of carrots from a bin near the door of the stable.

"So when it's over, does the horse get a diploma?"

"Sure. Cap and gown cost extra."

The small brown horse with the broken blaze looked over the door of the stall. Ethan held out a carrot. The animal's mouth snapped it up. He noticed the wrappings were off her back legs.

"How's her sprain?" he asked.

"Healing. I wish you could ride her before making your decision."

The warmth of her breath on his fingers was pleasant. He held out another carrot. What was the saying, you can't cheat an honest man?

"Hell with it," he said, "let's do something foolish."

At the kitchen table, as Nettie wrote out the bill of sale, Ethan showed them the picture of Archie Gatlin. She squinted and shook her head. Mac took the phone and held it closer to his face.

"Doesn't look familiar," he said. "Course we see dozens of folks every weekend. Can't say for sure I never met him."

"He drove a Jeep. Might have had fishing gear with him."

"Ask Mac about the Lipizzaner he rode when he was seventeen," Nettie said. "He can still tell you how she handled. Human faces he's not so good."

"And you?" Ethan asked.

"Cataracts. Sign both copies, please and thanks."

He took up the pen, looked the numbers over and signed, grinning at his own folly. The Sterankos' eyesight was fine. They'd seen him coming miles away.

39

Brenda Lee Page had spent the day traveling to Tacoma, where she'd spoken to Archie Gatlin's former landlord and looked through the dead man's apartment. A strikeout: the suite was rented to a family now, and none of Archie's possessions had been kept. The landlord told her Mr. Gatlin had been a gruff man who paid cash and kept to himself.

Next she'd visited the gas station in Castle Rock where Archie stopped on his way to Blaine. Another strike out. And a third when she convinced a park ranger to show her where Archie's Wrangler had been found. The stretch of forest was now the parking lot of a water processing plant.

To round out the day, Brenda Lee had hoped to speak with Miles Gatlin again, this time in person, maybe show him some photos of Ty. But when she phoned from the Steilacoom ferry, Miles's wife told her he was out. A fishing trip, ironically. Brenda Lee had given up and headed home.

She arrived at the station to good news. Assistant District Attorney Hayley Hokuto had worked out an agreement with Seth McCandless's lawyer. Seth would speak with them tomorrow.

"Why would he agree to that, all of a sudden?" Brenda Lee asked.

Ethan looked at the paperwork on his desk, avoiding eye contact. "We're writing him a letter of cooperation."

"We are, huh? This was your idea?"

"Sissy McCandless suggested it."

"Doesn't surprise me," Brenda Lee said. "Ethan, are you sure this is a good idea?"

"No." And figuring he'd rather have all her criticism at once, he told her about what Sissy had wanted for herself.

Instead of criticism, though, Brenda Lee laughed. Long and loud enough that he shut the door of his office.

"Star-crossed lovers, huh," she said after the laughter ebbed away. "I spend all day in the field with less than nothing to show for it. Meanwhile, all you have to do is flash that Robert Redford grin at a lonely woman."

Ethan started to object but she was laughing again. He supposed it *was* pretty funny.

Brenda Lee turned serious. "As I was driving, I was thinking about Rash's movements after the murder. How he left the wallet on Archie's corpse. What if that wasn't to confuse us?"

"Not sure I follow," Ethan said.

"The wallet made us think the body was Ty's, but he would know that eventually DNA would rule that out. What if instead, Tyler Rash meant to toss his own identity?"

"Become someone else?"

"It's not farfetched. He probably left here in Archie's Jeep. Once he ditched that, he was free to become anyone."

"If you were in the market to buy a new identity, Seth McCandless might be a good person to know."

"Or Sissy," Brenda Lee said.

Ethan couldn't deny that.

As they finished discussing their strategy for tomorrow's meeting, Brenda Lee spied the bill of sale on his desk.

"You didn't," she said. "Do you have any idea the fees involved for stabling and feeding a horse?"

"I do now," he said.

Brenda Lee looked at the price again, shaking her head. "The Trojans got a better deal on their horse."

* * *

Darkness was settling in earlier every night. One sure sign of fall's approach. The stores were advertising back to school sales. The Super Value even had plastic jack- o'-lanterns and tombstones on display.

Heck Ruiz and his wife stood at the supermarket's entrance, handing out MOONEY FOR MAYOR pamphlets. Ethan nodded at the officer as he entered, glad Heck wasn't in uniform.

Watching the families shopping together, he thought of his sons. He wanted to call them tonight. That would mean talking to Jazz, though, and he felt he couldn't do that until he'd absorbed her new living arrangement.

So absorb it, he thought, moving down the bread aisle. Tell her you'll give up Christmas and fly out for a weekend in December. Or don't and stay home by yourself. But be happy for her. You *are* happy for her.

And in truth he was. Jazz deserved a fulfilling relationship, a sex life. Someone to be kind to her. It had nothing to do with him, and didn't lessen his role in Ben and Brad's lives.

But it sure felt that way.

What was the name of that old Hank Williams tune? "My Son Calls Another Man Daddy." A bullet would hurt less.

You work so hard not to repeat the mistakes of your parents, he thought. Instead, you make all new mistakes. And you lose them just the same as your parents lost you.

The parking lot lights snapped on as the sunlight faded. He carried his groceries out of the store, thinking how pleasant it would be to not feel anything for a while. That had been the blessing of the painkillers. A seductive numbness. His emotions could feel so raw sometimes.

Someone was following him. Ethan intuited this before his peripheral vision caught the figure weaving between parked cars. Without breaking stride, he transferred the groceries to his left hand. He veered across the lot, away from his truck, toward the street.

Angling around a raised up F350, he used the reflection off the Ford's hood to check if his pursuer was still behind him. Yes, the small figure was still there.

Near the edge of the lot he stopped abruptly, as if realizing he was heading in the wrong direction. Shaking his head, muttering, he circled the large pickup. When the vehicle was between him and the person following, Ethan crouched against the wheel, set his bag down and unsnapped his holster.

The pursuer jogged past him, not seeing him. Ethan fell in step behind. He placed an arm on a familiar-looking messenger bag.

"What's going on, Jess?"

Startled, Jessica Sinclair whipped around. Wire legs and all-weather plastic spilled from the teenager's bag. Lawn signs.

* * *

Ethan drove her home, using the time to think of how to handle this. Officially he should question Jess Sinclair, perhaps even caution her. Theft, interference in an election. Jess was the daughter of the richest man in town, but she was also a teen, one whose life had been up-ended, in no small part because of Ethan himself.

Nothing he could say, no amends to make. As the Other Man, he'd been ready to accept Steph Sinclair and everything she brought with her, including her children. To break up her marriage. They'd been in love, the first person since Jazz to strike that chord in him. But Steph had chosen her family over their passion. He couldn't blame her for making that sacrifice. Or her daughter for holding a grudge.

"You might think taking those signs isn't a big deal," Ethan said.

"I wasn't."

"The contents of your bag say otherwise."

Jess shifted the messenger bag off the floor of the truck, resting it on her knees. "You don't understand."

"A lot of teens feel nobody understands them. That's normal."

"*You* don't understand. I'm putting signs up. You know, as a volunteer?"

Jess opened the bag and showed him the signs, the metal legs, and a bundle of ARLENE SIX CROWS FOR MAYOR pamphlets.

"I was gonna ask if you'd put one on your lawn."

"I had one," he said. "It got stolen."

"That's pretty funny. Stealing from the Chief of Police."

"I suppose it is."

The Sinclair home was on a bluff overlooking the bay, the largest and most expensive private residence in Blaine. Ethan drove down the long shaded driveway. On the gate were signs for both Mooney and Arlene.

"Couldn't have made your father very happy," Ethan said. "Isn't he one of the mayor's biggest supporters?"

"I don't care. And I'm not doing this to get back at him."

"No?"

Jess looked offended. "Arlene is a good candidate, and I believe in her campaign. Is that hard to understand?"

"Most eighteen-year-olds are into video games, not civic politics."

"I'm not them."

He stopped at the end of the drive. Jess hopped out, placed two signs on the seat. She kept the door from closing.

"The whole thing with you and my mom," she said. "I guess I hated you. I guess it wasn't your fault. Mei says you're all right."

"Some days more all right than others."

"Anyway, I heard about the bomb or whatever. Wanted you to know I guess I don't hate you anymore."

"That means a lot," Ethan said. "Good night, Jess."

She nodded and closed the door. Then ripped it open again, long enough to say, "Everybody knows it's the Docherty brothers taking signs. They're real creeps. G'night, Chief."

Everybody but me, Ethan thought, watching the young woman vanish into the warm light of the mansion.

40

The best part of delegating work: it often got done while your eyes were closed. Before bed, Ethan had phoned Mal Keogh to pass along Jess's tip about the Docherty brothers. In the morning when he arrived at the station, Mal was at his desk, a McDonald's bag next to the keyboard, finishing up a preliminary report.

"You get to bed yet?" Ethan asked.

"Too much to do. Mercy is keeping watch on the Docherty place." Mal swiveled his screen so Ethan could read. "Feel good about these guys, Chief."

Steve and Tim Docherty were twins, forty-eight years old. Their brother Curt was two years younger. All three lived with their mother.

Curt was on probation for an unregistered gun charge connected to a road rage incident. Steve had been a drunk tank fixture in Lynden. Collectively, the Docherty clan had filed a lawsuit against that town. Though poorly worded and ultimately dismissed, it amounted to a laundry list of infringements on their right to conduct business.

The brothers usually represented themselves in their dealings with the law. Curt had fired the public defender assigned to his weapons case. He'd earned two citations for contempt during the hearing.

"Remember a few years ago when somebody parked an RV on the beach and started selling beer out of it?"

"Vaguely," Ethan said. "Didn't people get sick?"

"Did they ever," Mal said. "Tim Docherty was brewing the stuff out of his mother's house—next to her hot water heater, turns out. He tried to argue the trailer was technically a home, and they were actually selling the jars, which only incidentally held beer. Arlene didn't go for it. Turned down their license."

The twins had lived in Lynden before moving home. Mal outlined some of their other schemes, including a public campground and archery school in their backyard, a music festival that shorted out power to their block, and even a private gas station selling siphoned fuel.

"The brothers see themselves as entrepreneurs," Mal said, biting into his McMuffin. "But they half-ass the paperwork and never learn from their mistakes. Arlene turned them down several times. I guess they see that as state interference on free trade."

"So which of the brothers vandalized her truck and stole her phone?"

"Take your pick. Now that it's light out, Mercy and I are going to swing by the Docherty place, try to talk with them. See if they consent to a search."

Mrs. Docherty had been at the book club meeting, he remembered. She hadn't seemed particularly angry with Arlene. Then again, she hadn't seemed all that happy with anything.

"Make sure to get some rest," he told the officer.

* * *

Brenda Lee was unusually silent on the four-hour drive to Clallam Bay. Ethan tried to engage his senior officer in pretrial strategizing, how best to extract the information they needed from Seth McCandless. When that failed, he asked if she thought the weather would hold. No reply. Brenda Lee had never been shy about voicing an opinion, but this morning she kept her thoughts to herself and her answers to one syllable.

Well, that was what car stereos were made for.

The last time Ethan had been to Clallam Bay Maximum Corrections Center, he spoke to Seth McCandless briefly out in the yard. Someone had been sending Ethan death threats; Seth had known nothing about them, but wished the would-be assassin good luck.

Today's interview was formal, in the white painted brick visiting room. Folding chairs were set up on opposite sides of a white steel conference table. Ethan and Brenda Lee shared one side with ADA Hayley Hokuto. Seth's lawyer, a sallow man named Corliss, sat across from them. The two attorneys did most of the talking.

At the front gate of the prison he and Brenda Lee had surrendered their firearms. Sitting there with an empty holster on his hip, a silent officer next to him, and the lawyers quibbling over the precise wording of Seth's letter of cooperation, Ethan felt at a loss. For all the good he was likely to do, he could have stayed at his desk and prepared for the election, or helped Mal and Mercy with the Docherty investigation.

Any luck? He texted Mal.

Too much luck came Mal's reply. *Mercy and I are writing up a warrant.*

He showed the text to Brenda Lee, who nodded disinterestedly. Her mood was troubling. Ethan kicked himself for not finding out what the problem was before they entered the prison. They would have only one shot at Seth. A distracted lead investigator was a liability.

Eventually the deal was struck. Seth McCandless was led in. A large brawny man with thinning hair, a smirk on his face that grew as he spotted the officers. Since the last time Ethan had seen him, Seth had shaved his beard and gained a few new tattoos. The convict whispered to his lawyer for a minute.

Aside from the eyes and the color of their hair, Seth and Sissy didn't look much alike. Still, it was strange to be seated across from an enemy whose sister he was taking to the Supper Club tonight.

The way Sissy had looked at him the last time they'd spoken . . .

Corliss cleared his throat and addressed Brenda Lee and Ethan. "Mr. McCandless has a good idea why you're here. How we'd prefer to do this, he will tell you what he knows about Mr. Gatlin and Mr. Rash. Then he'll answer a few pertinent questions. We feel that's the most efficient approach."

"Who decides whether a question is pertinent or not?" Hayley asked. Ethan had worked with the prosecutor before, and trusted her to press for advantage.

"Mr. McCandless is the best judge of that. If necessary, we can arrange for a follow-up—"

"Won't be any follow-up," Seth said. "Let's get this over. I was in juvie with Archie Gatlin, but I didn't know him that well. He did a couple jobs for my dad—and 'fore you ask, I don't know the details. Dad had a lot of pies in a lot of fingers, God rest his soul."

So that was the strategy, Ethan thought. Seth would tell them something, probably not the full truth, framing it around his father. Big Joe McCandless had been a smuggler, a Vietnam veteran, and a well-liked citizen of Blaine. Now he was a straw man for Seth to pin the family crimes on, a dead mastermind who insulated his children. Smart. Ethan would bet that Sissy came up with that strategy.

"When you say jobs . . ." Hayley began.

"Told you I don't know every detail," Seth said. "He grew into a real tough guy, old Archie. You sent him to get money outta someone, he'd come back with it."

"Allegedly," Seth's lawyer counselled.

"Right. That's just what I heard."

On it went. Seth had no idea what happened to Gatlin. Couldn't say when he'd last seen or spoken to the dead man. Archie Gatlin had been freelance muscle, occasionally working for Seth's father.

"So that takes care of Archie," Seth said through a mouthful of turkey burger. They'd brought in an early lunch. "Now the other guy. Tyler Rash. This one here knew him much better'n me."

Pointing at Ethan.

"Ten years ago he was working for your family," Ethan said. A guess, but he stated it as if it were fact.

"Don't know anything about that."

"You're a bad liar, Seth."

"Hell I am."

Hayley touched Ethan's forearm, silently bidding him to back off. She was right. On the other side of the table, Corliss did the same for his client.

Seth ate his burger sullenly, chewing with his mouth open. He munched the fries, then lingered over his Pepsi. Making them wait, demonstrating who was in charge.

"Should I go on now?" Seth asked his lawyer. "Or does Mr. Brand over there want to accuse me of anything else?"

Corliss looked at Ethan.

"Please continue," Ethan said.

Seth nodded, grinning at the victory.

"Ty was a kid I saw around town. He used to camp out in the woods near our place. One time some kids I knew found his campsite and waited till late at night. Then we, I mean *they*, hit his tent with paintball guns and slingshots. Chased him into the brush. Ran over the tent with their truck. Pretty funny, lemme tell you."

No one else was laughing. Seth belched into his fist and continued.

"Now when Ty got a little older, he and my dad transacted a little business."

"If you thought real hard," the ADA said, "could you make a guess as to the type of activity?"

"Courier service," Seth said with no hesitation. "The kid turned out to be a whiz at getting stuff from Point 1 to Point B. So I heard from my old man."

"Would these points have been on opposite sides of the border?"

"Fair assumption, ma'am."

"Go on," Hayley said.

"A guy like my dad didn't have a whole lot of employees. What he had was contacts, and he gave people opportunities to earn. Little Miss Canada has something to sell, and Mrs. America is buying, so my dad contacts someone like Ty and offers him a piece to get it done. Each of them duke my dad a little something, on account it's his reputation that makes sure it all goes tickety-boo."

"And did it always go tickety-boo, as you say, with Mr. Rash?"

"Always, yeah. Till it didn't."

Seth explained that his father had come to rely on Ty for regular monthly deliveries. Seth didn't know how the young man was moving things, only that it got done cleanly and with no questions.

"'Bout ten years ago something got screwed up on the Canuck side," Seth said. "They took delivery but the money never made it back to us, I mean back to my dad. Ty disappeared with it. Far as I know, nobody ever saw his carcass after that."

"Did someone associated with your father search for Ty?" Hayley asked.

"Sure. I did some of the searching myself. Tracked down his ma, asked old Mac and Nettie. Nobody knew squat, so I gave up."

"Could it be that your father hired Archie Gatlin to look for Rash?"

"Very possible," Seth said. "A situation like that, he'd be the go-to guy."

"And when Gatlin disappeared as well?"

"Nobody went to pieces over either of them. What I recall, we're not talking about some huge whack of money. Twenty, maybe thirty grand. A good payday but not enough to live on in South America or nothing." Seth paused to look over at Ethan. "Of course, maybe to you that's a lot of cash. To us it was one shipment by one guy. Cost of doing business. Dad moved on."

"When you read about the discovery of the body, what did you think?" The ADA had photos of the scene, which Seth McCandless glanced at with no real interest.

"Seems pretty clear that Ty shot Archie and ran. Sneaky devil, luring old Archie into the tunnel, maybe telling him the money was down there, then popping him in the head."

Seth's fingers formed a gun, and he blasted at them across the table, grinning.

Corliss began to wrap the interview up. Hayley Hokuto asked if either Ethan or Brenda Lee had any further questions. Brenda Lee shook her head, still distracted.

Ethan looked across at the felon. What Seth had told them was valuable. It put Gatlin and Ty on a collision course, but didn't explain what happened after the collision. Seth didn't know anything more. No clue where Ty was now.

"This happened ten years ago?" Ethan asked.

Seth made a joke of counting on his fingers. "Ten, nine, eight, liftoff. Need me to count for you?"

"Your father was dead by then, wasn't he?"

"Calling me a liar?"

Seth was out of his chair, shouting and striking his own chest. A pair of corrections officers were in the room almost immediately. They shoved the convict back into his seat while Corliss tried to calm him down. He stared at Ethan with hatred.

"You keep away from my sister," Seth told him.

Meeting over. Ethan and Brenda Lee collected their firearms and headed back in his truck.

"On a scale of one to ten," Ethan said, "I'd call that 'not very satisfactory at all.'" Brenda Lee didn't respond.

"Something's up, isn't it?"

"Sorry," she said. "Little distracted today."

They drove in silence for an hour. Ethan put a Roseanne Cash cassette in the stereo. When it started to repeat, he turned it off.

"How many weeks along are you?" he asked.

Without taking his eyes off the road, Ethan felt her gaze on him. Brenda Lee didn't speak. Her right not to. He swapped out Roseanne for Charley Pride.

Before they passed Bellingham, his phone was ringing. Ethan didn't answer, but a moment later Brenda Lee's chimed. She dropped the volume on the stereo and cupped her ear. The distant look on her face evaporated into one of concern.

"Problem at the Docherty place," she repeated to him. "Jon says backup requested. An all hands on deck situation."

As Ethan stomped the pedal, Brenda Lee fed the portable bubble light out the window and switched it on. The truck flew down the shoulder of the highway.

41

From what Ethan gathered later, the melee had started in a roundabout way.

The Docherty home had once been a nondescript two-story clapboard house from the 1950s, like the others on the block. As each brother moved back home, they extended or added to the structure. Steve parked a trailer along the side and constructed an overhang. Tim extended the back deck through his mother's vegetable patch and enclosed it to create a mud room. Curt, the baby of the family, dropped three plastic tool sheds along the fence to hold moonshining equipment.

Mercy Hayes and Mal Keogh served the warrant in the late afternoon, knocking on the door of the Frankenstein house. They were entitled to collect tools and clothing from the vehicles. There was no answer to their knocking, and none when they tried Curt's cellphone.

They began to search for the crowbar and knife. The bed of Curt's truck held takeout bags, burrito wrappers, soda cans, and a pile of grimy copper pipes. The cab was equally filthy, but attached to the dashboard was a camera. A lucky break, perhaps. The officers discussed whether the dash cam could be collected now or required a separate warrant.

In his trailer, Steve Docherty woke up to the sound of their voices. He moved aside the curtain in the trailer's window, saw two figures standing by his brother's truck. Steve booted open the door and rushed them, asking what the hell the officers were doing even as he barreled into them.

Mercy Hayes weighed half of what Steve Docherty did, was a foot shorter, and had both hands full of evidence bags. Her elbow came up defensively as the man approached.

"Sir, back off, we have a warrant," she was saying as he moved toward her.

Steve grunted but kept moving, propelled down the steep drive by momentum and gravity and a night of drinking straight vodka. It amounted to a body check, and squished Mercy Hayes against the side of the truck.

Mal had been looking in the front seat. He saw a large man ignore Mercy's command to halt and charge into her. Mal hurried around the front end to intercept the man.

"Private property of a tax paying citizen," Steve was yelling in a slurred voice. *Tash pain shushin.*

Mal told Steve Docherty to drop and surrender. Steve was talking too, unfortunately, giving instructions of his own. Mal took hold of the man's arm to steer him back. Steve roared and headbutted him. The move dazed both of them, and Mal hit the wheel well of the Dodge on his way down.

The lack of coordination would have been comical if it weren't leading to violence. Mercy recovered and alerted Jon Gutierrez to send backup to their location: 10–18, send anyone and everyone right now.

Mercy grabbed Steve from behind, keeping hold of him as Steve turned and flung her around, staggering into the street. Steve Docherty was belligerent and resisting arrest, but he still hadn't thrown a punch.

That changed.

Steve shook off Mercy and struck Mal in the chest. The two officers redoubled their efforts and tackled him.

Curt and Tim Docherty had taken their mother for breakfast. They pulled up in Tim's Chevy and saw their brother fighting two on one. They leapt out, leaving the truck in neutral and their mother sitting in the middle seat.

Heck Ruiz was next to arrive. He saw things deteriorating, and told Jon to put the word out for everybody.

An officer was under no obligation to fight fair. Heck waded in and was soon exchanging blows with both Tim and Curt Docherty. He clouted Tim on the knee with his baton, but the twin grabbed Heck's lapel and fell on top of him. Heck saw the man bare his teeth. The officer felt a sharp pain in his left ear.

Perched in the cab of the Chevy, Mrs. Docherty watched the situation between her family and the police devolve.

* * *

Ethan cut across lawns, driving over one of the neighbor's sprinklers. Approaching from the south, he saw the three officers brawling with three larger, wilder men. Steve Docherty was now swinging a pipe at Mercy and Mal, while Tim and Heck grappled on the ground. Brenda Lee Page jumped down as the truck nosed onto the Docherty's lawn.

Ethan's first impulse was to barge into the fray and join in, heeding the urge to crack heads. His second was to pull his firearm and impose order on the situation. He moved to the hood of the truck with those options in mind.

A third choice came to him, one that seemed counterintuitive and yet right. This was his officers' situation to control, not his. No one had escalated to deadly force. For most of them, this was their first brush with violence in a long time. Why not see how they handled it?

Ethan folded his arms and observed.

Out of breath, winded, and bleeding from the mouth, Mal Keogh steered Curt Docherty into the hood of the Dodge and snapped cuffs on him. Mercy Haze had a bloody lip, but grabbed Steve's elbow joint in an armbar, holding it until the man dropped the pipe. Brenda Lee pushed Tim off Heck Ruiz, who read the trio their rights with a hand cupped over his ear.

Score one for the hands-off management style, Ethan thought. Now he took charge.

Mal had sprained his wrist, and Heck's ear was too bloody to see if it was intact. Brenda Lee volunteered to drive them to the hospital. That would leave Mercy and Ethan to take the brothers to the station, book them and conduct the interviews. The evidence collection could come later.

He was proud of his people—a different sort of pride from what he'd felt as their coworker. His team. In a strange way, it was similar to what he felt as a parent.

As the officers split up, Ethan felt a sharp insistent tug on the sleeve of his uniform. Mrs. Docherty stood behind him, eyes pearling with tears.

"This is all my fault," she said. "I should be the one."

"I understand you worry, ma'am. We're going to take your boys to the station, but there won't be any more fisticuffs. My word on that." Assuming your sons don't start up again, he added silently.

The woman stared at the hood of her youngest son's truck. "It was my doing, Chief. I was the one who took that lady's phone. All of it was me."

42

A diminutive woman in a stiff wool coat, blowing on a cup of tea, Mrs. Docherty looked like the last person who'd find herself in the hard interview room. Seated in a stiff-backed metal chair, her feet didn't touch the ground.

Only hours ago, Mrs. Docherty had been in Ethan's home for the book club meeting. She had brought snacks. Now the same woman was confessing to vandalism, harassment and petty theft.

"All my boy wanted was a little stand on the beach," Mrs. Docherty said. "Curt's the youngest. He's never had the rough disposition of his brothers. He was born premature, you know."

Ethan nodded for her to continue.

"The twins can look out for each other, but Curt, he needs that little bit extra. He's crazy about making and selling his beer. It's good beer. The recipe he uses is from the 1600s. And nobody can explain to me why he's not allowed to sell it."

"Licensing," Ethan suggested.

Mrs. Docherty brought her thumb to the rest of her fingers in the gesture of a chatty hand puppet. "That's just talk," she said. "The rules don't get applied even. I see produce stands all over the place—corn, berries, pumpkins. You can't tell me all them have licenses and what-not."

"Alcohol is a little different," Ethan said.

"Not talking about alcohol. Just beer."

"All right," he said, happy to move onto a more productive topic. "Why harass Councilwoman Six Crows?"

"If anything, she was the one harassing Curt. Making his life harder."

Ethan let her explain.

"There's a new pizza place just opened in Bellingham. Curt took me. He's a good son. We brought a sample of his beer for the owner. If she liked it, maybe they could work out a deal to put it on tap at the restaurant. She promised she'd try it. Was practically a done deal. Curt was so darn happy."

Mrs. Docherty's hands spun the mug. Her eyes, focused on the handle, seemed to storm over.

"We had a very nice meal," she said in a faraway voice. "We left a good tip. And when we walked to the truck to drive home, Curt's growler of beer was sitting on the pavement next to the Dumpster. The manager hadn't even tried it."

"But how is that the councilwoman's—" Ethan began.

"She could have helped him out," Mrs. Docherty snapped. "Anyone else, that's what government does, helps 'em. But on account my boys don't dress fancy or talk good, they're somehow bad seeds. Miss Fancy Pants Lawyer knows the regulations, right? She could help him through the red tape. Instead, all she does is tell my boy, here's another form. He fills 'em out best he can, and she turns around and tells him she can't support his application."

"City council is more than one person. Those decisions are complex."

But the mother wasn't listening.

"We're not all built the same," she said. "The twins can look after themselves. But Curt needs that little bit extra."

Ethan leaned over the table as if the two of them were in this together. "Mrs. Docherty, I know you didn't break into Arlene's car. We have footage from surveillance cameras. Things will go easier for Curt if he confesses."

"You got your confession," Mrs. Docherty told him. And refused to say anything more.

* * *

Curt Docherty swore he didn't slash the tires of Arlene's car. Someone else must have done that using his jackknife, smashed her windshield with the crowbar he kept in his truck, and planted Arlene's phone in Curt's bedroom. He swore on his mother's life.

"Speaking of your mother," Ethan said, "she's willing to take the fall for what you did."

"But I didn't do anything."

"Are you really willing to stand by while the woman who raised you goes to prison?"

The youngest son of Mrs. Docherty shrugged as if the matter was out of his hands. "Guess that's a matter for a judge to decide."

Ethan sent him back to his cell. Even without his confession, the case against Curt Docherty was strong. His brothers would be charged for the violent altercation. They were in the drunk tank now. Ethan asked Mercy Haze to drive their mother home.

"Motherly love is a hell of a force," he said, sitting down across from Brenda Lee Page. "How did you fare at the clinic?"

"Mal's arm is in a sling, and Heck had five stitches put in his ear. 'That freaking loon bit a hunk off me,' he told the nurse. I've never heard Heck come that close to a four letter word."

"They did good work. You too."

Brenda Lee took a cloth from her desk drawer and began cleaning her glasses. "Poor woman. Her son gets turned down for a beer license and goes after Arlene. Makes her life hell. And when we catch him, his mother tries to take the blame."

"Part of your job as a parent is protection," Ethan said.

"In her place, would you do that? Take the blame for your kids?"

"Probably, yes."

"Even if it was something more serious? Murder?"

"Parental love isn't a rational thing," he said.

"That's a cop-out, Ethan. Answer the question. Your son commits a murder, would you be willing to take the fall?"

After pondering the scenario for a moment, he nodded.

"I would, yes," he told Brenda Lee. "The first time. But if he's cutting down people left right and center, then he's on his own."

Brenda Lee smiled and set her glasses back on her nose. "I worry I won't feel that," she said. "What I'm supposed to feel. And then what would that say about me?"

"On the other hand, you might find out you're more than you thought."

"Could be." She sighed. "At my age they call this a change of life baby. No goddamn kidding."

It was almost time to meet Sissy McCandless. Ethan headed out to the parking lot, thinking he'd just have time to shower and change. He heard Brenda Lee tell him to wait.

With a trace of her usual energy, Brenda Lee jogged over to the reception area. He watched her snap the stem off a violet resting in a vase on Jon's workspace.

"For your big date," Brenda Lee said. "The least you can do is bring the lady a corsage."

43

He chose the gray blazer because it best concealed his shoulder holster. Ethan showered and shaved, wasted fifteen minutes picking out a tie, then decided to go open collar. His reflection in the mirror looked adequate.

The date would be easier, in a way, if Sissy McCandless had an ulterior motive. Romance was too simple, with complications far too complex. He was chief of police, while both her siblings were in prison. Sissy herself had no criminal record. Part of his duty might be to change that.

His own feelings about her left him equally perplexed. Before the dream, he had only thought of her professionally. Hadn't he?

On second thought, a tie *would* look better. He dug out a blue houndstooth the kids had bought him.

It was time.

* * *

The Ocean Beach Supper Club was unrivaled for fine dining in Blaine. He was led to a table near the glass wall that looked out on Drayton Harbor. In early summer, the partition would be removed, and diners could sit outside, practically on the beach.

Tonight the sky was cloudless, but with September approaching and the rains more frequent, the patio tables were empty.

Sissy was late. He ordered rye and water and scanned the room. A slow night, only one waitress, a few couples and a small group of business types at the bar. Two women shared a table near the stone fireplace, one of them producing a plastic bottle of vodka from her purse. He watched it pass below the table as the waitress took their orders.

Stood up by a crook, he thought. And then there she was. Sissy McCandless entered the restaurant, looking nothing like herself. Or revealing herself, he wasn't sure. The oversized glasses had been replaced by thin black frames that accentuated her eyes. The dress she'd chosen was a simple check pattern with a plunging neckline, a white shawl over it. She smiled as he held her chair.

"You clean up quite nicely, Ethan," she said. "It's all right I don't call you Chief for tonight?"

"Work left at the door," he agreed.

"Excellent."

She ordered a dirty martini. When it arrived, Sissy tried it as if tasting liquor for the first time. Mildly surprised and pleased by it. As the daylight slipped away, the waitress brought out candles for the tables.

"What should we talk about if not work?" she asked.

"Dealer's choice."

"Music seems safe. What's the best concert you ever attended?"

"Merle Haggard at the Emerald Queen Casino. You?"

"Yo-Yo Ma."

"He's good," Ethan said. "Probably didn't play the Emerald Queen."

She smiled. "I have season tickets to the Seattle Symphony."

"That's where you go to cut loose, Seattle?"

"Sometimes," Sissy said. "I find it hard to be myself in a town as small as Blaine. Too many people know my family." Sissy inclined her head in the direction of the two women, who were now openly passing the vodka between them. "Imagine feeling that sort of freedom to misbehave. I'd be mortified."

"Free country," Ethan said.

"I suppose it is."

They split a Caesar salad for a starter. Sissy dabbed her bottom lip with her napkin between bites. Demure or self-conscious. He was aware of gazes from the other diners.

"Does it bother you?" he asked. "We can always go someplace else."

"I'm all right," Sissy said.

Behind her, the waitress had confiscated the vodka bottle. The two women snickered. One turned her water glass on its side. "Oops." The other laughed.

"Excuse me one sec." Ethan stood and walked to their table, leaned down and spoke to them. He kept his voice low. Their grins faded. As Ethan returned to his seat, the one who'd spilled her water stood and walked to the waitress, handed her a credit card and steepled her hands in a gesture of apology. By the time the salad was finished, the pair had left.

"I thought it was a free country," Sissy said.

"Still is. They were free to stay or leave."

She grinned conspiratorially. "What exactly did you say to them?"

"No work talk, remember?"

As they finished their steaks, they discussed the election. Sissy's evaluations of the two candidates lined up more or less with his own. He wasn't sure what to make of that. They discussed their parents, growing up with heavy expectations from their fathers. Joe McCandless had schooled Sissy's brothers in the family business. He mostly left his daughter to herself. Sissy's mother had died when she was young.

Having a bully like Seth and a sneak like Jody for siblings wouldn't have been easy, he thought. Seeing them encouraged by their father would poison the entire household.

"My ex was a fan of foreign movies," Ethan said. "Still is, I guess. When I was trying to woo her, I read up on the subject. A lot of old directors grew up without access to cameras or film. They spent their early years planning what they'd do when they got the chance to make something."

"Seems like a non sequitor," Sissy said. "I mean off-topic."

"I know what non sequitor means. Good word. It strikes me your childhood must've been like that a bit. Watching your dad and brothers make mistakes, miss opportunities. Thinking to yourself how you'd do things better once you had the chance."

"I thought we weren't going to talk work."

"I just meant in general terms."

"No you didn't, Ethan."

Sissy looked down at the last few bites on her plate. Nothing about her disposition seemed to change, yet he knew he'd offended her.

"You're right," he said. "I didn't. I apologize."

"Silly of me to think we could set aside who we are. There's really no hope for us, is there?"

"I don't know exactly how hope works."

"You like me, though, don't you?"

"Very much," he said. Meaning it, which surprised him a little.

"How does that Joni Mitchell line go," Sissy asked, "about coming from different sets of circumstances?"

"I don't hold your family against you, Sissy."

"I believe that. I believe you take people as you find them."

He nodded. Over Sissy's shoulder, he watched the waitress sop up the mess left by the two diners. "Where a person comes from, what they did in the past, who their folks are. Those aren't the sum total of a person. I don't think they have to define you."

"I hope that's true," Sissy said.

"You can make it true. Give up whatever you're doing on the side. Just run the travel agency and see how things play out."

"That simple, is it?"

He nodded.

"By that rationale," Sissy said, "if you loved your wife, you would have gone with her when she moved to Boston."

"I gave it some thought."

"How seriously, though?"

Ethan conceded the point. Over dinner they'd split a bottle of wine. He poured out the last drops into their glasses. "I have responsibilities here," he said. "Though maybe that's just what I tell myself."

"You're not alone in having responsibilities."

"A McCandless to the end?"

"Can't be helped, I'm afraid."

They finished their meal in silence. He'd disappointed Sissy and that fact sat heavy with him. As absurd as their situation was, Ethan had been enjoying her company.

"Should we ask for the dessert menu?" he offered.

"I'm not much for sweets. We can end things now if you prefer. I'll call for a ride."

"You choose the restaurant, I choose where we go after. That was our deal."

"Yes, but I won't hold you to—"

"Hold me like hell," Ethan said. "We're not going far, but it's a surprise. I think you'll like it."

44

At night the Steranko property was completely unlit, from the house to the stable and beyond to the dark green hill. Ethan had told Mac and Nettie he might stop by, though this was much later than he'd planned.

He felt reckless. Driving the truck after more than one drink was breaking a personal rule. As Ethan helped boost Sissy over the gate, he tried to think of how he'd explain this. Drunk driving, trespassing. Hardly fit behavior for a chief of police.

They held hands crossing the grass, Ethan taking each footfall carefully. They approached the barn and he snapped on one of the electric lanterns Mac kept there.

"That's her," he whispered, pointing to the stall on the right. "Trim Reckoning, though I'm allowed to change her name."

"Why would you?" Sissy said. "She's perfect."

With no hesitation she reached into the stall and brushed a hand down the muzzle appreciatively. The horse's breathing was steady.

"Amazing how they sleep standing up," he said. "I knew a corporal who could sleep sitting up, but he'd fall over in the night."

"A horse's legs are designed that way," Sissy said. "They sleep on three legs and rest the fourth, then alternate. Less energy than lying down."

"You know a lot about horses."

"Only what I've read."

He killed the lantern. The moon was on the opposite side of the barn, and they were in shadow. Before his eyes adjusted, he smelled Sissy's body wash, the perfume she'd touched to her neck. He felt her hands on his face, drawing him into a kiss.

His arms moved around her back, feeling the curve of her shoulder blade, the thin taut band of her brassiere through the fabric of her dress. She had left her shawl in the truck.

A light snapped on within the house. He felt Sissy bolt from his arms toward the fence, laughing. Ethan loped after her, vaulting over the fence and making sure to land on his good foot. Into the truck, backing down the empty street as the front door of the house opened. Like something teenagers would do, he thought.

Sissy's laughter, sharp and clean in the dark night, would stay with him.

At her door, they parted. No chance of another kiss. Both awkward but not quite willing to disengage. Sissy took his hand.

"Thank you for tonight," she said.

"I had a good time, myself."

Her hand was small but remarkably strong. He felt her thumb travel down his knuckles to the joints.

"There really is no reason we couldn't do this again," Sissy said. "Perhaps in another city."

"As other people?"

"Why not?"

"Hawthorne had a quote about wearing one face to the multitude."

"In a book about people who transgress," Sissy said. "And isn't the transgression what makes it exciting?"

"Didn't end up too well in the book, though."

Abruptly her hand left his. He missed her touch. Ethan was aware of the camera above her porch, and remembered the countless warrants that had been served on this property. Everything they'd set down in order to enjoy tonight was returning.

"Once a bad girl, always. Isn't that so?" Sissy's hand returned to his for a brief squeeze. "I enjoyed getting to play what might have been."

As she dug out her keys he remembered something. He dropped off the porch and reached into the back seat of the truck. He brought it to her. The violet Brenda Lee had given him. He'd wrapped the stem in a damp paper towel.

"Should have given this to you from the jump, but it slipped my mind," Ethan said. "I'm out of practice with dating."

Sissy spun it by the stem. "Lovely. This was a pleasant evening, Chief."

"Until next time, Ms. McCandless."

He waited until Sissy was inside and the porch light had been switched off. Then he rolled down the windows and drove home. Slowly the spice of her perfume dissipated in the night air.

* * *

At first the coyote pups had been downy and small, little more than sand-colored balls rolling across the grass. Now their heads were beginning to resemble their mother's. The ears sharp, bodies sleek on their long legs. Ethan had looked up how long a pup stayed with its mother. Around nine months.

"You think it won't happen to you," he called from the porch. Seated on the railing, he watched the coyote lead her offspring down the empty street.

He texted Jazz to say he'd be out for Christmas, and everything was fine, and he was happy for her. Slow to maturity, but I'm getting there, he thought.

Perhaps he had lied to Sissy. He believed in second chances, that a person could change their life with determination and a little luck. He believed that but didn't know if it was true. Wasn't everyone trapped by their families, their choices? Could Tyler Rash had been anyone else, raised the way he was? Could Sissy, or Ethan himself?

Life, he decided, was something like a deer trail. The path existed before you got there. Other feet had beaten the ground smooth, broken the branches. You could leave the trail, but it would be hard work fighting against the bush, with no guarantee where you'd end up. That was why most people kept to the trail. Pathfinding was a lonely occupation.

Ethan watched the coyotes for a while, then went to bed. In the morning, he left town before dawn.

45

A Thermos of black coffee and Loretta Lynn on the truck's old stereo. Tacoma was two hours away. Ethan kept to the center lane, watching the miles roll past. Thinking.

Something had been overlooked with Tyler Rash and Archie Gatlin. He wasn't sure exactly what. Being alone on the highway gave him time to chop away at the problem. To fit what he'd learned from Seth McCandless into what he knew.

South of Longview he found a rest stop and pulled over. Sat on the tailgate to finish his coffee and watch the sun rise. Archie Gatlin had been a plumber, which meant he was an early riser as well. Maybe he had done something like this on the day of his death. Archie Gatlin, the hired muscle who liked fishing, the dangerous man who'd been lured into a tunnel with no exit. There was always someone more dangerous, more cunning.

Past Seattle he saw the sprawl of Tacoma beneath a yellow morning haze. Airplanes taking off from SEATAC flew low across his windshield. A construction crew had erected scaffolding around the Tacoma Dome. Ethan located Gatlin's street, a block of apartment buildings done in apricot-colored brick.

Brenda Lee Page had already checked out Gatlin's apartment. For the sake of thoroughness, he poked around the building and the neighborhood. Gatlin had been a quiet sort, the landlady said. Nice to have someone who could do his own maintenance.

Ethan had a plate of machaca at a cantina near the building. The waitress didn't recognize Archie's photo. She was young and spoke Spanish to the equally young line cook behind the counter.

The woman who hired Gatlin on the day before his fishing trip still lived in town. She'd moved into a new house three years ago, and could only tell him that Gatlin did good work, didn't overcharge, and was a little too potty-mouthed for her comfort. "That man would apologize for effin' and jeffin', then go right back to cussing in very the next sentence. Uncouth, but a diligent worker. I haven't found anyone quite as reliable."

He drove by the woman's previous residence and debated going inside. A true bloodhound detective would. Maybe Archie had left behind a journal of his last days. Ethan knocked and rang the bell but there was no answer. He gave up on the journal idea.

All of this was pointless. A series of hopeless long shots. He drove on to Castle Rock, thinking at least he was putting more distance between himself and the wreck he'd made of his love life.

Why were matters of the heart so damn difficult at this age? The tinge of jealousy he'd felt over his ex. The note Vonetta Briggs had left him. Steph Sinclair leaving town. And now Sissy McCandless. For an all or nothing person, Ethan felt connected to each of them. Sissy most strongly, he had to admit, and also most dangerously.

The gas gauge in the Chevy was low. A nice coincidence. The truck was doing its part to follow Gatlin's last movements. Ethan pulled into the town's gas station, and retrieved the photo of Archie Gatlin's receipt. $60.42, paid at the till.

Archie had called his cousin from here—no, Miles had called Archie. The dead man had fueled up here just after three, telling

Miles he was en route for the 5:35 ferry. Instead Archie had headed up to Blaine and his death in the tunnel.

Ethan gassed up, then looked over the aisles in the station's refrigerated section. He bought sunflower seeds and a bag of Tim's jalapeno chips. The clerk was in his early twenties, and had only been hired a few years ago. His uncle owned the station. Ethan showed the clerk Gatlin's photo anyway. No recognition.

Behind the clerk was a wall of smoking products, scratch tickets and the like. Next to the checkout was a wire spindle holding headphones and charge cables in neon colors. The floor of the station was a pale gray linoleum, but beneath the spindle the tile was yellow and a shade lighter than the rest. Shielded from the sun for years by something. What had been there before?

He showed the photo of the receipt to the clerk, who nodded. "Yeah, that's from here. We upgraded our system, though."

"Would your uncle have been at work ten years ago?"

"Never took a day off till he retired. Uncle Ambrose always says you can be sick at work just as easy as at home."

"Quite a work ethic," Ethan said. "Could you call him for me?"

The voice on the phone was cured with age and whiskey, and spoke with a Louisiana accent. The clerk told Uncle Ambrose who Ethan was.

"Cops asked me back when he disappeared," the man said. "Didn't recall him then, and I'm no younger or smarter now."

"I have the same affliction," Ethan said. "How's your memory for prices? The receipt says sixty dollars and forty-two cents. That might be exactly what Gatlin spent on gas. If so, I'm out of luck."

"See where you're coming from," Uncle Ambrose said. "He might've bought fifty in gas and something else to make up the difference."

"Worth a thought. Road atlas, maybe?"

"We used to carry those, before everybody had their little phones. Good road atlas run you more than ten bucks. Most folks just buy maps, though. They're cheaper."

"Any chance you have a price list from ten years ago?"

"Only in my head, son."

A road atlas. A map. Two maps.

He took out his notebook, wrote *$60.42—50=10.42*. What would have cost ten dollars and change a decade ago? A sandwich and a soda? A six-pack? He tapped the pen against the counter.

What would Archie Gatlin buy at three in the afternoon en route to Blaine? A map? You couldn't miss Blaine if you stuck to I-5. Cigarettes? An air freshener?

The clerk attended to another customer while Ethan spoke into the phone. "Would a pack of cigarettes have cost around ten bucks?"

"Depends on the brand," Uncle Ambrose said. "Course you gotta factor in the smoke tax, three bucks and point two five cents. That leaves you with seven."

Ethan stared at the discolored tile where the display had once stood. His hand clutched the pen so tightly the plastic snapped. Ink on his fingers. He didn't care.

"Back in the day, you sold snuff, didn't you?" The owner confirmed he had. "Tell me, what would a tin of Copenhagen have gone for?"

"Seven and a quarter, plus two fifty-three for the tax, plus state tax of six point five percent."

He double-checked the math, looking up the tax rates, and thanked Uncle Ambrose for the use of his memory. Fifty dollars in gas plus a tin of Cope. The man who stopped in Castle Rock, who'd spoken to Miles Gatlin on the phone, had been Tyler Rash.

46

"I don't know that I follow entirely," Brenda Lee said over the phone.

Ethan had driven north from Castle Rock to Steilacoom, where he waited for the Anderson Island ferry. Ahead of him, the broad white vessel chugged across the narrows. The Chevy was one of a dozen passenger vehicles.

"Archie Gatlin was dead by the time his Jeep stopped in Castle Rock," Ethan said. "He never went south at all. Gatlin drove straight to Blaine, where he was killed by Tyler Rash. Ty took Gatlin's vehicle and his phone and drove south."

"I'll be damned," Brenda Lee said. "What about Miles? He would know his cousin's voice."

"Would he? The cousins didn't see each other that often. Ty could fake a bad connection, or say he had a cold."

"But Miles didn't tell me any of that when we spoke," Brenda Lee said. "Wouldn't that seem suspicious in light of Archie's disappearance?"

"I'll be asking him that, soon as this boat docks."

The heel of his good foot bounced on the floor of the truck. Ethan had heard pilots in Afghanistan talk about flying with night vision goggles. The NVGs allowed you to see in low light, but made it harder to judge altitude. What looked like a safe height to fly could be only mere inches from the ground. He felt like that now. He was seeing things he hadn't before, but the experience was disorienting.

Tyler Rash had worked for Seth McCandless, arranging transportation across the border. Something had gone wrong, and Seth held Ty responsible. A call went out to Archie Gatlin: drive up to Blaine and deal with him.

Gatlin had probably driven right up to the Steranko house, found Ty there alone, and marched him into the shed. Feeling in control every step of the way. Ethan could imagine Ty pushing aside the tools, reluctantly uncovering the tunnel's entrance. Offering to go first and retrieve the money. Gatlin, sensing a trap, insisted no, he would go first himself. Down in the tunnel, eyes adjusting to the dark, the shot would have come from behind. The pistol had to have been hidden somewhere in the shed.

Once Ty outfoxed Gatlin, he fled in the dead man's Jeep. Ty had stopped for gas and was probably surprised when Gatlin's phone rang. He bluffed his way past Miles and drove on, ditching the Jeep in the forest. From there, he disappeared.

In a way, Ty had done what Ethan's father only dreamed of: made a life for himself entirely off the grid. Ty earned money by building tunnels on contract, then slipping back into the wilderness. No one had missed him.

The ferry docked and let off its passengers. Ethan saw beach homes, a dock, and more cars waiting on the other side. About a thousand people lived on Anderson Island, which was under eight square miles. Its sister island, McNeil, had once held a federal penitentiary. Tracts of Anderson were still undeveloped, the properties a mix of cottages and small houses, with a few larger estates mixed in. A lot of the year-round residents were retirees.

With fall approaching, the summer residents had hoisted their boats onto trailers and battened down their cottages for the winter. The shoulder season, Ethan thought. The sky was remarkably clear, chilly in the late afternoon. Behind him rose Mount Baker, a white accent over the gray-green smear of the mainland.

Miles Gatlin's address was on Sandberg Road. Off the ferry, Ethan asked an elderly couple toting bicycles for directions. An excuse to suss out what Miles's neighbors thought of him.

"They're on the hippie side," the wife said. "Lotta fruits and vegetables, lotta canning. But nice folks. 'Specially Nancy."

"That's Mrs. Gatlin?" Ethan asked.

"Mmm hmm. You can't miss their place, it's the one with the jam stand by the drive."

In Ethan's experience, any location described with the phrase "you can't miss it" was begging to be missed. He found Sandberg Road, which cut across the eastern part of the island to Amsterdam Bay. The road wended through second growth forest. He saw the bay ahead of him, then spotted a small kiosk made of weathered cedar. An awning protected three shelves of plum and blackberry preserves. A small box with a slit in the top for money. The Gatlins' jam stand ran on the honor system.

The driveway was a steep quarter mile, carpeted with pine needles. At the top, an oval turnaround cut in the grass. The house was a long chocolate L with a mossy roof. Rustic but well-maintained.

Ethan saw movement through one of the windows. By the time he parked the truck in the small turnaround, a woman was standing in the doorway holding a paring knife.

"You get lost?"

She was around fifty, her white hair hanging down in a long plait. She wore a red wool sweater and quilted pants. Her face was pretty, eyes sharp and blue. She wasn't brandishing the knife, simply holding it. He had interrupted her kitchen chores.

"I'm looking for Miles Gatlin," Ethan said. "My name is Ethan Brand. I'm—"

"A cop," she finished. "They usually phone ahead."

"I prefer speaking face to face, ma'am."

"This about his cousin again? You people have been calling about that since the other day."

Ethan nodded. "We found Archie's body. My condolences, ma'am."

"Oh, none of that ma'am crap. It's Nancy. And I never met Archie, that's before my time. All I know is he's been a terrific hassle to Miles."

"A quick word with your husband, and I'll be out of your hair."

Nancy Gatlin gestured with the knife to come inside.

A beaded curtain separated the foyer from the living room. Animal hides and old saddle blankets covered the furniture. "On the hippie side," their neighbors had said. The Gatlins were handy people, makers and crafters. Crates of preserves were stacked in the dining room.

"Does anyone ever steal from your stand?" he asked.

"We're not that kind of community," Nancy said.

Past the kitchen was a long unfinished deck. Boards were piled on the lawn. Nancy jumped down from the kitchen doorway, stomping over the packed dirt and between the joists. She wore rope soled sandals and walked with a powerful, sensual roll of the hips. She moved fast.

"How close was Miles to his cousin?" Ethan asked.

"Not very. I gather Archie was a bastard."

"They went fishing together, though."

Nancy scoffed. "Miles'll fish with damn near anybody."

The garden ended in an uphill path, wooden steps cut into the steeper parts.

"Is that where he is now?" Ethan asked. "Fishing?"

"Foraging. Chanterelles are in season."

The path wended through the forest. Both of them were breathing heavily but Nancy didn't slow down. The ground was spongey, pocked with stones, and rose and dipped unexpectedly. Ethan's ankle began to bark with pain. Stubbornness compelled him to match Nancy's pace.

Nancy paused beside a felled redwood. On the ground near the log were several specks of gold. The cut stems of mushrooms.

"We're in the right area," she said. "He's foraging close to here."

"Should we call for him?"

"No need. Miles'll hear us long before we see him."

She vaulted over the log with ease. Ethan took his time walking around it. Nancy Gatlin was ahead of him about a hundred yards. He saw her stop by a thick birch and begin speaking to it in a low voice.

Only when Ethan got within a few feet did he spot the man, so well did he blend into the forest. Miles Gatlin's bald head jutted out of a heavyset frame. A pair of cloth carry bags were slung across his camouflage jacket. On a nylon belt was a machete, a mushroom knife, a can of bear spray, and a pistol in a worn leather holster. Miles had a bushman's beard, red and gold and gray. He wore aviator shades with dull brass frames that gave off no glint in the sunlight falling through the trees.

Miles whispered something to Nancy, who nodded and took the sacks from him. She headed back toward the house. Her pace seemed even faster than before.

Ethan watched Miles cinch his belt, turning the machete to the back and the holster flush against his hip. "That pig sticker digs into my leg when I walk. Easier to move this way."

"Easier to draw that pistol, too."

A yellow grin blossomed through the beard. "You don't miss a trick, do you?"

"Try not to. Mind removing your glasses?"

Miles's right hand swept up to hover near the pistol. It wavered there. "When exactly did you work it out?" Miles asked.

"Still am. Why'd you send me the bomb?"

"See how soft you'd got. Shortest distance between two points, Ethan. Unfortunately in this case, the shortest distance runs through you."

Miles unstrung the glasses, folded the arms and slipped them into his breast pocket, all with his left hand. His right delicately undid the snap on the holster.

Ethan stood still, waiting to see what Tyler Rash would do.

47

"When they start coming for your friends, that's when you know it's time to leave town. Nettie and Mac were real good to me. I wish to hell that business with Archie hadn't landed on their doorstep. Figured it was better I disappear. Care for a pinch?"

With his left hand Tyler Rash removed a tin from his breast pocket. He opened it one-handed and shook out a few flakes. All the while never taking his eyes off Ethan.

"Try to appreciate the spot I was in. My contact 'cross the border gets picked up by the Mounties. Disappears with the money. You know Seth McCandless. That family takes a shoot-the-messenger approach to doing business."

"So you shot first."

Tyler Rash tilted his head in a gesture of what-can-you-do. Odd to see his boyish features suspended in a middle-aged body. "End of the day, Ethan, what's it really matter? The dead are just as dead. None of us are saints."

"It matters. What about Miles Gatlin?"

The left hand pointed to the southwest. "There's a nice little creek not too far from here. Miles is buried beneath the bank. Planted a cypress on the spot."

"How'd it happen?"

"A mistake that turned out to be a gift horse," Ty said. "I was on the run, half out of my head, panicking, trying to put distance between me and what happened. I stop for gas and see his damn phone ringing. Out of reflex, I answer the damn thing. Turns out it's Miles, calling to see if Archie's gonna make the ferry. Even gives me directions to his place. You could say I took him up on the offer."

"You took more than that," Ethan said. "Touch your head with both hands."

Ty didn't move. "You gonna shoot me?"

"I'd sure hate to."

Ty nodded over Ethan's shoulder in the direction of the house. His eyes didn't move. No sound of footprints. A bluff. His expression remained casually indifferent. The same look from the photo, as if he'd been waiting for hard luck to find him.

"If it had to be someone," Ty said, and reached for the pistol.

Ethan's shot notched the trunk of the birch to Ty's right. The sound reverberated through the grove. Around them, a cloud of birds shook free of the foliage.

Ty hadn't flinched, but now he flung the pistol at the ground.

"By God you're fast. Hell of a warning shot, Ethan. I barely cleared leather."

His hands went up and he spun around. Was he surrendering, or mocking him? Ethan couldn't tell.

"Does Nancy know who you are?" Ethan asked.

"She knows enough. The name's not important. Not when you love somebody."

Not mockery. Ty had expected the warning shot. Ethan shifted ground, closer to the tree. "Kneel down, Ty."

"No, thank you. Bad wheel. Speaking of which, how's your ankle?"

"Aches a little, if I'm being honest."

"Not much fun getting older," Ty said. "Any chance of you and me coming to an arrangement?"

"What did you tell Nancy?"

"Fifty thousand. To start with, and more to come."

"What did you tell her?"

"I told her to put the mushrooms away. Then take out her scoped .308 and put the crosshairs on you. That woman can shoot, Ethan. Not as fast as you, but accurate as hell."

"Unless?"

"Like I said. We come to an arrangement."

Ethan moved in a slow circle, putting Tyler Rash between him and the house. He couldn't shake the feeling that Ty had anticipated this, too. The home field advantage.

"Watch your step, brother."

Ethan felt his foot nudge something. He dropped his eyes long enough to see that it was a gnarled segment of root. The branch above his head shattered. Only after did he hear the report of the rifle. He leapt back, seeking cover behind the trunk.

Silence replaced the echoes of the gunshot. When Ethan glanced up, he was alone.

A storm of panic threatened to overtake his nerves. Ethan took slow sips of air. First order of business, remove any close range threat. He craned his neck to scan for the pistol Ty had dropped. There it was, a few feet from his right, the dull metal of the barrel pointed at the house. Tempting to grab it, but that would bring him into Nancy Gatlin's line of sight.

His position wasn't secure, so the next order of business was to move. He sprang left, heading for the next closest tree, zig-zagging to make himself a more difficult target. Pain shot through his foot. He ignored it.

Ethan crashed down behind a twinned birch. Nancy hadn't fired a second shot. That could mean she was on the move, or she was waiting for a better target.

And Ty—had he run far? Ethan thought that was unlikely. A patient adversary was trouble. Now he had two.

Splitting his attention was something he hated to do, but Ethan removed his phone. Looking down as little as possible, he dialed the Pierce County Sheriffs. A smooth, authoritative voice answered. "Deputy Canning speaking."

"Canning, this is Ethan Brand of Blaine PD. I'm on Anderson Island, about two and a half miles southwest of Sandberg Road. Behind the property owned by Miles and Nancy Gatlin. That's Gatlin with a G."

"Why exactly are you—"

"Please don't interrupt. Both are armed and dangerous. Miles Gatlin is actually a man named Tyler Rash. With an R. Relay that to Officer Page when you get the chance, and send a tactical unit right away."

"Understood." He was grateful that Canning picked up on the urgency in his tone. "We don't have personnel on Anderson, however there's a fire station a few miles from you."

"Unlikely I can get there."

"All right. I'll call for a chopper. Our ETA is forty minutes to an hour, give or take. Can you hold out that long?"

A question Ethan was asking himself. He hadn't heard footfalls or breathing, hadn't stopped scanning his surroundings. Tyler Rash had spent his life in the woods, and the last decade in *these* woods. Who knew what he'd cached out here? What traps he'd laid?

Crouched, Ethan peered out to check if Ty's pistol still lay on the ground. He couldn't see it.

But there was movement down the hill. A figure in black wound up through the trees, carrying a rifle in the high port position. Nancy Gatlin, cutting him off from the road.

In a mad instant, Ethan was running.

48

His frantic burst of speed gave way to jogging, then limping. Ethan circled west. The trees grew shorter and closer together, the undergrowth more dense. Blackberry thorns ripped at his skin and snagged on his trousers and boots.

Exhaustion finally compelled him to rest. Sinking down to the carpet of the forest, he waited for his breath to return.

For a moment he was thirteen again, alone in an unfamiliar forest where his father had left him. Life sometimes had an ugly symmetry. He'd met Tyler Rash in the woods all those years ago. Now, one last meeting between them seemed inevitable.

The sun had declined, holding above the trees. A couple of hours of daylight left. Ethan considered his options. He could find a defensible position and try to hold out. Call that Option One. Unappealing—he was outnumbered, and even if Deputy Canning's people managed to reach him, their helicopter wouldn't be able to find him through the trees. The longer he remained in the forest, the more circumstances tilted in favor of his pursuers.

Option Two was to find a home or cottage where he could hole up. That would mean putting civilians at risk. No good.

Option Three, then. Head toward the water. Amsterdam Bay was close. From the shore he could signal to a chopper more easily, or find a way off the island. This was probably his best chance for escape. It would mean Ty's escape, too, though. Could he live with that? He wasn't sure.

That left Option Four. Ethan continued west, shielding his eyes from the sun, pausing at intervals to rip out a vine or snap a branch. Deliberately leaving a trail for Ty and Nancy to follow.

His throat was parched. He tried to ignore the shards of pain along his ankle and foot. Ethan began changing course, doubling back, turning north toward the Gatlins' property.

A good hunter wielded time and patience as weapons. Ty didn't have to pursue Ethan so much as intercept him. Go where your prey is headed but get there first.

Which worked two ways.

Despite all his advantages, Tyler Rash was prone to errors. Overconfidence, sloppy execution. The envelope bomb was an example of that. Ethan had been seeing the man as he used to be, a gifted teenager, bigger and wiser than himself. Distorted by adolescence.

Always come home, and always make sure your people come home. That philosophy had carried Ethan Brand through the corps, through injury and rehabilitation, into his job as chief. The times he'd failed were few, and each was burned into him.

Hell if he wasn't coming home now.

* * *

He passed the rubble of a dead campfire. Someone had carved the initials J+G in a trunk. A reminder that there were other people on the island, that civilization was tantalizingly close. He wished J and G well.

The ground dropped away into a sharp shallow gully, a trickle of water at the bottom. Ethan wet his mouth. In the reflection he saw only his silhouette. Was this the creek where Ty had buried Miles Gatlin?

He needed to improve his odds. Ethan streaked mud over his cheeks and forehead, the backs of his hands, his belt buckle and the eyelets of his boots. Nothing glinted.

The other side of the bank was even steeper. He crept along until the ground evened out. And paused. Exactly the spot where they'd expect him to climb up. Instead, Ethan passed it, found a tougher but negotiable spot shrouded with ferns, and clambered over the edge.

Moving downhill now, he saw where a one-lane road cut into the forest. On the other side was an A-frame cottage with an old blue muscle car parked out front. He steered clear of it.

A figure in black interposed herself between him and the road. Ethan dropped, his knees hitting roots. He slid behind cover.

Nancy Gatlin's white hair was visible through the foliage. She stalked cautiously, both hands on the rifle. A practiced hunter, given the way she moved. Aware of her surroundings, pacing with caution, pausing every few steps to look for sign.

Hunting an animal that could hunt you back was a different experience.

She moved on a diagonal, closer to him now and facing uphill. Within range and getting closer. If he fired and didn't drop her with the first round, Nancy would know exactly where he was. Even if he managed to wing her, there was still Ty to contend with.

Was he reluctant to fire at a woman? In Afghanistan, some of the most patient and deadly fighters on both sides had been female. Trust to tactics and be ready to fire if that proved necessary. Nancy Gatlin wouldn't spare him.

He moved along parallel to her direction. The terrain wasn't of his choosing, but Ethan kept an eye out as he moved. The geography would need to be just right. A tall tree with thick branches overhead. Some undergrowth. Even ground, but not too even. A draw would be perfect, what the Brits in Afghanistan had called "a re-entrant." A natural narrowing of the landscape so that all traffic moved through the same pass. He'd have to find it soon. Already the sky was beginning to blush, the sun prepared to sink into Puget Sound.

He found what he needed in a spot not far from where he'd first seen Ty. A twisted Garry oak in a small clearing above a cleft in the hillside. Blackberry vines crowding the brush a few yards away.

Ethan worked swiftly and mechanically, with no thought other than the tasks. Not even survival. He turned the volume on his phone up and set the alarm for twenty minutes. That might be too late or too soon, but he'd have to hope. Shimmying up the trunk, he wedged the phone into a forked branch, high enough that the leaves concealed it. Ethan dropped silently, landing on his good foot but feeling the pain in his left. He scraped the dirt nearby, then tore a piece of bark off the tree.

Now to hide.

He crawled amid the blackberries, tempted to pick some but knowing that would give away his position. Belly down, worming into the bush until he could just see the trunk without moving his head. The brambles caught at his hair. He felt a trickle of blood from the neck, but it couldn't be helped. Ethan snuggled down into the dirt. Becoming dirt. Waiting.

When he was positioned, he flung his keys so that they struck the tree, the jingle just loud enough. If Nancy kept to her course, she would hear it and investigate.

Shadows drew over him. The sun was almost gone. How much time had elapsed—ten minutes? Fifteen?

He sensed her proximity before he saw her. Somehow Nancy had swept behind him. Moving one foot directly in front of the other, nimble and light. Ethan didn't turn his head.

She took her time circling the small clearing, observing it from every angle. No doubt she had spotted the keys. Spiraling closer to the tree. He watched her examine the trunk. Noting the marks where a foot might have scraped away bark. Above her were scrawny limbs and branches, nothing that could support a human's weight. Or could they?

Twenty minutes. The phone blinked to life and music blared. Reba McIntyre, an old crush of his, singing "Is There Life Out There?"

His ankle hurt but it obeyed him. In one clean move he shot to his feet and pounced. Everything went into the swing, crashing down with the butt of the pistol, aiming at the back of her neck. Nancy turned and the blow caught her above the ear. She let out a grunt, teetered, crushing ferns as she fell. A small crescent of blood formed on the back of her head.

One small victory for the power of music, he thought. Thank you, Reba.

The rifle was beneath her and he tried to work it out, lifting one shoulder and then the other. Ethan let go of the barrel and pried Nancy's gloved hand off the stock. She was breathing but unconscious. Despite himself he felt relief at this.

A two-way headset had fallen out of Nancy's ear. Running a hand through her pockets, he extracted a utility knife, gum, spare batteries. He took it all. In the lining of her jacket was a pair of night vision binoculars. So that was their plan. Wait for nightfall, then stalk him in tandem. Smart.

Ethan broke the rifle over his knee. He bound Nancy's wrists with her belt, then took her headset, unsure if Ty could hear him or not.

"You're on your own now," he whispered into the mic. "No more warning shots."

49

It was a simple trap, designed to snare small animals. Nothing more than a loop of wire set in the bottom of a natural dip in the trail. His father had showed them how to make one. Ethan realized what it was the moment he stepped in it.

His mind had been on larger problems, and he hadn't expected a trap so near the Gatlins' own property. Probably meant to keep rabbits and squirrels out of their garden. If Nancy had taken him a slightly different route, they would have passed over it.

No excuse for carelessness, he thought. Ethan sat up. The fall hadn't hurt him but it had been loud.

He knew not to struggle. Reaching down with Nancy's knife, he carefully cut the loop of wire and peeled it from his ankle. It would have to be the left. His fingers touched something sharp. Ty had fashioned the snare out of barbed wire. The casual cruelty of that angered him.

Ethan crawled away from the trail before regaining his feet. The repairs to his ankle, the heel plate and insert, made uneven ground painful even in the best circumstances. The injury would add to that, and hinder his movement.

He was close to the garden and could see the outlines of a trio of rain barrels, staked rows of beans and corn. The sun had been replaced by a thumbnail moon that teased out behind fast moving clouds.

Ethan skirted the edge of the property, gritting his teeth through each step. He didn't know if Tyler Rash had returned to the house. For all he knew, Ty could be off the island already. Not a bad idea.

But if he had to guess Ty's strategy, it would be to pick off Ethan when he tried to rendezvous with his rescuers. The house would be their logical first stop. Ethan had an idea of what he'd find in the house. More importantly, what he'd find under it.

There was a first aid kit in his truck. He approached the turnaround from the far end and saw that his Chevy was gone. Had Ty taken the truck? Or had Nancy simply moved it out of sight? Ethan used the binoculars to lens the brush around the property. It felt strange to see the familiar Washington State plant life tinted an unnatural green by low-light amplification. He associated that color with the desert.

He spotted the familiar dented fender of the truck. A tarp and a few fir branches had been draped over the bed. Sloppy work. Even a person in a hurry could have done a better job of camouflaging the Chevy. Ethan zoomed in on the door and saw why.

Wire had been wrapped around the knob of the driver's side door lock. He couldn't see what the wire connected to. A bomb, most likely. But why leave anything visible?

Ethan turned the binoculars toward the house. Near the corner of the porch, a pair of the same binoculars stared back at him. Below them a bearded mouth, grinning.

He meant to leap but his leg gave out and Ethan tumbled as above him automatic rifle fire strafed the undergrowth. He rolled, losing the binoculars, eyes readjusting to the darkness. Disoriented and blind, he kept low and kept moving.

"How's that for a warning shot?" Ty called.

A floorboard creak broke the silence, followed by the front door slamming shut. Ethan heard a window pane being bashed out. Tyler Rash, ready to make his last stand.

The sound began as a drone, steadier than a speedboat engine but about the same timbre. As the noise grew closer it grew fuller, too. Soon Ethan could pinpoint its direction. The spotlight of a helicopter appeared above the trees.

A four-seater Bell hovered above the road, its nose below the rotor, scanning the property for human figures. Forty minutes to an hour like hell, Ethan thought. It had been over two hours.

The spotter would have a good sense of the terrain. They would know the Gatlins' address and the boundaries of their property, and would likely start there. It occurred to Ethan, as he began moving in the direction of the chopper's path, that Ty might want this very thing. All he needed to do to ensure his own survival was eliminate Ethan. If that meant waiting for the chopper and sniping off his adversary as he approached, so much the better.

Ethan knelt and waited, watching as the chopper worked its way along. If he had a lighter or matches he could start a fire, attract attention with smoke. He opened his phone, holding the screen so his body shielded the glow. Several missed calls from Canning, two from Brenda Lee. He texted the Pierce County deputy that he was near the house, then headed back into the brush. The chopper's spotlight could only help Ty's aim.

Ethan doubted whether his former friend was truly committed to going out like this. Making a show of breaking the window, preparing to hold off a siege, could be a ploy. What was Ty's real plan?

He dragged himself along the side of the house, around to the garden. The rain barrels were about the right distance from the house. Ty wouldn't make the same mistake twice.

The helicopter was lowering and he heard his name over a loudspeaker. Ethan watched the aircraft sink, dropping onto Sandberg Road. It would take the deputies minutes to reach the house.

There was a grinding pain in his leg now, and his boot dragged as he moved, but he headed toward the barrels. His guess was correct. Everywhere else on the property the grass grew in long wild bunches. The ground around the bushes, though, was smooth, the grass even and neat. Artificial turf, he reckoned.

Ethan lay prone across the field, took a two-handed grip on the pistol and aimed. The rough circle of grass near the barrels rose and shifted. A head teased up from the opening, looked around and dropped back. Hands emerged. Elbows. A torso pulled itself out of the ground.

He fired twice, saw the figure slide back into the opening. The shots were loud and the ignition of gunpowder bloomed fire. He wasn't sure if he hit his target or if Ty had evaded the shots. Ethan shifted position, covered the tunnel exit and waited.

Noise from the front of the property. Canning was calling to him. The deputies had made it to the turnaround.

Ethan's attention remained focused on the tunnel. He didn't see the explosion. But he felt a sharp concussion and heard the spray of glass and wood. When he looked, he saw smoke rising from the front of the house.

50

His instinct was to rush to Canning's aid and see what damage the explosion had wrought. But he couldn't tear his focus off the tunnel for any length of time. Ty might very well have an entire underground network, with multiple means of escape. He could be encroaching on Ethan's position right now. Or escaping.

Or he might be dead.

Ethan took his phone out and dialed Canning. "Anyone hurt?" he asked.

"No fatalities, thankfully, but a lot of splinters and headaches." The deputy sheriff was practically yelling into the phone. "What about on your end?"

"Less than a hundred percent," he admitted.

"You're certain Rash is still on the premises?"

"Below the premises, if he's alive." Ethan explained his position and the location of the tunnel.

"I have more personnel on the way, including a breaching team. I also spoke with Officer Page. She told me who Tyler Rash with an R is. She's on her way down, and she wanted me to tell you that you should have waited for her."

"She's wrong," Ethan said. "I should have stayed home and sent her instead."

He extracted the magazine from his service weapon. Five rounds remained, but he swapped it for the spare.

"Do you know what a double delay is?" he asked Canning. "Tyler Rash knows. It's a small explosion meant to draw a crowd of onlookers, before triggering a larger one."

"That blast felt plenty large enough up close," Canning said.

"Keep your people back from the house. The truck, too."

"Understood. And what about you?"

Sleep, he thought. A nice meal, a few CCs of morphine to numb his ankle. A Woodinville whiskey, neat, a little Sam Cooke and someone to hold tight. But sleep above all. Precious sleep.

"Do you have a view into the house?" he asked Canning.

"We do now that the front wall is gone."

Standing felt like a greater feat than any labor of Hercules. Ethan used the light of the phone to examine the tunnel entrance. Deeper than the one in the Sterankos' shed, at least eight feet, but as narrow as the other had been. Metal rungs were punched into the supports. A dark spatter on the top rung. He'd hit his target after all.

"Come on up, Ty," he called. "There's no way out of this that's any good, other than turning yourself in."

Faint laughter seeped out of the exit. Tyler Rash was alive. Waiting down there.

"You'll have to come down and help me, Ethan. I'm a bit incapacitated."

"Forgive me if I don't believe that."

"Worth a try." Ty's voice was low, difficult to make out. "Did you know I found him?"

"Who, Archie Gatlin?" No matter where he stood Ethan couldn't see the bottom of the tunnel.

"Nah, never set eyes on Archie till he was dead."

"Till you killed him, you mean."

"Same difference."

"Who did you find, then?"

"Jack."

Ethan didn't, couldn't respond. Exhaustion muddled his ability to comprehend.

"About three, four years ago I took another go at finding his camp. We had the wrong lake, Ethan. Our whole search was off by about two hundred miles."

A coughing fit broke off his words. When Ty resumed speaking his voice was softer. Ethan made out the words "other side of that mountain" and "kayak across, like Jack did."

He leaned closer to the tunnel, trying to hear, then heard nothing but the bark of a pistol. Ty's shot was wide, winged at the sound of Ethan's voice. Reeling back from the exit, Ethan saw a fissure in the nearest water barrel.

"You want to know where your father's buried, you'll have to come down here."

"You're lying," Ethan said.

"Only one way to find out."

Yet another trap. Was he being baited with a lie or with the truth? Ethan felt a teenager's anger and doubt. Exactly what Tyler Rash wanted him to feel.

He shouldn't be considering the idea. The tunnel provided his adversary with limitless opportunities for ambush and surprise. Entering the den of a wounded animal was an invitation to slaughter.

"Maybe you're right," Ethan said.

He tore the lid off the barrel and put his shoulder against the side, treating it like a tackling dummy. The barrel tipped. Its contents cascaded down into the tunnel. He heard the flood of water, a note of surprise as it washed over Tyler Rash. Then the frantic splashing of someone crawling away.

Before he could talk himself out of it, Ethan was descending the ladder.

51

A different type of darkness. Ethan crawled with pistol in hand, finger out of the trigger guard. With his free hand, he felt along the tunnel. Mud clung to his clothing. Like moving in a dream, he thought. His effort and speed felt completely unrelated.

His knee hit something metal. Ty's binoculars, abandoned in flight. Hopefully the water and Ty's swift retreat would prevent him from laying any traps.

The ground of the tunnel was muddy, but became drier as he moved farther in. The air colder and stale. Ethan tried to think what he'd do in Ty's position. If there was another way out of the tunnel, he would take that and run. Fighting through a number of deputies would be much more difficult than dealing with Ethan alone. He felt ahead for changes in direction, but the tunnel was a smooth straight bore through the earth. No turns or sidings.

One of the support beams was cracked and hung at an angle. He scurried beneath it, unsure if it was a trap or the work of time and moisture on the wood.

The tunnel began to incline. Moving forward took more work. The last few feet were almost a ramp, leading to a small circular portal feeding horizontally into another chamber. Light ahead, shadows around the opening. They dispersed. Below the house now, he reasoned.

Ethan paused to listen, heard nothing, then stormed up the ramp with as much quickness as he could muster.

Two facts imprinted himself as he dropped out of the tunnel. He was in a basement or cellar, its walls lined with shelves of preserves. He was also alone.

As his eyes took in the light bleeding from upstairs, he saw that the contours of the room were narrow, at odd angles. Directly ahead of him was a short carpeted staircase. The floor of the cellar was unfinished. Near him was a potbellied stove, pushed away from the wall at a forty five degree angle. He guessed the stove would be used to conceal the tunnel's entrance.

He hadn't heard Ty on the stairs. The floor was packed hard enough that all he could make out was a fait set of prints toward the stairs. Yet the dull gray carpet on the staircase itself looked unmarked. A wet and possibly bleeding man would leave more of a trace. Wouldn't he?

Looking up, Ethan saw ancient copper pipes running between floor timbers. No air ducts. No other way out. Nor was there any depression or crevice in the floor. He examined the shelves but they hid no secret passageway.

Damn him, Ethan thought. Ty had managed to escape. To beat him.

But if Ty hadn't taken the stairs—

Ethan put his hand on the bottom step. He lifted. The lower half of the staircase raised up from the floor on a hinge.

The instant he recognized what it was Ethan dropped back, flattening against the shelving, aware he'd stumbled into an ambush. Rifle fire perforated the steps, smashing jars, panging off the stove.

A panicked move, Ethan thought. Ty had emptied a high-capacity magazine. He would be reloading now. Ethan slammed his left palm into the staircase, raising it in one move, and as he did took one-handed aim at the target in front of him and shot twice.

Tyler Rash lurched, the rifle and spare magazine slipping through his hands. His throat made a gurgling noise. Beyond the wounded man, Ethan could see a narrow passage leading along the front of the house.

"Think that did it," Ty said.

His shoulder had already darkened with blood. The two chest wounds were only perforations in the camouflage jacket. Ty turned his head and spat, looking up at Ethan, unable to smile and yet something amused in his expression. His hand moved steadily toward his holster.

"Careful," Ethan said.

Too late for careful. Ty's hand was moving on reflex.

This should have played out differently, Ethan thought. The two of them should be closing down a roadhouse somewhere. Swapping lies and life stories. Telling off-color jokes. Raising a High Life in remembrance to Jack Brand and the rare good times. This shouldn't be how it happened.

He watched Ty's fingers grip the pistol and raise it with intent. And Ethan shot him center mass. He couldn't have improved on his aim. Ty convulsed. Now the wounds were blooming, the material soaking through. The heart pumping out its last beats.

Ethan kept his gun at ready, knowing a trick was beyond the dying man but unwilling to take the chance. He saw Ty's arm drop.

"Want to ask," Ty managed. "Your father."

"If you want to tell me."

Ethan listened to the dying declaration. He kept listening for minutes after Tyler Rash was dead. His hand let the hinge of the staircase fall, submerging Ty in the darkness. He felt two hundred years old.

The smell of canned peaches and pears filled the cellar. Ethan climbed the steps until he saw the roving glare of flashlights. He waved and called to the deputies. Two hundred years old and then some.

52

Deputy Sara Canning turned out to be a trim woman in her thirties with a ponytail of frizzy red hair. She treated his ankle herself, as Ethan stretched out on the back seat of a Sheriff's Department 4x4.

"Just to make sure I have the sequence," Canning said, "you came to interview Miles Gatlin about a suspect, only Gatlin turned out to *be* the suspect. He chased you. You shot him. That about sum things up?"

Not remotely, but Ethan didn't argue. There was no summing up that he could fathom. Tyler Rash was dead. Ty had killed others and now been killed in turn. Death never felt like justice to Ethan Brand. It only ever felt like itself.

A wad of explosive the size of a family bible had been fitted beneath a floorboard in the front hallway of the Gatlin house. The deputies had disarmed the tripwire that would trigger it, and were now clearing the rest of the property. Reinforcements soon arrived and began searching the grounds.

Canning removed his boot, saw the heel plate. She didn't grimace but frowned in concentration.

"A lot of that is old damage," Ethan said.

"Guess it has to be. And you get around on it OK?"

"I get around."

Canning swabbed the leg and wrapped the ankle, giving him an aspirin. She had arranged a special ferry just for Ethan, and accompanied him across the water herself.

"The body we recovered has a valid driver's license and credit cards in Miles Gatlin's name," she said. "Even a fishing ticket. Living off the grid the way Miles did, it was probably not the hardest identity to steal."

As Miles Gatlin, Ty had created more of a life than he had as himself, at least on paper. Even down to a marriage. Which reminded him.

"What about the woman," Ethan said, his voice a croak.

"Nancy Gatlin." Canning uncapped a bottle of distilled water. "Birth name Nancy Leigh. Any chance she's actually someone else as well?"

He could only swig the water and shrug. He knew nothing about her, really.

"My team has the location you gave me, but so far no sign of Nancy. Hard to search in the dark. A K-9 unit is on its way, though. We'll pick her up."

He fell asleep in Canning's truck. When he woke up, a weak gray light was streaming over the peak of Mount Baker. Canning was turned in her seat, holding out a takeout cup.

"Not sure how you like your coffee, but this is reasonably fresh." She pointed at his foot. "You want another aspirin?"

"Desperately."

Ethan took the lid off the coffee, careful not to drip on the seat. He watched the steam rise. After an ordeal, the little miracles were what a person appreciated most.

"You know I'll have to hang onto your weapon until this is officially resolved," the deputy said.

"And my truck?" Ty's decoy bomb had been removed from Ethan's Chevy.

"That too. Off the record, so far everything's as you said. Clean shooting from the looks of it."

There seemed to be something more Canning wanted to say. Ethan took three of the painkillers and washed them down.

"I don't like to second-guess another officer, but my boss is going to want answers. Like why you went to the island alone. Officer Page told me you and Mr. Rash had a pretty storied history. Is that true?"

Ethan nodded but didn't attempt to explain.

"Rash didn't say anything before you shot him? Or after?"

Through the windshield he could see the terminal. In the weak morning light he could only make out one vehicle waiting on the dock for them. It looked like a department cruiser. Brenda Lee Page would be at the wheel.

Ethan thought over what Tyler Rash had told him. He didn't want to lie to the deputy, so he said nothing. After a moment Canning's radio blared. She spoke into it quietly.

"The damnedest thing." Canning craned her head back in the direction of Anderson Island. "My team found the spot where you ambushed Nancy Gatlin. We found a broken rifle and a belt that had been chewed through. For now, that woman is in the wind."

* * *

In the entire time he'd known Brenda Lee Page, they had never hugged. Brenda Lee wasn't the hugging type. But when the ferry docked, and she helped him limp from one department vehicle to another, she held onto Ethan's neck for an extra half-second. The gesture seemed to embarrass her.

"I should be mad at you for having all the fun without me," Brenda Lee said.

Instead of driving straight home to Blaine, he told her there was a stop they had to make first.

53

Emily Heller opened her front door but kept the screen shut. She looked over Ethan in his ragged clothes and the dark windbreaker the Pierce County Sheriffs had loaned him, standing in her driveway next to Brenda Lee. Tyler Rash's mother placed a cigarette between her lips.

"Only reason you'd be back is if he's dead," she said. "Was it you killed him?"

"I'm afraid so."

Ethan insisted on telling her himself. He knew once he got home he wouldn't have the strength to do much of anything. On the drive to Olympia, he told Brenda Lee what happened and what the dead man had said. Ethan imagined how Ty's mother might react. He expected tears, the tough act to fall away. But Emily Heller was tough all the way through. She lit her smoke and stepped out, the screen clattering behind her, not inviting them in.

"Looks like Ty put you through the wringer," she said. "The wringer and a whole lot more. You want to tell me how it happened?"

He told her the truth, not justifying himself, or downplaying Ty's criminal actions. Ethan was still too close to the moment. A proper reckoning would come later.

She listened calmly and intently, smoking and nodding to show she followed. The only part of his story that seemed to surprise her was about Nancy. Hearing how her son had married under Miles Gatlin's name, Emily's expression softened. When Ethan was finished, she asked what happened to the woman.

"The deputies still haven't found her," Ethan said.

"Nice to think Ty had a little happiness in his life. And you took that away. How's it feel?"

"That's not fair," Brenda Lee said.

"I don't know how it feels," he answered.

What he felt was too much. The exhilaration of cheating death, of surviving. That was accompanied by a supreme exhaustion, the hunt being over and taking everything he had. Beyond that, a sorrow and a stark emptiness at watching the light wink out of a soul. Even worse when the dead man was someone he had known for decades.

Known, and yet never known, not really. Tyler Rash died an enigma to everyone, his mother included.

"Seems Ty did better in the love department than me," Emily said. "Still looking for my Prince Charming."

"Before he died," Ethan said, "Ty told me he found my father's remains up in the wilderness. He told me you knew something about how it happened."

"He did, did he? About Jack?" Emily blew smoke and lobbed the filter toward the curb. Dressed in sweat pants and a Rolling Stones T-shirt. Already lighting another cigarette. She drew on it, thinking.

"I must have told Ty that I felt Jack was the one. The one that got away from me, I mean. A few days after your mother brought Ty back to me, Jack came by to check on him. We struck up a friendly conversation. After a while we became more than friends.

I was working at a Dairy Queen back then, and he would walk me home sometimes. For a while he was even thinking about leaving your mom."

Ethan wasn't sure how much of that to believe. "What happened between you?" he said.

"The night before Jack flew up to camp he stayed over with me. You didn't know that, did you?" Emily smiled. "His gear was sitting by my front door. I didn't want him to leave."

"So what did you do?"

"I was so young back then. In love."

"What did you do, Emily?"

Instead of answering, she retreated into the house, batting the screen door aside. Ethan followed her into the living room. Emily walked to the bookcase and reached on tiptoes to the top of the case, taking down one of the old tins she kept there as decorations. She passed it to him. He recognized the Senator tobacco logo.

Inside were ancient cotton swabs and yellowed bandages. Waterproof matches, sewing kit, scissors. A blister pack of water purification tablets. Nestled at the bottom, half a tube of very old liniment. It still smelled faintly of camphor.

"All I wanted was something to remember him by," Emily said.

Without Jack Brand's first aid kit, what had his last days been like?

Ethan closed the tin, thought of keeping it, but passed it back to the grieving woman. The answer was enough. At one point in his life, he imagined that the knowledge would fill some empty part of him. Instead, it was an eyedropper in a dry well.

Leaving the house without goodbye, he hesitated before climbing into the cruiser. Tyler Rash's mother observed him from the doorway.

"It was him or me," Ethan said.

"Always was," she called back. "From the very start. And it was never gonna be him, and Ty knew it."

*   *   *

Brenda Lee dropped him off at home, insisting on helping him onto the couch. She turned down a beer but accepted a glass of water. His father's file caught her attention, and she scanned the clippings.

"I guess when you're healed up, you'll make arrangements to bring back his remains," Brenda Lee said. "Ty told you the location, didn't he?"

Ethan nodded. Ty had buried what was left of Jack Brand and his campsite. The spot was secluded and wild. A lonesome place for a grave, but more fitting for his father than the family plot in Blaine, where Ethan himself would probably lie one day.

"No," he said, "I don't suppose there's any point in disturbing him."

Brenda Lee rinsed out her water glass. "Well, if you change your mind and want company. In any case, I hope it's some sort of closure."

Ethan didn't respond right away. When he did manage to speak, he found that Brenda Lee had been gone for some time. He was alone.

"Feels more like I lost something I never knew I had," he said to the empty house.

54

Blaine was at its best and most beautiful in the fall. Life seemed to slow and hurry at the same time. The lick of chill in the sea air, the grousing at the counter of Lucky's about how the Super Value already had their Christmas decorations up. Hot coffee, boots and scarves, the trample of leaves and the absence of summer traffic. The days held a fragile beauty.

That fall was no exception, and yet to Ethan Brand it felt gray and unremarkable. The Pierce County Sheriffs took a month to investigate the shooting, retracing his movements. They probed for guilt, for admission of mistakes. They delayed their final report.

All of this he barely registered, as if it was happening to someone on the other side of the Pacific. Most of his duties as chief could be handled from his desk. Brenda Lee Page and Mal Keogh stepped up to handle public interactions. The town was accommodating, sympathetic.

His doctor examined the ankle and told him it was bursitis. In the future he'd have to rest at the first sign of swelling, or risk losing further mobility. The doctor wrote him a prescription for painkillers. Ethan pinned it to his refrigerator.

The swelling in his ankle went down. Soon he was moving around with the barest of limps. It didn't matter. In the days before returning to the field, there was no place special he had to go.

Vonetta Briggs sent him a get-well-soon bouquet. No signature, but he recognized the shade of lipstick she'd kissed to the card.

Brenda Lee Page had made peace with the life growing inside her. She marked off her maternity leave months ahead, and performed her duties with her customary diligence. Occasionally he caught her reading books on classical music and the developing brain, or scrolling through websites of baby names.

Mal Keogh would start in Portland in the new year. Mal rode out his final months with a cheerfulness Ethan hadn't seen in the young officer before. Mal and Brenda Lee, never bosom buddies, seemed to get along more easily now.

All was well. The town was moving merrily toward the holidays and the end of the year. And yet when Ethan came home from work, he would sit in the dark and see Tyler Rash bleeding out, whispering his final words. Sometimes an image of Jack Brand would join them, receding into the woods. Ethan would stare at the prescription on the fridge for a good while before creeping to bed.

Loneliness was a large country with a vast population, a country that granted citizenship for life.

* * *

The night before the report was due, Deputy Canning called him. Nancy Gatlin had walked into a station in Puyallup and surrendered.

"Rash told her you were sent to kill him," Canning said. "She knew Rash wasn't Miles Gatlin, but claims she didn't know anything about his crimes. Could be lying, I suppose."

"She knew about the booby traps and bombs," Ethan said.

"Sure. All part of their survivalist lifestyle. Living off the land, ready for the end of civilization. She's a tough customer, Nancy. If she hadn't turned herself in, I doubt we would have caught her any time soon."

"So why did she?" Ethan asked.

"Her mother's sick," Canning said. "Nancy wants to be out of jail soon enough to take care of her."

Ethan rubbed the bridge of his nose, trying to process the information. Was there an ulterior motive in this, or was Nancy Gatlin sincere? He decided it didn't matter.

"I doubt she knew about the murders," he said after a moment. "If you can cut her a break, I'd appreciate it. I owe that much to Ty."

"We'll see what we can do," Canning promised. "As to your shooting."

He readied himself for the news. "Go ahead."

"Clean," Canning told him. "You're cleared for duty with no restrictions. The panel agreed there was nothing you could have done differently."

Ethan wasn't sure of that. A feeling was growing in him. A sense that he'd left something unfinished.

* * *

Since the department was short staffed, Election Day coincided with Ethan's return to the field. The voting went smoothly. When the results were in, Arlene Six Crows was the new mayor of Blaine.

Over a late dinner at Lucky's after the polls had closed, Ethan studied the chess board and saw a hop for his knight that would tempt Mei's queen off the back rank. A sacrifice. He double-checked, then moved. Mei was chatting with Jess Sinclair, and barely gazed at the board. As soon as her hand left the queen, Ethan slid his kingside rook up the board to checkmate.

"No freaking way," Mei said. "Darn, Chief, took you long enough but you did it. Another match?"

Even victory wasn't enough to thaw him.

* * *

The thaw didn't come till mid-October. He was home on a day off, watching *Rio Bravo* for the thousandth time. Ethan looked up to find Sissy McCandless in his living room.

"Your door was unlocked, and you didn't answer my knocking," Sissy said.

He hit pause and stood, conscious of his stubble, the raggedy jeans he wore.

Sissy ignored his appearance. She sat and accepted a beer, which she didn't touch. Her outfit was cool and casual, and she'd traded her librarian's specs for the smart thin frames. She looked good.

"I have a favor to ask," Sissy said. "First, though, I'm going to say something you might not want to hear. Killing that man was right. Necessary."

"Wish it was that simple, Sissy."

"It *is* that simple. What's more, you know that. Ty would have killed you, and anyone else, and gone on with his life in good spirits. You know I'm right, and you know the alternatives to shooting him were far more unpleasant."

"Maybe," he said.

"You're a good person, Ethan, so you're not fond of killing, but what bothers you is how little you're bothered by it. What that might say about you. I'll tell you what it says: that you prefer life to death and are willing to make hard choices and live with them. Living is the thing. That's a strength."

Sissy reached across the coffee table and squeezed his hand. A romantic gesture, he thought at first, and then the pressure increased.

Her grip was surprisingly strong. It earned his full attention. Sissy let go, smiled and folded her hands.

"Now for my favor," she said. "Asked on behalf of my employee, Cliff Mooney."

"What does Cliff want from me?" Ethan asked, genuinely puzzled.

"He's worried about his uncle. Of course, being Cliff, he would never admit that in so many words. But he—"

"Grunted a few times and drew on the wall of his cave?"

Sissy laughed. "I was going to say 'intimated to me.' Our former mayor is moping about on his boat, refusing to see anyone. If you could find an occasion to drop in on him, both of us would appreciate it. It's not good for a person to shut themself off from the world. Life is too damn precious, isn't it?"

55

On his next day off, Ethan found occasion to pay Mooney a visit. He pulled the Chevy up to the marina and took the gangplank down. Boarding the *Sassy Bess,* he rapped on the cabin door, ignoring the flats of empty Corona bottles and the bags of trash on the deck.

Eldon Mooney squinted out from the doorway. He took in Ethan in his new jeans and blazer. An outfit worthy of dropping in on an elected official, even one who'd recently lost his post. Ethan aimed his best grin at the former mayor.

"Did you come here to gloat?" Mooney said.

Ethan shook his head. "I read somewhere that football coaches and the heads of movie studios are the only people who know, the moment they're hired, that one day they'll lose their jobs. Success always runs out. Being mayor might be like that. Maybe chief of police, too."

"Movie moguls and coaches get paid a lot better," Mooney said.

"That's a fact. Do you have a spare hour or two, Your Honor? I need help from somebody business-minded."

Mooney was in his underwear, wearing a grubby shirt from the Tillamook Dairy. A rip in the fabric over one nipple. He scratched his ear. "I really wasn't planning on going anywhere today."

"So I gather," Ethan said. "Normally I'd ask Brenda Lee, but she's got her hands full these days. I'd really appreciate your help."

While Mooney dressed, Ethan carted the beer bottles and garbage bags to the shore. Sure, he'd mostly invented the errand as a means of drawing Mooney out of his sulk. He supposed Sissy McCandless had done the same for him. Some types of melancholy were too deep to cure. Other types, what you needed was to feel useful. Connected to the rest of humanity.

The mayor emerged, blinking at the morning light. He reminded Ethan of Mole from *The Wind in the Willows*. His mother had read that book to him. Maybe this winter he'd read it to Ben and Brad.

"What's so important?" Mooney asked as the Chevy pulled away from the waterfront.

"Tell you on the ride over," Ethan said. "What do you know about horses, Your Honor?"

* * *

Trim Reckoning had graduated with flying colors, according to Mac Steranko. "That little mare has the gentlest disposition now, without losing her feistiness. Hard to believe she was ever raced. No bucking, no biting. You'll be able to put your boys on her back with just about no risk."

"Just about?" Ethan asked.

The old man removed his ball cap, his version of a shrug. "Well, she's still a living creature, and they can always surprise you. But I'd trust her with my own kids, if I had any."

Mac led the horse out of the stable and walked her around the pen. Trim Reckoning cantered easily. Her leg had healed fully and was giving her no trouble.

Ethan had decided to build a stable on his empty lot. He'd already ordered the components. If the weather cooperated, he could have it up before the boys arrived for Christmas.

That morning, Ethan had phoned Jazz and told her he needed to see his family this year. Travel wasn't an option. Rather than fly to Boston, why didn't they all come here? All four of them, that is—the kids, her, and her new guy?

"You wouldn't find that terribly awkward?" his ex asked.

"I can survive terribly awkward," Ethan said. "I can survive anything except not seeing my family."

Now he watched Mac Steranko help the mayor onto the back of Trim Reckoning. Mooney and the horse took a turn around the small pen. Ethan had told Mooney his ankle hurt too much to make the ride himself. A slight exaggeration.

"Does she seem OK to you?" Ethan asked.

"Seems just fine." Mooney's face had broken out in a broad grin.

When he dismounted, Mooney peppered Nettie Steranko with questions about horse prices and stabling fees. The former mayor brushed the horse's mane, running a hand over the broken blaze. Captivated, Ethan thought, just as he had been. Mooney began asking if the Sterankos might have any other horses they'd be willing to part with.

"Well, Your Honor, at our age, our nags are very dear to us," Nettie said. "But maybe we can work something out."

Minutes later, Mooney was following Nettie inside the house to haggle over the price of a strawberry roan. From boats to horses, Ethan thought. He hoped the mayor had sense enough not to mix the two.

Mac Steranko echoed his thoughts as they watched Trim Reckoning move about the pen. "Seems Eldon found himself a new hobby," Mac said. "Give you three-to-one odds Nettie sells His Honor that big frog-walker, too."

On the drive over, Ethan had noticed that the Sterankos' shed was gone. A backhoe had filled in the tunnel. All trace of the crime scene had been returned to grass and soil.

He knew he had to bring up the subject of Tyler Rash, but dreaded doing so. The Sterankos had already been told of Ty's death, but they deserved to hear the details from the man who killed him.

"About Ty," Ethan said, stumbling his way through the story one more time.

The dead man's mother hadn't reacted with tears. Mac Steranko did.

"I wish things hadn't shaken out the way they did," Mac said, wiping a weathered cheek. "If I'd paid a bit more attention, maybe the boy would have turned to me before things went bad."

"He did turn to you, though, didn't he?" Ethan said.

"What do you mean?"

"Ty told me something in the forest. He said, 'When they start coming for your friends, that's when you know it's time to leave town.' In a way, Ty was running for you as well. Wasn't he?"

The old man didn't respond. He whistled to the horse, who cantered over to their side of the pen.

Ethan spoke softly. "Which one of you shot Archie Gatlin in the tunnel?"

Mac's eyes didn't move from the horse. In an even voice he said, "What makes you think it wasn't Ty?"

"Gatlin was a trained enforcer. No way he'd go first into a tunnel with Tyler Rash at his back. But he might do that with someone he didn't think posed a threat. Where did the pistol come from?"

"Ty kept it in his bedroll," Mac said, gripping the reins. "Nettie saw it one day when she took him his breakfast. When he left for the second time, we kept the shed the way it was, in case he came back."

"And four years later he did," Ethan said. "How did it happen?"

"That man Gatlin came by the house. Said he knew Ty stayed with us sometimes. Ty owed money, and if he didn't pay, Nettie and me would be on the hook. Gatlin knocked me over like I was a feather. Made me take him out to Ty's shed."

"Only Ty wasn't there," Ethan guessed.

Mac nodded. "Gatlin knew there was a tunnel. Guess he thought Ty kept the money stashed there. Gatlin went down, only it was dark. He asked me to pass him a flashlight."

"And instead you brought the gun."

"I remembered it was there," the old man said. "I knew Gatlin wouldn't stop, even if he found the money. He'd hurt us, and he'd wait there for Ty and hurt him, too. He was barking at me to hurry up with the light... You've never heard anything like it, Ethan, the report of that gun in the tunnel. My hand jumped so bad, the second shot was practically an accident."

"How did Ty's wallet end up down there?" Ethan asked.

"Ty came to see us that afternoon. He'd heard Gatlin was in town. He found me by the shed, told me he'd clean things up, seal the tunnel so it was like it never happened. Ty knew he'd have to disappear, so he placed his wallet on the body, closed up the tunnel and drove off in Gatlin's Jeep. Made a point of not telling me where he went."

Mac opened the pen and led the horse back to her stall. Ethan walked beside them. The inside of the stable was dark. The old man fastened the gate and wiped his eyes.

"Someone had to look out for that boy," Mac said. "Someone had to stand for him."

THE END

Acknowledgments

Blaine is a real border town in Washington State. Ethan Brand's Blaine bears certain similarities in geography and history, but is ultimately a fictional place, populated by fictional characters. They also choose their mayors a little differently. Any similarity to real people is coincidental, and all errors are ultimately mine.

I owe a debt of thanks to my agent, Chris Casuccio at Westwood Creative Artists.

Thanks to my editor Marcia Markland and the publishing team at Crooked Lane.

Thanks to Mel, Brad, and Adam for the inspiration, and for introducing me to Ernie the horse.

Thanks to Nathan Ripley for the encouragement.

Thanks to my family.

Ultimately everything I write is for C.R. Thanks to her.

And to you for reading this.

Nolan Chase